D1706813

# TAMING

## THE

# WILD

# HIGHLANDER

TERRY SPEAR

Copyright © 2013 Terry Spear

All rights reserved.

ISBN: 1483933032
ISBN-13: 978-1483933030

PUBLISHED BY:

Terry Spear

Taming the Wild Highlander
Copyright © 2013 by Terry Spear

All rights reserved. No part of this book may be reproduced or transmitted in any form or by any means, electronic or mechanical, including photocopying, recording, or by any information storage and retrieval system, without written permission from the author, except for the inclusion of brief quotations in a review.

Discover more about Terry Spear at:
http://www.terryspear.com/

# DEDICATION

To my Highland readers who love Highlanders, their kilts, wind, and what is and isn't beneath the kilt! Keep those imaginations running wild and I will keep writing about those hunky Highlanders!

# Prologue

Leaning against an ancient oak on a summer day, the warm breeze catching his plaid and lifting it playfully, Angus MacNeill, at six and ten, quietly watched the daughter of the chief of the Chattan clan. Dressed in a blue léine and plaid brat, Edana Chattan dangled her legs over the edge of a massive rock overhanging a loch near her clan's castle, her reflection caught in the rippling water. She looked... contemplative. Which struck him as odd.

Other girls her age were chasing butterflies amongst the heather in full bloom, or giggling in small groups of two or three, most trying to catch one of the lads' attention. Like his cousin's. Or his. Or his brothers', who were all older than him.

The girls ranged in age from two and ten to his age. Edana Chattan was four and ten. She didn't look lonely, *exactly*. Just dreamy-eyed as if she were happier to be in a world of her own. He couldn't help being curious about her. Not after he'd heard some of the others telling him tales about her curse.

Birds twittered in the heather while the clanking of steel against steel sounded in the background.

His older brother, Malcolm, left the sword practice to stand beside him. "Why dinna you talk to her?" Malcolm's dark brown eyes sparkled with a knowing gleam as he brushed his dark hair out of his eyes.

"She seems happy by herself." She was so bonny—the sun shining on her dark hair, a reddish cast to the strands making it appear even more fetching. Angus had seen her smiling at her brothers, her father, and her mother, but at no one else, and for some odd reason, he wished her to bestow a smile upon him.

Her smile, when she offered it to her close family, was like sunshine on a cloudy day, engaging, charming, enough so that when he saw her smile, he smiled, too. Yet when she'd caught him spying on her and smiling at her, she'd quickly lost her own and burrowed into herself again.

"You know about her, do you no'?" Malcolm asked, as if to warn him to take care around the lass.

Aye, he'd heard the rumors. The lass was touched by the fae. He shrugged as if it was of no consequence. But it was. He didn't know what she could do, in truth, but some had said she had caused deaths in the past. She would warn of it, and then the person would die.

He wasn't sure what to believe. Her five brothers were practicing swordsmanship with Angus's older brothers, and he himself had only stopped to take a break. It was hard work training against the older lads.

Malcolm folded his arms and studied Edana. "You have watched her for the three days we have been here whenever you have the chance."

Aye, he had. Waiting for her to do something—to show her fae abilities. To learn if the rumors were true.

"I havena." Angus couldn't help but sound irritated. He hadn't realized Malcolm had seen him observing the lass.

Ignoring Angus's professed claim of innocence, Malcolm said, "She has noticed you studying her as well. Go speak to her. Let her know you see her as a friend, not foe."

"Are you weary of sparring with the other lads?" Angus gave his brother a pointed look, trying to convince him to leave well enough alone.

"Mark my words, if you dinna speak to her before we leave, you will regret it." Malcolm stalked off to rejoin the practice battle nearby in the grassy glen.

Angus didn't think his brother was right. The only thing he would regret was if he couldn't learn if she truly was cursed by the fae. He looked back at the rock, but she'd disappeared. His heart beat irregularly, and he glanced quickly around the area for any sight of her, trying to quiet the fear he had that she'd truly just vanished into mist and drifted away.

Then he caught sight of her. She was vehemently arguing with a group of lads and a lass, her eyes narrowed, her lips pursed, her red-brown hair hanging loose about her shoulders. He thought to stroll over there and settle things between them because he had a cooler head and he was older. But she quickly reacted to their taunts. The next thing he knew, she had slapped the older girl's cheek and struck a lad in the stomach with her fist.

Before anyone could react, she ran off like a sure-footed red deer.

And then he learned she was truly one of the fae.

# Chapter 1

*Eight years later, Rondover Castle, Clan Chattan*

Heart pounding, Edana Chattan woke to the sound of her brother Kayne's urgent plea. *Manacled, dungeon,* was all she heard, though she felt he'd said more, but she couldn't clearly recall the words he'd spoken. As if she'd been dreaming and upon waking, she couldn't capture the words as they slipped away.

It took her a moment to fully wake and realize she was at home on her feather mattress, covered with furs and the lovely quilt Kayne had brought back for her after fighting in the Crusades.

She sat up, trying to make sense of what she'd heard. Her brothers, all five of them, were on their way to see their cousin McEwan. They wouldn't be here at home. She must have heard Kayne's voice in her special way. A plea to rescue him.

Were all of her brothers in the same predicament?

Her skin chilled and not just from the coldness in the chamber. She climbed off the bed and shivered. Then she lit a candle. Her maid and companion, Una, was sleeping soundly on her pallet and Edana was careful not to disturb her, not wanting to explain the trouble to her right this very moment.

Edana quickly found her shoes in the rushes and slipped them on. She lifted her wool brat off the wooden bench sitting near the hearth. After fastening it with her brooch, she headed out of her chamber for her father's. Would he believe just her word without some kind of proof that her brothers were in trouble?

*He just had to.*

Her footfalls echoed softly off the stone walls in the corridor. Her candle cast eerie shadowed lights along the way. When she reached her father's chamber, she knocked.

There was no answer. He was a heavy sleeper, but she had hoped she could wake him from *this* side of the door—much less dangerous that way. She opened the heavy oak door and it creaked a bit.

She paused, waiting for a response. Nothing.

She peered in. "Da," she said, quietly.

If her father was disturbed in the middle of the night, he was known to jump out of his bed and grab his sword, fully prepared to attack an enemy—as many times as he'd fought in battles over the years.

She called out a little louder, "Da."

Still, he didn't awaken. Her skin pricked with trepidation, she walked toward the bed, her shoes crunching on the rushes.

She looked around for his sword, then spying it resting on the small table beside the bed, she tried to lift it with one hand, while she still held the candle in the other.

She'd hoped to move his weapon far from his grasp should he mistakenly think she was an intruder there to attack him before he fully woke. His claymore proved too heavy. She pushed it on the table as far away from the bed as she could without knocking it off on the floor. The hilt scraped the wood a little. She glanced back at the curtained bed, but her father didn't stir. She considered the brown wool fabric cloaking her father from her view, praying he didn't have another sword hidden in his bedding. Worrying her bottom lip, she stiffened, then pulled the curtain aside.

And froze.

He *wasn't* alone.

Shocked and appalled, Edana couldn't stop her mouth from gaping.

His back to her, he was naked, his arms around one of the scullery maids, the covers down about their ankles. Zenevieva opened her brown eyes. They widened at first, but then seeing it was only Edana, she smiled maliciously.

Her heart thundering in her ears, Edana dropped the curtain back in place before her father discovered what she'd seen. Thankfully—as much as she shook—she hadn't dropped the candle, or spilled hot wax on her father. She turned on her heel and hurried out of his bedchamber, upset and angry with him and with Zenevieva, but worried about her brothers still.

After what she'd witnessed, she considered not bothering to tell her father when he woke this morn about what she'd heard. Instead, she could gather a small escort to accompany her to find her brothers and do this strictly on her own.

But she couldn't do it. She always—well, most always—had done the right thing when she'd grown old enough to know right from wrong.

She would see her father and tell him what she'd heard Kayne reveal to her. Then she'd decide what to do next. She feared her father would dismiss her concern and not do anything about it. Just as he had rejected her alarms on many other occasions. Did denying the truth make it go away? No, but he would rather ignore her than deal with her strange curse. Or gift.

She returned to her chamber, removed her brat, and slipped into her green léine, then fastened her brat over that. It was still too early for her to get up for the morn, though some servants were moving about below stairs, but she couldn't sleep any further.

Rubbing the sleep from her green eyes, Una raised her head from her palette and frowned at Edana. "What time is it? 'Tis no' time for us to rise. Is it?"

"My brothers have warned me they are in trouble." Edana slipped one of her chemises into a leather pouch.

"What?" Una asked sharply, jerking aside

her covers and untwisting her chemise from around her legs before she jumped up from her pallet. She considered Edana's pouch. "You... you are packing."

Una's hair was a light brown with no hint of red like Edana's, and she stood taller. Which meant Una didn't have to reach up so high nor did a clansman have to lower his head so far to kiss her. Not that Edana had any experience with that. No lad had wanted to kiss the witch, and when she grew older—though Una had said she was bonny often enough—no man had come close to even attempting to kiss Edana. But she had seen Una kissing one of the guards once.

"What is wrong?" Una asked, quickly getting dressed.

"Kayne called out to me and said he was imprisoned in a dungeon. Or at least I fear his words meant that."

Una paused to look at her. "And Gildas?"

Edana *knew* Una liked her second eldest brother, though she'd denied it often enough. Una was two years younger than Gildas, and she was two years older than Edana. Both of them would be too old for any man to wed if they did not marry soon.

"I...I dinna know. They could all be in the

same dungeon. If 'twas only Kayne, the others would have come home to let us know. Kayne wouldna have needed to send word to me."

"Sometimes you said it happens anyway. That even if someone else is there to aid the stricken person, his or her fright is..." Una waved her hands about in a familiar gesture of trying to describe the bizarre way Edana could hear someone's terror. "...forced into your thoughts."

"Aye," Edana said, dejectedly as she continued to pack.

"Have you told the chief? Are we going with his blessing?"

Edana's eyes filled with tears. Her mother had died only last winter. How could her father have taken Zenevieva into his bed this spring? The woman didn't care for her father. Edana had overheard Zenevieva complaining often enough about her father's faults—he was too harsh, too demanding, too *old*. Did she think she could worm her way into his bed and then become his wife? Even if he was too old? And thereby elevate her position from working in the kitchen?

Edana had heard from Cook often enough how lazy Zenevieva was and how if she didn't move more quickly, she would beat her.

Her eyes blurry with unshed tears, Edana ground her teeth, trying to keep her emotions in check, and looked Una in the face. But she couldn't say the words.

"What is wrong?" Una asked, her anxious expression changing to alarm. She seized Edana's hand. "Your brothers... they are all right?"

"I dinna know." She looked away from Una. She couldn't keep the secret of her father and Zenevieva sleeping together even though she was ashamed of her father and didn't want anyone to know the truth. Una would continue pestering her until she told her what had happened.

"What, then? Tell me."

Straightening her shoulders, Edana faced Una. "I went to speak to my father about what Kayne had revealed to me. My father was with Zenevieva in his chamber."

Eyes wide, her lower lip dropped, Una stared at Edana. She finally found her tongue and whispered, "Nay."

"Aye." Edana hastily brushed away the tears she'd managed to keep at bay until now. It was as though spilling her secret had opened the way for the tears to spill as well.

Una pulled her into a warm embrace. She was supposed to be Edana's maid and companion, one of the guard's daughters, but once she had come to live with them, she had become more like a sister. She was the only one who had treated Edana's abilities with a mixture of awe and concern. Never with disbelief. Nor had she regarded Edana as if she was cursed like others had, though most attempted to hold their tongues when she, her brothers, and her father were within hearing. Her family would not have approved of such talk.

But that was one of the reasons Una was her maid—to ensure that Edana remained chaste. Even though an older woman normally served in that capacity as a younger woman might easily be convinced to look the other way if Edana had wanted to see a lad in secret. In truth, no man wished to touch Edana in that manner anyway, so her father must have decided she would be safe enough with a woman nearly her age.

"They were…," Una said, leaving the rest of her words unspoken.

"They were *together*."

Una pulled away to look at her, ripe

speculation written all over her face. Eagerness. Morbid curiosity.

"We must prepare to leave if my da says he willna do anything about my brothers." Edana did not wish to speak another word about the matter concerning her father and that woman.

"He…didna see that you saw him with…Zenevieva?" Una asked, sounding uncertain whether she should bring it up.

Edana took a deep breath and released it. "Nay…but Zenevieva did."

Una's eyes grew wide again. "Och, she is the devil."

"She would say, and has said, that *I* am."

"Nay. You are…gifted." Una looked at the floor for a moment, then back at Edana. "You must tell no one."

"I hadna planned to. No' even you."

"Nay, telling me was the right thing to do. Zenevieva would like naught better than to claim she has your da's heart. If you say anything about this to anyone else, word will spread that she has been in his bed."

"Do you no' think she will do the deed herself?" Edana asked, infuriated.

She wasn't happy her father would lay with any woman, but Edana had to be reasonable. If he found himself another wife, Edana wanted it to be someone she cared for. Trouble was that because of her abilities, no one cared for *her*.

"First we deal with the issue of your brothers. Then we take care of the other matter."

"What would your plan be?" Edana asked Una because she was older, even though Edana always had her own plan in mind. More than half the time they both had the same notion.

"You will tell your da about the message from Kayne as you had intended. And then if your da does naught about it, we find a couple of guardsmen who dinna have duty for a couple of days and nights. Aye? Think you we can locate your brothers before then?"

"That was my thinking on the matter. Which is why I confided in you in the first place. Because your da is a guard, you know the men better than I do."

"Aye." Una licked her lips as if she was nervous about something. Then she said, "If Seumas wishes to go, you must say nay."

"Seumas?" Then the reason dawned on Edana. "Because he kissed you and you kissed him back?" And Una didn't want him knowing she wished to rescue Gildas.

"Nay. He would most likely attempt to stop

us from leaving. As to Zenevieva? Once we, well, *you* tell your brothers about that, they can deal with her."

"My...brothers?" Edana could do a lot of things, but tell them she'd found their father naked in bed with another woman? Her body grew hot with humiliation.

"*I* canna tell them," Una said, packing the rest of what they'd need on their journey, evidently suspecting the same as Edana—her father wouldn't do anything and they would be forced to leave with a small escort without his consent. "He is *your* da and *you* saw him with her, no' me."

"Do you think *I* could tell my brothers that I had spied my da and Zenevieva in bed together naked?" Edana whispered.

Una's mouth dropped open. "God's wounds. In truth?"

Edana took a deep breath and nodded. She thought Una had realized...

"I thought they would have been covered up. Mayhap wearing something. Naught at all?"

"The covers were down around their ankles." Edana felt her face warm, but Una's face blushed in color, too.

"You shouldna have seen that."

"Aye," Edana said. "'Tis my fondest wish I hadna. Are you ready?"

"Aye. Should your talk with your da prove useless, I will have to ensure we ask two of the guards who wouldna tell *my* da of our mission, or we willna be going anywhere."

\*\*\*

Later that morning, Edana joined her father at the high table to break their fast, having an awful time meeting his eye. Though he seemed to be suffering from the same condition. Had that horrible woman told him Edana had seen them naked together? Her whole body felt it was on fire, she was so mortified.

Her father was speaking to one of his men, ignoring her. She touched his arm to get his attention. She couldn't wait for the meal to end to tell him what her brother had said to her.

Glowering, her father turned cold blues eyes on her, his dark brown brows pinched together.

"Da, I need to let you know what Kayne told me," Edana said, attempting to keep her voice steady.

"Is that why you sneaked into my chamber this morn?" he asked, his voice angry, but low.

He *knew*. Zenevieva, the witch, had told

21

him.

"*Never* enter my chamber without my permission again," he growled low for her hearing only.

She wanted to crawl under the table, yet she tried to bolster herself with the notion she'd embarrassed her father by catching him with Zenevieva in his bed and that he hadn't wanted her to know. Now he didn't have any idea how to deal with her concerning the whole horrible matter.

Despite telling herself that, she felt her eyes fill with tears. If she stayed a moment longer, those same tears would be flowing down her cheeks. He'd always adored her—or so he had acted—because she was his only daughter.

When her mother was alive, he'd had enough love for them both. Now that her mother was gone, she assumed another woman would take her mother's place and Edana would no longer matter to him.

Feeling guilty, ashamed, and unworthy, she dropped her gaze, which instantly made the tears begin to roll down her face. "May I be excused?" she asked, her voice soft, choked, as she refused to look at her father.

"Aye, go," he snapped, as if he wished

never to see her again.

She quickly left her chair and headed out of the great hall. If she could have done so, she would have obliged him. Una jumped up from the bench she was sharing with others at one of the lower tables and hurried after her.

"You didna get his permission, did you?" Una asked gently, as she redirected Edana from the spiral stairs to her chamber, and out the door of the keep instead, heading straight for the stable.

"Nay. He knew I saw him with Zenevieva. The woman told him."

Una sighed. "I knew that witch would. I was watching you the whole time, saw your da speak to you, and witnessed your reaction. He was angry."

"Aye, and he had every right to be."

"You have always gone to your father's chamber if there is a great need. He has always welcomed you to speak with him no matter the time of day or night. Even if he chose not to believe what you had to say."

"No longer. He said I am never to enter his chamber again without his permission. Though I would never wish to after what I saw."

"So we go without your da's permission?"

"He wished me gone. Out of his sight. We will find my brothers and my da can do whatever he wishes to do with the scullery maid. 'Twill be none of my concern."

Yet it would be. Even thinking he would be with that hateful woman where her dear sweet mother once had lain with her father made her heart shrivel.

"I... already spoke to two of the guards. Seumas is coming with us, through no fault of my own," Una warned.

Alarmed, Edana glanced at Una as they crossed the inner bailey to reach the stables. "You said he wouldna let you go."

"I thought so. But he wanted to come, knowing we would go anyway. He overheard me talking to the other guard. Seumas said he believed you."

"Good. Then let's be on our way." Mayhap she could convince her brothers, if she could rescue them, to talk their father out of his folly. Though she would not tell them she had seen him naked with the scullery maid.

*\*\**

Standing in his older brother's solar at Craigly Castle, Angus MacNeill stared at James in disbelief. Aye, James was laird of their clan and he could set any task before him and Angus would be obliged and honored to carry it out. Normally. But this time, Angus was desperately trying to come up with another solution to the problem. His brother's angular jaw was set as he sat at his table, and Angus was certain he wouldn't be able to change his mind. Not when he looked *that* determined.

Their cousin, Niall, as much a brother to Angus and the rest of his brothers, was quietly waiting near the doorway to see what would happen next, not about to get himself tasked with such an assignment. He had a slighter build, not as muscular as Angus and his three brothers, but he had the same quick wit and smile, his dark hair much curlier, his eyes a darker brown. Gunnolf, their Norseman friend, blond with sharp blue eyes and sturdy features that said Viking warrior, was leaning against the wall, wearing a smirk.

"I canna see why Edana's own brothers wouldna be the ones to fetch the wee lass home," Angus said.

His dark gaze on Angus, James shook his head. "Her *da* sent her brothers on an errand, and they willna be returning for a fortnight. In the interim, you would reach their lands sooner than they would."

"Surely Tibold has other clansmen he could send to retrieve her, who are in the area and could find her more quickly." Angus would stick his life on the line to protect a beautiful young woman. But the time it would take to travel to the chief's lands, in Angus's estimation, placed the lass at greater peril.

"She needs…special care," James said.

Angus frowned at his brother, knowing fair well the special care he mentioned. Angus was certain forcing her to return home would mean tangling with the lassie—and that would not be a good thing. Not that he didn't want to see her again—he did, but under better circumstances. He just didn't want his family to know how much so. Nor did he want to upset her in any way.

Even her name meant fiery, and she had a temper to match. He'd never been able to banish her from his thoughts since that fateful day when she'd proved she was one of the fae. Her dark brown hair had a reddish cast to it, and that made her look all the more wild when she became angered. She had bewitched him from the very beginning.

"Why did she run off?" Angus asked.

"Her da didna say."

"Did he no' know?" Angus asked, suspecting it had something to do with her fae abilities.

"He just sent a messenger, Angus. The lad only told me what her da requested of me."

Angus had a few adventures under his belt, and many more that he was interested in enjoying, but this one bothered him more than he wished to say. Niall was excited about going on more adventures also—now that he wasn't tagging along with Dougald, which invariably meant a stay in a dark, dank dungeon—except he also looked reluctant, wary.

Gunnolf was ready for *any* adventure, even if it landed him in a dungeon. And even if it had to do with Edana. In fact, Angus thought their friend looked hopeful that James would send him if Angus managed to talk his way out of this.

"So send Niall." Angus waved his hand at his cousin, who looked as though he didn't want the task any more than Angus did. He swore Niall paled a little at being included in the conversation.

"He is more afraid of the wee lass than you are." James's eyes sparkled with dark humor.

"I am no' afraid of the lass," Angus said vehemently. He wasn't. More than anything, he didn't wish to upset her. That wasn't the same thing as being afraid of her as much as he felt concerned about her feelings.

Straightening his back, Niall protested, "Nay, I am no' afraid of the lass. *I* will return her to her *da*."

Deep down, Angus wanted to be the one to find the fae woman and send her home. He still feared distressing her when she must already be in such a state or she wouldn't have left the keep without her father's blessing. He was certain James would command he go anyway, and then the matter would be out of his hands. But if James chose Niall to go? Angus would have to go nevertheless. Just to see that the task was handled in as proper a manner as possible, considering who the girl was.

James paused, considering the notion for only the briefest moment, then shook his head and rose from his chair, his decision made. "You will go, Angus. You are the only one of my brothers who is available. We have been friends with the Clan Chattan forever. The chief has asked our help, specifically, for me to send one of my brothers. And as such, you are assigned to the task. I wish this matter taken care of at once. You will gather as many men as you deem necessary."

"To locate the wee lass and return her to her castle?" Angus snorted. "I will need no one." At least he didn't want anyone to see what would happen when he tried to make the girl mind. She was an untamed wildcat, and he still wasn't sure what she could do with her strange abilities. He paused, another concern coming to mind because of what they had witnessed of her in the past. "She didna run off alone, did she? Surely someone is with her."

"The chief didna know for certain. He is trying to account for everyone. He hopes she has an escort, but no matter what the situation is—escort or no'—he wants her returned home at once."

Angus folded his arms.

James sighed in the way that said he was deeply exasperated with his brother. "You will gather an accompaniment of men, your choice as to the number and who you wish to take with you."

"Aye," Angus finally conceded. He glanced at Niall, who looked somewhat relieved it wasn't his job, but a little worried that Angus might choose him to go. "Then since Niall is unafraid of the lass and wishes some adventure, and Gunnolf doesna believe in our Gaelic mysticism, they will come with me."

"Good. Dinna tarry. Every day the lass is missing, the more her da believes some harm has come to her."

After having fought in the Crusades alongside his brothers, Angus would prefer *that* to the task at hand. "We will go now."

And with that, Angus, Niall, and Gunnolf left his brother's solar to ready themselves for the journey. "Dinna look so worried, Cousin," Angus said to Niall, as they headed to their chambers to pack. "You said you would find and return her yourself. Just dinna rile her."

Gunnolf chuckled. "We probably willna land in a dungeon this time, Niall. Which will be a good thing. Dougald usually is the one who can get us out of one. And he willna be with us."

The Norseman was always game for an adventure, and he looked pleased to be going on this one. Niall looked unsure, as if he had spoken too soon about rescuing one wee bonny lass. But this was one that Angus would have preferred someone else deal with.

# Chapter 2

Lightning and the resounding boom of thunder shook the ground as Edana and her escort traveled away from Rondover Castle while she continued to listen for her brothers' pleas, praying their silent entreaty could aid her in finding them. A low cloud hung overhead, while the wind and cold and a wet drizzle persisted in stalking her party. Seumas stuck close to Una, while Kipper rode beside Edana.

"Have you heard anything more, lass?" Kipper asked. He and Seumas were about the same tall height as her brothers, but Kipper was heavier, older, mayhap in his thirties, his face more weathered. Seumas was nine and twenty, the same age as Edana's oldest brother.

"Nay," she said, shaking her head. She'd heard Gildas cry out, cursing unlike she'd ever witnessed before, and she had let her party know. But not about the cursing.

They deviated in the direction she thought she heard his voice. It was as though the words were spoken aloud and the hearer could pinpoint the speaker's location. But his voice sounded still far too distant.

Then the weather worsened, the sky turning a murderous greenish-black. Before they could prepare themselves for the torrent and with no shelter that they could find, the ominous skies let loose a drenching rain. Chunks of ice intermingling with the rain fell from the heavens. Lightning forked into the low lying hills and thunder boomed almost on top of it. Heart pumping, Edana attempted to get her horse under control as the others were struggling with their own mounts.

The rain and chips of ice were coming down so hard, she couldn't hear anything but the roar of water in her ears as her horse galloped off, threatening to dump her and be on its way.

"Nay, Nana," Edana shouted, trying to get the mare to slow down before she injured a leg, took a tumble, and Edana was thrown.

"Nana, whoa!"

But the horse continued on its hell-bent course across the glen, not minding her master, the mare's only interest—survival.

Which was Edana's as well, but she feared she would not make it if she couldn't get Nana under control.

She seemed to have galloped for miles before her frightened horse calmed a bit. Edana was soaking wet, her brat that had once served as a hooded cloak of waterproof wool, had slipped from her head during the wild ride. The rainwater saturated her hair and ran down her neck, managing to soak her léine and chemise.

The mare finally slowed to a canter, then to a walk as the rains lessened, the lightning still intermittingly illuminating the sky and the thunder booming or crackling nearby.

Edana considered where they were—at the forested edge of a stream, and thinking she knew their location, she headed north. Or should she have gone south? Somewhere along the river, a shieling was built into the side of a rock face and that would provide welcome shelter. Hoping her escort would think to go there, she could dry her sopping wet clothes also.

She began calling her companions' names, but no one responded in the chilly rain. She clucked at her mare to encourage her to move a little faster as they climbed the slight incline through the trees lining the stream.

In the blinding rainstorm, she knew for certain she had lost her escort. The two men of her father's guard were not scheduled to serve on duty for three days. Una had feigned visiting a sick aunt at a croft several miles away. Kipper had only agreed to go with Edana, fearing she was right and her father wrong and wished to aid her. If they could locate her brothers before her father could send out men in search of her, all would be well. Seumas joined them because of Una, not wishing anyone else to be with her. None of them wanted Edana searching the countryside for her brothers unaccompanied.

Yet now she was alone. Not that she feared being on her own. She was used to being by herself until Una came to stay with them three years earlier.

Cold and wet, she heard her brother Kayne call to her again—*Drummond*, was the only word she could make out. Her youngest brother. Was he all right? She prayed it was so and tried not to worry as she could do nothing but continue to look for them in the morn. When her brother's name had swept across her thoughts, from the sound of it, she was certain she was headed in the right direction still.

If she continued to follow her brothers' cries, she hoped to discover their whereabouts before long. She refused to return to the keep until she knew where her brothers were being held or her father would most likely lock her in her chambers for a fortnight when they were scheduled to come home.

Movement in the woods made her heart quicken. If it had been her escort, they would have called out to her.

On foot, the two men suddenly appeared, dark beards, long wet hair, dirty tunics, plaids just as filthy, muddy from all the rain. Thieves. The one had ice blue eyes. She didn't have time to see the other's.

"Look what we have here," the blue-eyed man said, grabbing for her reins.

She kicked out with her foot as hard as she could, hitting him squarely in the chest, knocking him off-balance. He tripped backward over a downed tree and swore words she'd never heard before. Getting the better of him had been pure luck because he had not expected her to fight. She couldn't let these men get hold of her.

The other man was laughing at his companion, but when he attempted to grab her reins, she managed to unsheathe her sword—the small size fashioned just for her by her father's armorer—and slashed at the brigand. To avoid the slice of her blade, he dove back so quickly, he lost his footing and fell on his arse in the mud.

She charged off. On foot, they'd never catch up to her. But what if they found her when she tried to sleep during the night?

Her heart thundered as she pushed her horse onward at a gallop until she felt it was safe to walk her again. If it wasn't for the fear her brothers could be in danger if she did not find them, she would return to the safety of the keep. She felt she had no choice but to continue on.

For now, she headed for the haunted shieling where she could sleep under a thatched roof this eve and hoped to reach it before gloaming.

Alone with her thoughts, she wondered if the guards who had accompanied her knew about her father and Zenevieva. The woman would most likely spread the word about her being with the chief if she had not already done so. Despite the cold seeping into her bones, for an instant, Edana felt hot with anger.

Had she told everyone that Edana had spied them together? So that if their clansmen and women did not believe her, Zenevieva could say Edana was her witness? Edana wouldn't put it past the woman. What if Edana declared she *hadn't* visited her father's chamber? That Zenevieva had lied about the whole sordid affair? Who would they believe if she told everyone she had not witnessed her father in bed with the scullery maid? But what if her own father admitted to having been with the woman? Then everything Edana did to cover up what she'd seen would be for naught.

Edana clenched her teeth to try to stop the shivers racking her body. Soaked to the skin, she was freezing. She hoped she'd reach the shieling soon. And tried to think of anything but of how upset she was with her father and Zenevieva. Edana prayed she'd hear something more from one of her brothers.

She had to concentrate on the darker concern. Her brothers *weren't* coming home. Not when they were manacled in a dungeon somewhere. She'd felt their anger, heard their pleas directed at her to find them and free them, could almost see them.

*"Edana, manacled, dungeon, blindfolded, help,"* Gildas suddenly said. Torn, she knew she needed to head in a more westerly direction, but she had to find the shelter and stay there until morn.

She rode forever, it seemed, before she

spied the abandoned stone shieling built into the side of a hill near the stream she had been following. Relieved, she sighed, looking forward to sleeping in the shelter and not slumbering under the stars or mist or drizzle while the chilly breeze cloaked her this eve. And hoped her escort would also find their way here before long.

Stiff with cold, she dismounted, then pulled her horse into the byre built against the side of the stone shieling. The family had died during a winter snowstorm, and most others she knew talked about the place but would not draw near. She had never felt anything but comfort here. For now, she was miles from home after weaving her way back and forth across the moors and glens, trying to pick up a signal from her brothers.

She prayed to God they would still be alive by the time she reached them.

*** 

Angus ate a chunk of bannock with Niall and Gunnolf, huddled together for a brief moment in the gloaming mist before they headed out again, not even bothering with a fire. Once they'd reached the Chattan's lands, they'd searched everywhere for the wee lass. They'd been in one drenching rain shower after another, and had only a quick respite to grab a bite to eat before the next downpour, he was certain, the way their luck had been holding out.

Angus had the sinking feeling, Edana had come to harm. He should have known how difficult it would be to find her. Yet, he'd had it in mind she would have given up whatever her reason for leaving home and returned by now. But a farmer they had come across who worked for the chief said the lass was still missing.

"Why do you think the lass left the castle as she did?" Niall asked Angus.

Angus drank some of his mead. "James said the chief didna know. But I suspect her da *did* know and was afraid to say."

"Something to do with her being *special*?" Niall asked.

"Aye, I am certain of it. If you had a daughter who had run off on some fae errand, would you tell the men who sought to find her and bring her home that was the reason she had disappeared?" Angus asked.

"Nay. I would keep her motive for leaving a secret," Niall agreed.

"Aye. As would I."

"So why did he no' send his *own* men?"

Niall asked.

Angus raised his brows at his cousin. "Her brothers would be one thing. Mayhap the Chattan's men are afraid of her."

"'Tis a good thing we are no'," Niall said with a smug smile. "I never knew what she actually did. Do you?"

"Nay, no' exactly. When we visited the one time while you were sick in bed, she was extremely distraught. From what her maid told us, lads and lassies alike had teased her about her abilities for years. But that day, Edana was frantic to get help for a lass she feared was drowning. Three lads and a lass taunted her, told her the girl pretended to be injured and drowning to see if the witch would know the truth or no'. Edana slapped the lass provoking her across the face and punched one of the boys in the stomach before she ran off to the river nearby. I have never seen such a wildcat in action before."

And Angus hadn't known what to think, but he had been worried about her.

"No one from the Chattan clan bothered to follow her. Her brothers had ridden off to race with some other lads before they knew of the trouble. We were concerned for Edana's safety.

We were no' sure if what the others said was true or no'. James took charge of us, like he always did, and told us we were going after the lass. We searched for a good long while before we heard her sobbing. I expected to see her sitting by the river, her pride wounded, crying. But what we found was something altogether different. She struggled to pull a much older and bigger girl from the water, her body wedged between two boulders, reeds tangled in her hair, her brat and léine soaking wet and weighing the girl down."

Niall took a deep breath. "The lass was dead. I remember now. But we never knew how Edana discerned the girl was drowning. Was it like Lady Anice who sees something of the future?"

"Nay, no' like that. 'Tis something different, though I know no' what. Gunnolf ran back to the keep to tell the chief the news. Dougald and I carried the dead girl home. James and Malcolm, being that they were older, had to subdue Edana. She was terribly distraught that the others jested about her abilities and ultimately their sport had caused the lass to truly drown. Edana didna wish to return home."

"So that is why you didna wish to go on this

mission. You already know how much of a challenge the lass will be," Niall said, wisely.

"If 'tis anything like the last time, aye. And you see why James sent *me* this time? He knew what we are in for."

Gunnolf was quietly contemplating their words, and Angus turned to him. "What think you, Gunnolf?"

"Chattan asked James to send one of his brothers. He undoubtedly knows you are the only one left at Craigly Castle. You dinna think the chief has something in mind other than just bringing the wee lassie home, do you?"

"What other reason could there be?"

Gunnolf shook his head.

Angus frowned at his friend. "Speak your mind, mon. What other reason would it be?"

"Mayhap he believed because of the kindness you and your brothers showed to the lass before—now that she is full grown—you would fall in love with her once you set eyes upon her again and wish to marry her. When no others would."

Angus stared at Gunnolf as if he'd become the jester for King Henry's court. He shook his head. "'Twas James and Malcolm who took the lass in hand and returned her to the keep."

"Aye, but 'twas you who asked about her welfare the three remaining days we were there when she refused to take meals in the great hall," Gunnolf said.

"And before that," Niall said, "I heard Malcolm say the lass had caught your eye."

She had, and Angus had regretted every day since then that he hadn't spoken to her beforehand to offer his friendship as Malcolm had said he should.

Angus mounted his horse, considering the notion, then dismissed it. "Nay. He knows the lass would be safe in our hands and that we have aided her before. Naught more."

"*Ja*," Gunnolf said, trying to look serious, but a teasing light shown in his eyes.

Angus didn't believe for one moment that Chattan thought Angus would have any interest in the lass beyond locating her and returning her home. It wasn't the first time Gunnolf had come up with an outlandish saga to explain a situation—and he had turned out to be wrong. Angus wondered if Gunnolf's storytelling was a gift handed down to him by his own family, way before Gunnolf ended up with the MacNeills.

He kicked his horse. The others quickly joined him and they were again on their way.

Angus hoped they would find the lass soon, not believing she could make it this far on her own. They had slept on and off, tired beyond measure, but they wouldn't stop until they found her.

Some hours after they'd begun their journey again, they smelled smoke from a peat fire carried on the chilly breeze. Like before, they headed in the direction of the shieling, to speak to the inhabitants, to see if anyone had seen the wee lassie recently. Praying that they would have some success in learning she had returned home on her own.

\*\*\*

Hearing horses approach, Edana quickly roused from a troubled sleep, worried sick about her brothers, unable to reach them with her special ability. And concerned beyond measure for her traveling companions also. Were they safe? She had hoped they would have thought to come here and been here long before this.

Naked and wrapped only in one of her wool blankets, having discarded her brat, léine, and chemise next to the fire to dry earlier that eve, she listened carefully to the hoof beats. Three horses approached, she believed.

She'd barred the door, but would it be

enough?

She quickly stumbled from the pallet she'd made of her remaining two wool blankets. She glanced around the dark room lit only by the small peat fire that helped to take the chill off the stone shieling. The one-room abode was furnished with only a table and two chairs. Hoping this would do, she shoved the table across the stone floor. The table legs scraped against it, and she cringed, knowing whoever approached would hear her moving about. Well, and the smoke from the fire would clue them in that someone was within.

Her mare. Och, they could take her horse. She loved her mare and could not allow anyone to steal her. Beyond that, how could she go much of anywhere without her?

She could never find her brothers in time if she were on foot.

# Chapter 3

Her heart beating wildly, Edana pulled her spare chemise out of her bag and slipped it over her head. She stood near the table shoved up against the door and listened to the sounds of the horses approaching, their hooves clomping on the muddy ground, and tried to judge how far away they were. They were a good distance still, mayhap.

What of her horse?

She couldn't leave her alone in the byre. What if the men decided to steal her? She had time to take care of her mare before the travelers were upon her. She believed.

Wishing she'd thought of it sooner and hoping she wouldn't get her only dry piece of clothing too wet, she hurried to pull the table away from the door, the legs scraping again, making her cringe at hearing the noise she was creating. If the riders heard it, they would think her mad, moving furniture back and forth in the middle of the night. But she would not allow them to steal her horse.

She yanked open the door and looked out into the ghostly gloom. She saw no one. Judging by the sound of the horses' hoof steps, they truly were a ways off.

Heartened by the knowledge, she rushed to move her mare from the byre, the rain having turned to a thick wet mist. Darkness cloaked the byre, and in a panic, Edana fumbled around, trying to grab her mare's reins. Spooked, her mare reacted skittishly, shaking her head, sidestepping away from Edana.

She whispered to her, "Nana, come." She cooed to her, speaking encouragingly, soothingly until she had moved her out of the byre and hurried her to the door of the shieling. Edana was instantly cold all over again and shivering.

When she tried to move her mare into the shieling, Nana balked.

"Nana, come," Edana said again, her voice hushed, pleading, comforting—although terror filled her as she tried to quiet her own fears.

Finally, the mare took a step, her hooves clicking on the stone floor, and then another step and another, until she was all the way inside. As soon as Edana had moved her far enough into the room, she squeezed by her to close the door. Then she again barred it and shoved the table against it.

Brushing her hands off, satisfied she and her mare were perfectly safe, she watched the door, listening as the horses grew closer. No one said a word. She suspected the travelers would be male, and no woman would be among them.

With every step they took that brought them closer, she felt her heart beat a little faster.

The horses stopped right outside the door. The table secure against it, she stepped back, watching it, afraid whoever had come might attempt to break it down.

Nobody said anything, but the horses nickered and whinnied. And her mare, traitor that she was, called back to them.

"There is a...horse inside the shieling," a man said with a Norseman's accent, sounding half surprised and half amused.

Had the Norsemen invaded their shores again? She stepped farther away from the door, her heart racing.

A soft knock on the door followed.

She barely breathed, her hands to her chest, her eyes fixed on the door.

"We are looking for someone," a man said, his heavenly voice, deep and intriguing, though commanding.

She tilted her head to the side. Where had she heard that voice before? Deeper than she remembered it. More manly.

"We are looking for a lass by the name of Edana," the same man said. "We wish to speak to you and learn if you know anything of her whereabouts."

They knew her. They'd come for her.

They did not wish to talk. They meant to turn her over to her father. Who were they? No one from her own clan. At least she did not recognize the man as someone from her clan.

"Nay!" she said. "Go away. The woman you seek isna here." She made her voice sound much older, gruffer, scarier. They would not think she was Edana. Then she realized her mistake at once. They had not believed she was here. They had only wished to learn if the occupant of the shieling had seen her.

*** 

Recognizing the woman's voice, no matter how much she tried to disguise it, Angus shook his head at Niall and Gunnolf as they waited for him to decide how to handle the wildcat locked in the shieling.

They didn't know who the shieling belonged to, but no one would take a horse into it unless she was a madwoman, or a lass who was trying to protect her mount.

God's knees, he didn't know how he was going to get her to open up so he could speak with her. He stared at the door, sure she stared right back at it from the other side.

He couldn't believe she'd moved her horse into the shieling!

He tried to reassure her first that they were friends, not foe. "'Tis Angus MacNeill, my cousin, Niall, and friend, Gunnolf. Do you remember us? We have been friends of your family's clan forever. We wish you no harm. Let us in so we may speak."

"Nay, 'tis the middle of the night. I am sleeping. Go away."

This time she didn't bother to use her old woman's voice, which didn't serve to deceive him in the least anyway. "You are no' talking in your sleep. Open up."

She didn't respond.

"I dinna want to ruin a good door, but I will if it means getting out of this cold, wet weather to speak with you."

She still didn't say anything. He knew she hadn't returned to her pallet to sleep. Instead, she was waiting, tense, worried, wondering what he would do next.

He wasn't sure. He wasn't going to tear down the door unless he had to.

Gunnolf and Niall moved the horses into the byre and were wiping them down as Angus continued to stand in the thick chilly mist. "We are no' leaving. So you can let me in now or later, but we are no' going—"

"You are planning a siege? Of a shieling?"

He heard Niall and Gunnolf chuckle in the byre. He couldn't help but smile himself.

"Is this how you train for grander glory?" she asked, as if getting her second wind.

His cousin and friend laughed.

Though Angus couldn't help being somewhat amused, the night was late and he was cold and wet and tired. He folded his arms and glowered at the door, wondering if the lass would have matched wits with him when they were young. Again, he regretted not having spoken to her back then. "No one need lay siege to a castle when the treasure lies within a shieling just waiting to be plucked."

That shut her up. He certainly didn't mean

that *he* saw her as a treasure. More that someone in her clan would. Her father at the very least. Not that Angus didn't find the lass intriguing and bonny. But at this very moment, he saw her as the wildcat of his youth.

Even Niall and Gunnolf remained silent as they waited for her response.

"Angus?" she said very sweetly.

*Finally.* He hadn't thought she'd respond, but she still wasn't moving the furniture that had to be blocking the door, if that was the cause of the noise they'd heard emanating from the shieling upon their approach.

"Aye?" he said.

"You have come to the wrong shieling."

His friends laughed.

"Open up, Edana," he said, louder this time, demanding. He'd ridden far too long in bad weather, worried sick about her, to put up with any games she might wish to play.

She didn't open the door. Of course. She was a wildcat and witch all in one.

Angus called out, "Gunnolf, ride to her da's castle. Tell him we have found the lass if they want to come and get her."

This would be in her father's hands then. Her father could break down the shieling door, toss the lass on a horse, and take her home where he could lock her in a tower room.

Angus's job—locate the lass and protect her—would be done.

"*Ja*," Gunnolf said, and led his own horse out of the byre.

Angus was certain she'd open the door to the shieling. But if she *didn't*, his plan would proceed.

Gunnolf mounted his horse, the leather creaking as he seated himself. He waited for Angus's signal to ride off.

Niall watched them, waiting to see what happened also.

When she didn't open the door, Angus said, "Make haste, Gunnolf. At least you will have a warmer place to bed down the rest of the night while her father sends men to come for the lass."

"*Ja.*" Gunnolf nudged his horse forward, then began to trot away.

Angus waited for Edana to capitulate.

She didn't.

Niall raised his brows at him. Well, it had been a worthy idea, Angus thought.

The clip-clops of the horse's hooves grew more distant.

"Tell him to stop!" Edana cried out.

Angus smiled, then tossed over his shoulder, "Gunnolf, the lass is opening her door to us. You may return your horse to the byre."

*And hers, once she opened the door.*

While he listened to a table scraping across the stone floor away from the door, he envisioned the girl of his youth and wondered just who had won the battle.

***

Edana should have known a Highlander who had fought in the Crusades would outmaneuver her, though she thought he might break down the door rather than attempt to outwit her. She had to admit she admired him for not doing so.

Most men she knew wouldn't have bothered with any attempts to secure her concession, but barged right in and forced it on her. Not that she still didn't suspect Angus might do just that once he gained entrance to the shieling.

She waited, dirk in hand, because they weren't going to take her back to her father. Unfortunately, she'd have to tell them her reasoning for being here, suspecting her father had not told Angus and his companions what it was—although how could her father have told anybody when he hadn't allowed her to have her say? If she had managed to tell him her errand and he had revealed this to Angus and his friends, they most likely wouldn't have come.

Angus didn't shove the door aside like she expected him to as if he was waiting for an invitation.

In exasperation, she let out her breath. She hated to have to invite him in as if it was *her* idea. "Come in!"

Angus pushed the door open, but he did not step inside the shieling. Dripping with water and filling the doorframe—much taller than she remembered him to be—he appeared menacing and dark, despite his words of friendship. He glanced into the room. What did he think? She had a whole army of men waiting in here with her, ready to wage war with him?

He raised his brows to see her armed. Then he smiled at her horse. "The byre wasna warm enough for her?" His smile was amused, his dark brown eyes taking in her whole appearance, and she realized her damp chemise was clinging to her body.

Her whole body instantly warmed, but she couldn't grab one of the blankets to wrap around herself and still hold her dirk readied for a fight.

She wasn't going to respond to his comment about her mare either. He knew full well why she had moved Nana in here.

"I told you we wished you no harm, lass," Angus said, moving around her to reach Nana's reins, and Edana quickly stepped back, his size and closeness making her fearful.

In that brief instant, she felt his body heat radiating toward her, smelled him—rainwater, leather, man, and horse. And took another deep breath of him.

He clucked at her mare to get her to back up because there wasn't any way to turn her around inside the small room. She was looking a little wild-eyed, and Edana thought she would have to take over and coax her horse out of the shieling. But Angus was gentle with the mare, speaking with her as if...as if he was coaxing a woman into bed!

Though why she should think such a thing all of a sudden made her whole body burn with chagrin.

"Gunnolf, will you take the mare to the byre?" Angus called out, as he finally backed the horse outside.

"*Ja*," the man said. He took the mare's reins and said to her, "You are a fine horse, but you are still meant for a byre."

Thankfully, Angus did not comment further about the horse.

Now that her mare was gone, the place would have seemed comfortably large, but with the broad-shouldered, tall man standing inside the room, it appeared piteously small.

The last time she'd seen Angus, she had been a young lass and he had been but a lad. He was a full grown man now—his dark hair nearly black because it was sopping wet. His dark eyes took in the dirk she still held, and she felt foolish then as she saw his fine sword. Yet, she didn't set her dagger aside no matter how insignificant the weapon seemed compared to a warrior and his claymore.

He grabbed a chair, and she took a step back. But what he did next, shocked her. He removed his plaid and laid it over the chair next to the fire. And then, *the brigand*, he began to slip off his boots.

"What are you doing?" she asked, hating how breathless she sounded. His damp shirt clung to all his manly parts, his muscled chest, arms, and thighs, even his groin—revealing a part of his anatomy that was growing in size.

Fascinated, she had a devil of a time

shifting her attention away from it—as much as she knew she should. She swallowed hard and lifted her gaze from considering his rugged body to see a small smile curving his mouth.

"Drying my clothes. You wouldna want me to catch my death, would you?"

"'Tis no' my fault that you were daft enough to ride in a rainstorm."

"May we come in?" Niall asked from the doorway, like Angus, having to dip his head to enter. His hair was dark brown, curly, and short. He was lankier than Angus, the two of them being the same age.

He didn't wait for an invitation and did exactly what Angus had done. Began stripping.

Her face had to be crimson as she quickly looked away.

Gunnolf didn't ask to be invited. The blond-haired, blue-eyed Viking entered, shut the door, then barred it.

Unease slid up her spine as she instantly felt trapped.

Finding no more chairs to leave his plaid on, Gunnolf moved the table. Her clothes were lying on the hearth, as close as she could get them to the fire. And they took the only furniture to hang their clothes?

She shrank back from all the half-naked men. Before she tripped on her blankets, Angus stalked toward her, startling her, and seized the dirk from her hand. She sat down hard with a thump, attempting to put distance between them.

"We can talk now, or get some sleep first," Angus said, as Gunnolf and Niall began laying out their blankets.

"Sleep first," she quickly said.

As tired as they looked, she had every intention of slipping away while they slept. She hoped she could unbar the door without making any noise. She even thought of setting their horses free, but the horses might suffer for it, so instead, she would leave the shieling far behind while the men slept away the rest of the night. She would continue on her way to find her brothers, and she might locate the guards and Una while she was at it.

Niall tossed Angus his blanket, and the brute laid it right next to hers! Touching hers, overlapping hers.

"Nay, move it farther away," she snapped.

Angus said, "I am a very light sleeper. If you move, I will know it. I dinna want to tell your da I had to tie you up."

"He would be furious."

"He would be satisfied if he knew it meant I returned you home safely."

Angus spoke the truth. Edana would still try to slip away. Then she saw the Norseman consider where he had placed his blanket. He shook his head and moved the wool cloth right next to the door.

With his big body, or any of the men's lying there, she had no chance to slip out unnoticed. The blue-eyed devil glanced at her as he reclined on his blanket and winked, then shut his eyes to sleep.

Likewise, Niall moved his blanket so that it was at her feet. She was blocked in by walls on two sides and Angus beside her, allowing her no real escape, trapped. Angus watched her as she considered how she was surrounded.

"Satisfied?" he asked with a smirk.

He knew just what she'd been planning. She turned away from him to face the wall, closed her eyes, and tried to sleep. The room was cold, most likely because the men's plaids were blocking the heat from reaching this far into the room. Which was why *she* had spread her clothes out on the hearth!

She felt his warm body press up against her. She stifled a squeak, tried to move closer to the stone wall, but found the male figure shifted again, seeking warmth—*from her.*

"Quit trying to get away from me, lass," Angus whispered, as he wrapped his muscled arm around her, holding her still, possessing her. "You are shivering, and I dinna want you to grow ill. I will share naught more than a little heat with you."

She tried to tell herself he was like a blanket warmed on a summer's day and not a man she should stay well away from. But she couldn't. She'd never felt a man's intimate touch, even if Angus *wasn't* attempting to be intimate with her. She couldn't resist the urge to pretend he was holding her like a man would hold a woman—wanting her, yearning to kiss her— like she'd seen Seumas kiss Una—desiring to make love to her.

Realizing she'd been holding her breath, she tried to let it out without moving at all, because she thought his staff was growing hard, bigger, and she didn't want to think about what that meant. Well, mayhap a little. She believed her body was making his react in an interested, masculine way. That pleased her because she didn't think she could cause anyone to respond to her in such a manner.

She should have reviled the way in which she succumbed to enjoying the heat he shared with her, but she was glad for the extra warmth. She decided then she had to try and convince Angus and his friends how important her mission was, and maybe they'd accompany her while she searched for her brothers. And maybe he'd share a little more heat with her while they travelled—if only to ensure she didn't grow ill on the journey.

Somehow she had to convince them she wasn't crazy.

# Chapter 4

Sometime during the night, Edana had turned and was half sprawled over Angus, his blanket and hers combined to give them extra warmth, although as much as her slight body was pressed against his, he was plenty hot.

When he'd seen her as a young lass, contemplating the water in the loch from her stone perch, she'd been bonny, her hair a dark brown with a cast of red, her skin ivory—except when she'd fought with the others and then her cheeks had been positively rosy. Like she'd been when he'd perused the way she'd grown into a woman. And he saw her fully—the damp chemise clinging to her breasts, her taut nipples pressing against the cloth, the outline of her legs, the way the cloth had dipped provocatively between her legs at the juncture where his gaze had lingered on the shadow of dark red hair—fascinated.

She was beautiful—soft, warm, smelling of woman, freshly bathed after the drenching storm she'd been through. Why anyone *hadn't* already made her his wife, he didn't know. Then he reconsidered that notion. She had abilities that might chase off the most stalwart of suitors.

She'd been shivering when he first had pulled her against his body, though he wasn't sure if it had all been due to being cold and damp, or some of it was feeling his body so close to hers. Which he couldn't make behave no matter how hard he had tried. Not that he'd tried very hard for very long. He'd finally given in to the feel of her pressed against his groin, thought of what it would be like to enjoy every bit of her as a man would a woman—if she were his wife.

Her full breasts pressed against his chest now, his tunic and her chemise not in the least bit of a deterrent for feeling every bit of her. Her head was turned toward the closest wall, her light warm breath fanning his bare chest where the ties on his tunic had come undone.

He heard movement by the door and turned his head to see Gunnolf stand, stretch, then grin at him. Niall was securing his plaid, shaking his head. Smiling. The two left the shieling to take care of personal matters, while Angus was stuck beneath the fae who was making his staff ache with need.

He should have set her aside and put distance between them, but as much as he hated to admit it, he rather liked where she was right now.

He closed his eyes and wrapped his arms around her, intending to rise and dress so he could get them on their way and return her home forthwith. In just a few minutes.

When Gunnolf and Niall returned later and rummaged around as they built up a fire, they woke Angus. He couldn't believe he'd fallen asleep again. The lass hadn't moved an inch and must not have had much sleep since she'd left her castle.

Gunnolf and Niall shook their heads at him, but were smiling as they worked on the fire.

Could he help that the lass liked to use his body as a pillow and a source of heat? How had she managed to travel this long all on her own? He, for one, had the first good night sleep in a while.

He was certain Niall wished he had come alone and found the lass instead, and been in Angus's place. Mayhap Gunnolf also.

The men were as quiet as they could be, making porridge for them, until she stirred.

She looked down at him as he lay beneath

her, her expression surprised—lips parted—that had him thinking of kissing her—then her expression turned horrified. Blue eyes wide with disbelief.

She quickly pushed at him as she hurried to get away from his body—making him groan out loud as his friends chuckled under their breaths. She acted as if *he* had pulled her on top of him because *he* had been cold. Just as well that she moved off him in a hurry, though she'd been none too gentle. He needed a walk outside—to cool off. Though he wasn't certain he could move just that moment.

She shifted her gaze from him to his friends and closed her eyes as if she was even more alarmed to see that both had known how Angus and she had slept the night.

Angus got to his feet, crossed the floor to the fireplace, and grabbed his plaid off the chair. Neither Gunnolf nor Niall said a word, their small smiles cast in his direction saying it all. They knew he was in no mood to talk. He hurried outside to cool his heated blood.

He was certain, though the sleeping arrangements had worked well enough last night, the questioning as to why she had run off from her father's keep, would not go as well.

\*\*\*

Edana didn't think she'd ever been more embarrassed in her life. She couldn't believe that she had slept not only in Angus's arms, but on top of him for who knew how long. And both his cousin and friend had witnessed it, too!

Though to avoid Angus being shackled to her in matrimony, she assumed none of the men would breathe a word of this to anyone. Or at least she hoped they wouldn't. She *certainly* wouldn't.

Once Niall and Edana were settled at the table, Angus and Gunnolf standing nearby as they ate their porridge, she felt an uncomfortable awkwardness. Not only because of having slept with Angus in the way in which she had. Worse, though they would never learn the truth, she loved having slept with him in that manner. She'd never slept so soundly in all her life. Well, after she finally quit thinking about the way his hot, hard body had been pressed to hers.

All three men's eyes were on her, and she knew they were trying to figure her out. How could she tell them she had the most urgent business, and that she knew barely anyone from her clan would listen to her entreaties? But she couldn't tell them why she didn't speak to her father about it. How he hadn't wished to hear a word from her after what she'd done—walked into his chamber and caught him naked with Zenevieva.

Most likely Angus and his companions would take her straight back to her people to let them deal with her.

She couldn't go back. Not with her brothers' lives at stake.

Angus watched Edana eat her bannock, fidgeting the whole while, glancing at the door, like a deer among hunters. He suspected he and his companions would look that way to her— big, menacing, outnumbering her three to one. He couldn't believe how much he'd enjoyed her warmth and soft body this morning, when he should have wished to push her away and keep his distance from the fae creature.

She darted another glance at him, and he finally broke the silence. "So tell us why you ran away from your clan, Edana."

He had been concerned that someone might have wronged her, but that no one, her father included, had believed her, and so she had run away before she suffered any further abuse at the hands of the knave.

But she hadn't appeared unduly afraid of Angus or his friends. He thought she would be if she'd faced a fiend and feared he and his friends might treat her in the same ruthless manner. Except that she had known each of them once. Still, they were all grown men now, no longer green lads.

Yet, he didn't believe he had the scenario right.

She was slowly eating the oatmeal porridge now, and he thought it was to avoid answering his question, or maybe the bannock had helped to satisfy her hunger. Her stomach had been rumbling well before she awoke this morning so he knew the petite lass had been hungry. But when he'd investigated her leather bag, he'd found cheese, smoked fish, and bannock aplenty, so he suspected she was eating very little to last as long as she had planned to wander.

What was she thinking? Traveling out here all by herself?

Aye, some thought she was touched in the head and would avoid her at all costs. But those who didn't know who she was, or know something of her fae oddity, might very well take advantage of the bonny lass. He had still envisioned her being only four and ten, the last time he'd seen her. Smaller, less filled out, her hair lighter, but her blue eyes had still caught his attention. He had a time tearing his gaze away from the vision she had become—all woman, and all soft curves.

She finished the last of her porridge and swallowed hard. Then she turned her gaze on him, and he felt lost in her blue eyes again, so vibrant they forced him to stop before he took the last bite of his bread.

"If I tell you why I left the safety of my home, you willna believe me any more than anyone else would," she said.

Angus was afraid of that. If someone had harmed her, and no one would protect her, he couldn't return her to her clan. He had to at least learn the truth of the matter before he put their clans' friendship at risk over the lass though, or James would be furious with him. If she had been maltreated, he would speak to her father, attempt to prove she was sincere, and ensure her safety prior to leaving her there.

He hadn't had time to respond to her declaration that they would not believe her plight as he was chewing the last of his bread when she shook her head, her reddish-brown silky curls slipping around her shoulders, the same lovely strands that had curled about *his* shoulders this morning. "You willna believe me, but I canna go back."

Angus had to know the facts. If she felt freer to speak of some personal matter with him alone, he'd ask Niall and Gunnolf to see to the horses. He couldn't take her to Craigly Castle without having a damn good reason. Last time one of his brothers took a lass from another clan to their ancestral home to have his brother decide what to do with her, James had made Dougald marry her!

In a flash, he thought about being tied down to a wife, who had curious abilities. He attempted to tell himself he was not interested in such an arrangement in the least. Until he'd found her sleeping on top of him this morn, and he couldn't help but wish for something more. Which was daft. He swore she cast a spell over him every time he saw her.

"Do you wish to speak with me in private about the matter?" he asked, trying to sound gentle and encouraging. He thought he sounded much too warrior-like instead because if someone had attacked her, he would be dead by his hand.

Niall and Gunnolf watched her closely, waiting for her answer.

"Mayhap one of them will believe me when you willna," she said softly.

Well, that put him in his place. "Then tell us what happened."

She didn't. Instead, she stared at her flask of mead as if that would give her courage.

"Lass, did someone make untoward advances?"

Her head snapped around, jaw dropping, eyes widening, and her skin grew flushed. Either he'd hit on the truth of the matter, or he'd shocked the lady to the tips of her shoes.

"Och, nay," she quickly said, refuting the whole awful notion. "'Tis my brothers who are in harm's way, and I must find them."

Her brothers. They had been on their way to see their cousin McEwan from what James had said.

She rose from the chair and began pacing across the small shieling, but away from him and his friends. Once she started speaking, she didn't stop. Pacing back and forth, her hands doing some of her talking, she was so animated and concerned for her brothers, he stood motionless, fascinated. His attention focused on the way she moved, the lyrical quality of her voice, the way her blue eyes flashed with worry, and then shifted with heartfelt eagerness. Her skirts moved around and between her legs as she walked, her actions mesmerizing.

"Did you hear what I said?" she asked, suddenly stopping, facing Angus.

His gaze shifted from the outline of her breasts to her face, her now narrowed cat-like eyes, and her pursed soft pink lips.

As if she'd been speaking to Niall instead, he said, "Aye, you have some fae gifts."

Angus stared at Niall. What had the lass said?

Gunnolf finished his mead and stood. "'Tis obvious those are no' the only gifts the lass possesses." He smirked at Angus as if knowing he had missed the whole conversation.

Angus wondered if Gunnolf had been watching him while Angus couldn't get his eyes off the lass.

"So we take the lass back to her castle now, Angus?" Gunnolf asked.

"My brothers are rotting away in a dungeon some place, and you dinna care?" Edana asked, her tongue sharp, but tears filled her eyes. A few spilled down her cheeks, and she brushed them angrily away.

Niall cleared his throat and glanced at Angus, his expression beseeching him to take care of this before she dissolved into weeping fully. Gunnolf was the only man Angus knew that seemed immune to a woman's tears. If Angus knew more what the lass had said, he could respond, but he was afraid she'd weep even harder if he asked her to repeat her words all over again. Though this time he would pay attention.

"If you knew where they were being held," Gunnolf said, "we could attempt to free them. But you dinna know that, *ja*?"

She looked at Angus, appealing to him to be the word of reason, to say he would help her in her time of need. What had she said?

"How do you know your brothers are incarcerated in a dungeon?" Angus asked.

She threw her hands heavenward. "Were you no' even listening? And you thought to dismiss your friends and hear my plea alone?"

Mayhap he would have listened more astutely then. Or…mayhap not. The woman was beguiling.

Niall sat up taller. "She said she has a fae ability to speak with people who are close to her."

Angus raised his brows at Niall. Wasn't that what they were all just doing? Speaking…to each other? How was that special?

"In her head, Cousin," Niall said, sounding exasperated as if from a look he had discerned Angus had mistaken his words. "Not like what we are doing now."

Angus tried not to frown at the lass, but he wasn't quite following the gist of the conversation.

"I canna speak to my brothers," she said, sounding exasperated that Angus was not the only one who had missed what she had said.

Angus felt a wee bit vindicated.

"I can hear them calling out to me. Pleading with me to send help to free them."

At first, Angus hadn't believed that his brother Malcolm's wife, Lady Anice, could see future events, but he'd witnessed enough of her visions that had come true, that he'd become a believer. And his brother Dougald's wife, he truly believed could commune with ghosts. So mayhap if they had special abilities, Edana had them also.

Yet, he still had a difficult time imagining she could experience such a thing as *this.*

"Where were your brothers going when they were captured?" he asked, as if he thought the scenario might be true, not humoring her, but thinking they might check into the matter—after they left her with her father—to set her mind at ease.

The relief and thanks in Edana's expression surprised him. No matter what was going on, she truly believed in what she had told them.

She quickly sat down at the table again. "They were to return in a fortnight after seeing our McEwan cousin. But somewhere along the way, they crossed paths with someone who took them prisoner. I only know my brothers wouldna have done anything wrong to have deserved such treatment. They have to have been mistaken for some others."

"I dinna understand how you can know this," Angus said.

Sounding vexed—though whether with him or with herself, he wasn't certain—she let out her breath. "I...I dinna know how I can only capture some words and not others. Or how I can discern who has spoken them as if every thought had a voice of its own. But I know they were not said aloud. They were willed to me when the person in trouble thought them…breathed emotion into them…focused on the words and called out in distress. My brothers *are* in trouble."

Angus and his companions didn't say a word. He wasn't sure what to believe.

She folded her arms and looked absolutely cross at him. "Not even my brothers had wanted to trust in my abilities, even scoffed at them, although I suspect they did so in part to assure our clan that I am no' touched by the fae. That I am a great storyteller, naught more. Except for one thing. What I warn my clansmen of always is the truth and comes to pass. And no one can explain that away. For years though, I have kept my abilities to myself and attempted to help people without revealing how I knew they needed it. No' that they didn't suspect the truth."

She expelled her breath. "But now, my own brothers are desperately seeking my help. At least I believe they are and not that they are just thinking the thoughts and I am receiving them not due to their own attempts to reach me."

"Your da asked us to find you. Did you tell him what you had heard?" Angus asked.

"He doesna like it when I discern things I couldna possibly know. And he ignores them for the most part. He worries about my revelations, but he doesna give into them. I had no intention of remaining at the keep while the clan believes my brothers will return in a fortnight when I know better. I will locate them on my own if I have to. The closer I am to where they are incarcerated, the better I can hear their pleas, and I will finally be able to isolate their location. Once I do, I can tell my father *exactly* where my brothers are being held prisoner, and then he can send men in to free them." She waited for Angus to agree or disagree.

What bothered Angus most was that he was certain she had not talked to her father about this or he might have posted a guard to ensure she did not run off on her own.

"You didna tell him what you had witnessed, did you, lass?"

She pulled her hands into her lap, tilted her chin up, giving a haughty and stubborn look that was utterly appealing, and said, "He wasna interested in what I had to say."

He studied her—the determination in her expression, no hint of dishonesty. She wasn't lying, yet something wasn't being. He wasn't sure what, but he wanted to know.

"You tried to talk to him."

"Aye," she said quickly as if she didn't wish

to discuss the matter further.

"And he wouldna listen to you."

"Nay."

Angus rubbed his chin, the stubble softer now. Then he folded his arms. "You tried more than once? When he wouldna listen?"

"He was more concerned about other matters," she said, dismissively.

"Such as?"

Her face reddened. Out of the corner of his eye, he saw Niall quickly glance at him.

Angus *knew* there was some other reason for her being out here alone. And he didn't like it. "Who were the men you were with?"

At that, she raised a brow. "Are you serious?"

Aye, he was. Only mayhap he had not gotten the scenario right this time either. "Your da will want to kill them when he learns who they were and that they took you beyond the keep without his permission."

Her face paled a bit. "They…they know I speak the truth. They wanted to help me find my brothers as much as I did."

"To earn your favor?" Angus asked, unable to curb the harshness in his voice. Neither of the men should have ever left the keep with the chief's daughter, except with his blessing. And he suspected one or both of the men were sweet on the lassie.

Her cheeks blossomed with color again. He'd never seen a woman wear emotions on her face as much as she did.

"Of course, no'!"

He didn't believe her. He couldn't imagine any man not wanting the lass…well, except maybe because of her peculiarity. "And now because of their actions, you were alone and vulnerable. What if someone had come upon you and had wished you harm?"

"I dinna worry about being alone. I have my sword—which I already used on a brigand—and I have my dirk. I had no choice. Not when my brothers need me."

Angus stared at her in disbelief and snapped his jaw closed. How could she have survived an encounter with someone who wished ill of her? "Tell me, what manner of man did you dispatch with your sword?" He couldn't imagine unless the man was small, drunk, and half starved. And unarmed. Mayhap a green lad. He couldn't visualize her fighting with her wee sword either.

"Similar to you in build," she said.

He didn't believe it.

"Of course I was taller, seated upon my horse."

Angus wanted to curse out loud. The woman could have gotten herself killed. "And if there had been more of these big ruffians to attempt to stop you?"

"More than the two might have given me difficulty," she agreed.

"Two?" Angus said in disbelief.

Gunnolf grinned. "She would make a good Viking bride."

She gave him an annoyed look.

Niall shook his head. "She doesna need a man to escort her. *She* can be the escort."

"Did you injure them?" Angus asked, ignoring his friends' jests. His stomach knotted at the notion she could have been injured or killed.

"Their pride, I warrant."

"Then they are no' dead?" He knew she couldn't fight a man and take his life.

"Nay."

"Then they are still out there."

"Aye, aye. Are you willing to help me?" she asked.

"A dungeon," Niall said, skeptically. "You promise we willna end up in one, Angus, if we attempt to prove the lass's claim true and run into trouble of our own?"

She reached over and took Niall's hand and squeezed it. "Thank you. When do we ride out?"

When had Niall taken charge of their destiny?

"We will return you home and ask your da about the route your brothers took. We will see if there are any keeps along the way and verify that your brothers are not locked in any of them. When we find them, we will send word of them home."

She frowned at Angus, and he could tell his plan was not agreeable to her. "I will go with you."

"Nay, you willna, lass. Your place is home with your da."

"You need me. I can listen for my brothers calling to me, but I fear they will weaken the longer they are in captivity. We can find them faster if I go with you."

"'Tis too perilous for an unmarried lass to make the journey such as that. We canna take you."

"You are no' returning me home."

"Aye, we are. Your da wishes it of you, and we will do as he asks." Angus was beginning to think his plan of last eve had been better. Ensure the lass didn't leave the shieling and have her father's men come for her. Instead of him and his companions having a fight on their hands, her father's men could have dealt with her.

Yet, he wouldn't have given up the memory of warming that sweet body of hers all night long for anything, and as daft as the notion was, he would do it all over again in a heartbeat.

She stood abruptly, then seized her brat and wrapped it around her. "'Tis time to go then."

Angus glanced at Niall and Gunnolf. They both gave him wary looks that confirmed they didn't believe the lass was ready to give in that easily.

"Good," Angus said, and proceeded to put out the fire. "Let us be on our way."

So why, if he was doing the honorable thing for the lady, did he feel he was not?

\*\*\*

As they rode to Rondover Castle, Edana kept worrying the reins in her hands, the horrible prospect of seeing her da filled her with dread. She would do anything for her brothers. She wouldn't be stopped in her quest to help them.

She knew the men didn't believe her. Not

truly. And they didn't trust her not to run away either. She wasn't surprised when Niall led her horse and Gunnolf and Angus stuck close to her flanks.

The day was cool, the fragrance of orchids clustered on the grassy flanks of mountains drifted to her on the light breeze. The mist in the distance was growing thicker, closer.

She took a deep breath. Would Angus and his friends really search for her brothers as they said they would? Or was it only a ploy to get her to agree so she'd return to her home without causing them any grief?

She feared she wouldn't be able to slip away from her castle again. And she was certain when she entered the inner bailey, she'd be taken in hand and shuffled off to her chamber where she'd be locked for a fortnight. If only to prove she was wrong and her brothers would return on time without further complications.

She knew Angus would return her home and she couldn't save her brothers if he did. She fought the tears that welled in her eyes. Her brothers had protected her, humored her, loved her, just as she loved them. She couldn't imagine them being tortured or starved, cold and sick in a dank dungeon.

A couple of tears trickled down her cheeks. She wiped them brusquely away. She didn't wish these men to think she was some sniveling maid who couldn't keep her emotions under control. But the worry kept plaguing her. By the time her father sent men to look for her brothers, they could be near death or dead.

She had nothing to bribe Angus and his companions with either, though she'd even considered that. Yet, could they be bribed? She highly suspected they could not. They seemed to be honorable men, coming to her father's aid just because he'd asked them to, based on the clans' friendship over the years.

She glanced at Angus. He was observing the path ahead of them, appearing to be lost in his thoughts. "Will you truly look for them?" she asked softly.

He turned to her and appeared so sincere. "Aye, lass, on my honor."

She believed him. But she wasn't satisfied. She feared Angus and his men could be too late. "If you inquired at any of the castles, how would they respond? 'Nay, we dinna have the Chattan men chained in our dungeons?' If I were close by, I would know the right of it. If they lied, you would travel onto the next castle,

85

believing them not to be manacled in the last one. How would you ever divine the truth?"

Angus nodded. "Your reasoning is sound, Edana."

Was it? Only if Angus truly believed in what she said.

"But I canna in good conscience take you with us," Angus continued.

She pondered that for a while as their horses clip-clopped across the glen, the now thick mist making her feel as though ghostly walls had been erected where they could not discern what lay beyond.

Did he worry about her reputation? It didn't matter whether it was in tatters or not. No one would marry her. She would be living with her father, and then her eldest brother when he became chief, if the wife he took agreed, until the day she died.

That was the trouble with having these cursed abilities of hers. She couldn't banish them from her thoughts. She had to help whenever she could. Some were afraid of her because of them.

"You dinna have to worry about my reputation," she finally said.

Niall turned back to look at her. She

realized both Gunnolf and Angus were staring at her.

"No' that I have any, mind you. A reputation." She sighed, afraid she was not getting her point across. At least she didn't think so with the way the men waited for her explanation. "My reputation is no' in tatters, I am meaning. 'Tis just that..." She ran the reins through her fingers. "'Tis just that...well, no one will ask for me and so you need no' concern yourselves that anyone would likely fear that my character is damaged. You have no need to worry that anyone would believe that you had caused my ruin. No' that I am saying 'tis ruined, mind you. Just that no one will believe it could be spoiled."

There, she said it. Shouldn't that set their minds at ease?

Gunnolf cleared his throat, grinned, and looked straight ahead. Niall was smiling, shook his head, and watched the forest they were growing nearer.

Angus likewise was wearing a conceited smile, and she let out her breath in a huff.

This was not going at all as she planned.

# Chapter 5

"'Tis all your fault you had to take a gamble on the whore, Drummond," Kayne Chattan said, annoyed with the youngest of his four brothers, and the most reckless, "if you hadna given into that wench and made such a muck of it."

"I didna tup her. I kissed her in the darkened corridor of the tavern, aye. But naught more. And I didna ask you to fight my battles." Drummond closed his blue eyes, his dark curly hair lying on the rotting blanket. "And you know verra well we all thought she was what she professed to be."

Kayne grunted. "And that is supposed to make it right? We had the fortitude no' to give into the whore's solicitation. You should have left well enough alone."

Halwn tied his dark brown hair back in a tail, the next youngest brother, and he nearly always agreed with Drummond. "He is right, Kayne. He only kissed the woman, though why, I still canna fathom. How were we to know she is a chief's mistress? *She* should be in chains, no' us."

"Drummond didna have to lay a hand on the wench!" Kayne retorted.

"Before long, McEwan will send out men searching for us when we dinna show there," Gildas—the second to eldest brother—said, his blue eyes sharp. "What is done is done. So take heart."

"And if his men reach this clan's keep, whichever that may be, and he preserves the secret about us being down here?" Kayne shook his head. "Have all of you been attempting to reach our sister?"

Drummond gave a soft snort of derision.

Kayne fought the urge to hit him, although Drummond already sported one black eye. Mayhap he needed another to knock some sense into his thick skull. "Edana may give us hope when we may have no other."

Drummond opened his eyes and glowered at Kayne. "'Tis no' that I dinna believe in her strange fae abilities, but God's wounds, we dinna want her traipsing about the land, searching for us. If she speaks of it to Da—and you know she will—he willna believe her. We have gotten ourselves into this; we will have to get ourselves out of it."

"We? *You* got us into this horrendous mess," Kayne said. Age-wise he may be the middle brother, but felt he was as much the voice of reason as his two older brothers.

"Need I remind you once again, you didna need to fight on my behalf. Had you no', you could have told our da what happened to me." Drummond closed his eyes.

"Mayhap Drummond is right," Egan said and Kayne had to agree with his eldest brother, despite not wanting to concur with anything Drummond said. "'Twould be a mistake to call Edana, if 'tis even possible. Da wouldna believe her. And you know what she would do if he doesna act on her revelations."

"Run away," Kayne said, rubbing his bristly chin. Hell, he had been trying to reach her ever since he'd gained consciousness. "What say you, Gildas?"

Their second eldest brother seemed deep in thought. "I only wish we knew where we are."

Kayne knew what he meant. Gildas had been trying to reach Edana also, and if he could tell her where they were being kept hostage, she could have their father send men to find them. After the day the lass had drowned in the river, all of his brothers had become believers. Because of her peculiar abilities, poor Edana would never find a husband. But that didn't mean she would be safe from men who could wish ill of her.

They didn't know exactly how her abilities worked. She had admitted being uncertain herself. But she'd alluded to hearing people's emotions and their thoughts when they found themselves in peril. Not one of the brothers was in immediate peril. But with the chilly conditions, no garments, and lack of food or drink, they could all grow ill at any time and die.

"She willna give up on us," Gildas said reverently, his fingers interlocked on his chest as he rested on his blanket.

"Edana? Then you think she is looking for us this very moment?" Drummond said. "If any harm comes to her…"

"She loves us," Hawln said, with a scoffing sound. "Unconditionally. Even when we didna treat her well because our clansmen hadna."

"Speak for yourself," Kayne said. He and Gildas had always been her champions.

"I stuck up for her," Hawln said. "Nearly drowned a lad for making fun of her once."

Drummond ran his hands through his hair, but didn't say anything.

Halwn shook his head. "You can pretend you didna champion her cause but I witnessed it on a number of occasions, Drummond. Even if no mon ever wants the lass for a wife, she has stolen all our hearts."

"Aye," Kayne and Gildas said.

Everyone waited for Drummond to say something. Then he said very gravely, "Which is why we shouldna attempt to reach her as we could verra well put her in harm's way."

\*\*\*

Riding through the thick mist on her way home, Edana felt defeated as Angus and Gunnolf continued to flank her, Niall still leading the way. Then she heard someone speaking. A faint voice. Trying desperately to hear what he was saying, she closed her eyes. Gildas. What was he saying? "*Stay home.*"

Stay at home? Nay! They worried for her. Nay! She wouldna give up. His voice sounded so far away, she knew she was moving away from him.

"My brother Gildas just spoke to me," Edana said in a rush to Angus and his companions.

Everyone reined in their horses and stopped.

"I canna…I canna speak with them. I wish I could ask them the questions we need answered. I only know they canna tell me which keep they are being held in. But we are riding away from their location."

She couldn't believe Angus and his friends had actually stopped to hear her out. Did they trust in her? But what if her brothers no longer tried to reach her? What if they realized they could put her in danger by doing so?

She closed her eyes, willing Gildas to say something more. *Please,* she pleaded. *We have help. The MacNeills.*

Nothing. She knew it didn't work that way, although every time she'd had one of these one-sided conversations, she'd attempt to draw them out—to have her own say, to learn more so she could help the person in trouble.

Niall did not pull her mare along. And Angus did not tell the others to keep moving. He was waiting for her to do something.

*Oppida*, Kayne said, the woman's name brushed across Edana's mind. "Oppida!" Edana said. "My brother Kayne just gave the name to me." Though she couldn't be sure if he was so angry with the woman that his emotions had helped send the name to Edana or not, or if he actually had tried to give her the name. "Does the name mean anything to any of you?"

Niall said, "No' me."

But Angus looked at her so strangely that she thought he appeared to have seen a banshee. "Angus?" she asked.

Gunnolf said, "We encountered this Oppida. Well, actually heard of her."

Edana's hopes instantly rose. "You know her? You know where my brothers could be?"

"At Lockton Castle. 'Tis Dunbarton's keep. Dougald and I stayed there for a spell," Gunnolf said.

"Then we must go there."

Angus said, "We must return you home first and let your da know where they are, if they are there at all."

"He willna believe us. No' unless we know for certain."

Angus looked at Gunnolf for confirmation.

"We heard tell Oppida was the chief's mistress. She visits taverns looking for payment for her…services. When the chief learns of it, he throws the mon in the dungeon who dared…" Gunnolf stopped mid-sentence.

"My brothers wouldna have been with such a woman," Edana said vehemently. None of the men said anything, which infuriated her. Did they think she did not know her brothers that well? After she'd seen her father with Zenevieva when she would have defended his honor to the death, maybe she didn't know her brothers any better. But she wouldn't admit to that. "They wouldna! Just because you and Dougald had been—"

"Nay, lass," Gunnolf said quickly. "I mentioned we had heard tales of the woman. Dougald and I attempted to stop Dunbarton's men from raiding sheep on our lands. We found ourselves vastly outnumbered."

"Oh," she said. "My brothers wouldna have been doing such as they were on their way to see our cousin, the McEwan. They wouldna have been... Well, they must have been doing something honorable as well, and Dunbarton threw them in the dungeon. They must have heard about the woman as you did and thought I might share the information and someone would know then where they are."

"What think you?" Niall asked Angus. "I believe going for reinforcements might be in our best interest. Beyond that, seeing to the lady's care by leaving her with her da is probably the best idea, do you no' think?"

"Quite a squabble ensued between Dunbarton's five bastard sons as to who would rule the clan next when he died. We dinna have much to do with them, and they havena been raiding our lands of late," Gunnolf said. "So we dinna know which one is now laird."

"But you and Dougald have already been in their dungeon once. Dinna you think if they see you, they will want to put you there again? And us because we will be with you, and of course we will fight to keep you from going into the dungeon in the first place," Niall said, clearly sounding as though he was afraid he'd end up in a dungeon again.

Angus said, "If Keary rules in his father's place. I believe he will listen to us. He did aid us in freeing you and Dougald, Gunnolf. But we will still take the lass home first."

"We will be heading in the wrong direction and add four more days if no' more to our—your journey—if we go to my da's keep. Four more days of abuse!" Edana exclaimed, her temper flaring.

"We take you home, Edana. That is my final word," Angus said.

If her brothers were truly at Dunbarton's keep, she had done her job. Angus would enlist her father's help, and somehow they would convince their laird to release her brothers. So why was she not happy with the prospect?

What if they had some of the scenario wrong? What if Oppida was somehow the key, but the keep Gunnolf thought they were being held at wasn't the correct one?

"Are you certain they would be holding them at Dunbarton's keep?" she asked. "That Oppida is still at Lockton Castle when Dunbarton no longer lives? That she isna some other chief's mistress?"

Angus didn't say a word. Neither did Gunnolf.

She pursed her lips. Then she wondered just how difficult it would be to get them released. "Gunnolf, how were you and Dougald set free?"

"The first time?"

Eyes wide, she asked, "You we thrown into the dungeon more than once?"

"*Ja.* The first time, a lass freed us."

"A lass?"

"Aye. She gave the guards a sleeping draught and helped us to escape. But we were captured again and the next time we needed extra help."

"I wasna there, but James led a force to help free them," Angus said.

"Why were you no' there?" she asked, believing he would have been there to help his brothers.

"Angus was injured in a swordfight with some of Robert Curthose's men," Gunnolf said. "He couldna fight for a fortnight, but his injuries healed, and he has use of his sword arm again."

She glanced at Angus's arm, not having seen him favor it in the least. But now she worried he might be injured if he was unable to keep up with the other men.

"'Tis properly healed," Angus said, giving Gunnolf an annoyed look.

But she still worried. "Your brother, James, laid siege to Lockton Castle?"

"James had some assistance. Once he and his men were shown the secret tunnel, they made their way inside."

Her spirits lifted at once. "You can sneak them out. Good. Aye, you will need my da's men to assist you."

"We canna just force our way inside," Niall said. "We have to learn if her brothers are even there."

"Aye, 'tis true," Angus said.

"How will you be able to do that with a group of men? They will surely realize you mean to wage war on them. Especially when they see my da's men, if they know which clan my brothers belong to. Or I suspect they might."

"We will come up with a plan," Angus said, sounding as though he was attempting to appease a bairn and wished to end this discussion.

She meant to speak not another word to them all the rest of the way back to the keep, though it would take them two days, but she couldn't help herself. "What if my da doesna believe you? That my brothers are being held in Dunbarton's dungeon? What if he thinks you will cause trouble with a clan we havena had problems with before? What if he says no' only is he no' sending men, but he doesna wish *you* to visit Dunbarton's keep on my brothers' behalf either?"

But worse, what if they had it all wrong and her brothers were not shackled at Lockton Castle?

# Chapter 6

As Angus and his companions crossed the glen, the foaming burn running through the center of it, they paused their horses to drink of the fresh water and fill their flasks. He felt unsure about what to do concerning Edana as she stretched her legs, bending over to add water to her flask. So surprised, he stared, mesmerized as he considered her lovely backside. It didn't matter that she was wearing a brat over her léine. Just the way she was bent over made him harden.

*Och.* He quickly turned away, but caught Niall and Gunnolf watching her, all smiles. He frowned at them and once they saw his scowl, they busied themselves with filling their own flasks.

The lass belonged at home, not with the men who were not family and when she had no female to accompany her.

He glanced at the Scots pine towering nearby and the craggy peaks of mountains, spearing low-lying clouds, predicting they would soon have more rain.

Shortly thereafter, they remounted their horses and continued on their way.

The nagging thought kept pulling at his conscience. She could be right. That even if they convinced her father to allow them to take men with them, what if they couldn't persuade the current Laird of Lockton Castle to give up her brothers? What if the laird wouldn't admit to having the brothers incarcerated at his keep? Worse, what if they discovered her brothers were not even there?

His mind made up, though he could not believe he'd come to this decision, he hollered, "Hold!"

Everyone stopped.

"We go to see the Laird of Lockton."

"We canna take her with us," Gunnolf said, frowning.

"She will be my wife," Angus said.

Her jaw dropped.

"We will pretend you are my wife," Angus clarified. "We will ask for Highland hospitality and see if we can learn for certain that Edana's brothers are there. Once we learn the truth, we can take the news to Edana's father, and he can send men with us to convince the laird to release her brothers."

"What if the lady herself ends up in the dungeon?" Niall protested.

"We will endeavor to keep her safe," Angus said, not believing anyone would take such measures with the lass.

"Sorry, Niall," Gunnolf said, already agreeing to the plan that could lead to their downfall. "'Tis an adventure when you journey with any of the MacNeill brothers. Have they no' warned you?"

"I thought Dougald was the only one who landed his friends in a cell with him," Niall said glumly.

"Mayhap 'twas one of the other brothers who was the cause before," Gunnolf said, with just a hint of a smile. "Malcolm and James had their turn also."

"If you mean the time that Da arranged two marriages for Malcolm at once," Angus said, "'twas Da's fault, no' my brothers."

"*Ja*, but if Malcolm had agreed to wed the daughter of that clan chief, none of us would have ended up in the chief's dungeon. 'Tis good that James finally convinced the chief to free us as the lady that Malcolm finally wed is the perfect one for him," Gunnolf said.

Edana cleared her throat and they all looked at her.

"How can I ever thank you?" Edana asked, so gratefully, she looked as though she would come out of her saddle to hug Angus. Tears swam in her eyes, but they were tears of joy and relief.

He wanted that hug, truth be told. But he was on a mission so important, he couldn't allow a bonny lass to distract him.

"But you must promise to guard everything you say, Edana, so you dinna give our purpose away," Angus warned. "'Tis a role we must all play."

"Oh, aye, you have nothing to fear on my part."

She looked so eager to aid them in locating her brothers, Angus frowned.

Why did he not believe her?

*** 

Edana could have embraced Angus she was so relieved that not only had he believed her, he agreed to take her with them. She hoped Kayne would attempt to speak to her again. She prayed they would learn for certain that her brothers were locked in the dungeon without her escort getting into any trouble themselves.

"There is one little problem with all of this," Angus said. "Gunnolf has been there before, as he has mentioned. Gunnolf isna one to forget easily and any number of Dunbarton's men might recognize him. We may encounter trouble because of it."

"Then mayhap we should leave him nearby and see for ourselves if they have my brothers there first," Edana said.

"If you wish it, Angus, I will wait. Should you no' return by an agreed upon time, I will seek Chattan's help."

"That is a wonderful idea," Edana said brightly. "Even if my da is reluctant to come to my brothers' aid, believing they are still safe and riding to see our cousin McEwan, he willna balk at demanding *my* release."

Angus frowned. "You willna try to get us placed in the dungeon so that Gunnolf will seek your da's help, would you?"

She was shocked he would even consider such a notion. "Surely you jest, Angus. I have no wish to reside with my brothers in a dark, dank cell even for a heartbeat."

Even so, if she could be with them, she would give up her freedom, knowing Gunnolf would bring a rescue party.

Angus looked unsettled as if he knew just where her loyalties were. "Just so you know— they most likely will be naked."

She gaped at Angus, then quickly closed her mouth and stared straight ahead. She didna wish to see her brothers naked, even though she had seen Gildas's bare arse when he was tupping a maid by the loch when she'd chanced upon them. Thankfully, neither had seen her dash away from the scene of their impassioned romance. At least she hoped not.

Chin up, she continued to look forward, her cheeks heated despite the chill in the air. She would do anything, she reminded herself, if it meant getting her brothers freed.

Then she frowned, coming to a conclusion she didn't wish to consider and turned to Angus. "They wouldna do such a thing to a woman prisoner, would they?"

Niall's eyes rounded, his mouth gaping as he turned to see how Angus would respond.

Gunnolf did not say a word, though she assumed he'd know, as many times as he'd been in one. Angus flushed a little. "Aye, lass. No' always, but sometimes, aye."

Her brothers would be furious with her

captors and with her!

She would do most anything to secure their release. Mayhap not that.

*\*\**

God's knees, Angus *knew* Edana must have been thinking of getting herself thrown in the dungeon so that Gunnolf would go for help and her father would damn well provide it.

He hoped mentioning that captors sometimes stripped women prisoners of their clothing would make her reconsider such a notion. He wished to help her in her quest, but not at the expense of them all losing their freedom. Even for a brief time.

They traveled until late that night and made camp near a burn streaming white, alder mixed with downy birch, and rowan leaning over the burn's banks. This time he knew she would not attempt to slip off on her own because they had agreed to ride with her to locate her brothers. Small consolation as he had other concerns now. The difficulty was that he did not want her sleeping by herself, cold and shivering in the chilled night air. They had no tent, no way to keep out the damp mist cloaking them.

Yet, wrapping her in his body heat and sharing hers with him could be a habit he would not be willing to give up so easily once they had accomplished their mission.

While Gunnolf watched over the lass and made a fire, Angus and Niall gathered more kindling in the tangle of brush to last the night. "You are no' making a mistake by calling the lass your wife, are you, Cousin?" Niall asked.

"'Tis just a ploy."

"Yet with our customs—saying it is so, makes it so. 'Tis just as binding as marriage in a kirk." Niall struggled to untangle a fallen tree limb from the brush.

Angus went to help him as Niall wasn't making much headway. "Aye, I know, but she agreed to the ruse only in an attempt to learn where her brothers are. She wouldna keep me to my word when we are only pretending to be husband and wife."

After the way they had been together during the night already, had her father seen them, he would have forced the marriage to take place, he was certain. But she had assured Angus, he need not concern himself with such. And he believed the lass.

Niall shook his head as they pulled the limb free, then gathered more twigs and downed branches. "Seems to me you are playing with fire. What if she agrees with this plan of yours and doesna wish for anything further to come of it? But her da has other designs?"

"What do you mean?"

"That when he learns you have declared her your wife, he wants it to be so."

"He wouldna wish that on his daughter." Angus didn't think.

"You are no' such a disagreeable knave as that," Niall joked.

"I dinna mean that. Because he cares for her, he would want the lass married to someone she loved who loved her in return."

"Aye, but what if he knows no one will even make such an offer, ever? And he has the chance to have a MacNeill, brother to a laird, wed to his one and only daughter, who he cherishes, even if she is a bit different. He knows we are all honorable. He wouldna believe you would be anything but your charming self with the lass. Why do you think he has asked James to send one of his brothers when he knew you were the only one still there? And as of yet—unmarried."

Again, the inference being that Edana's father had plans other than just having them find her and escort her to his keep. Maybe even the reason her father would not send his own men to fetch her back.

"I...dinna believe it," Angus said, heading back to camp with the armload of wood, although both Gunnolf and Niall's words gave him pause.

"Believe it or no', but I am just warning you in the event you want Gunnolf or me to take the lass home while you wait for us. Or better yet, if we are able to free her brothers, they can return her home and leave us out of it altogether."

A prudent man would consider Niall's words of concern and might even agree with him. So why was Angus fighting the notion that he would not want anyone to escort her safely back to her castle but him?

After eating porridge and a trout Gunnolf managed to catch, Edana was quiet, staring into the fire. Angus observed her for a while, watching the orange flames cast flickers of light across her sweet face.

Her unplaited hair rested over her shoulders and reminded him of that day so long ago when she looked into the loch, her expression contemplative.

"I will take first watch," Gunnolf said, breaking into his thoughts.

"Aye," Angus said. Before he could say he would take the next, Niall piped up.

"Me after that," Niall said.

"Are you ready to bed down for the night, lass?" Angus asked, standing, then stretching. He didn't remember a time when he felt so uncomfortable. He wished to keep the lass warm, but didn't wish to offer in front of Niall and Gunnolf. He didn't wish to embarrass the lass. Before, he had lain next to her to prevent her from trying to leave the shieling, then offered to keep her warm when she was so chilled.

But now…

She had already brought out her blankets and hesitated as she considered the fire again, her gaze catching his.

"Is this…where you want me to sleep?" she asked.

Gunnolf had left to provide guard duty. Thankfully. Niall fetched his blankets and laid them on the ground next to the fire opposite from where Angus and Edana stood.

"Aye, the spot is clear of rocks. Close to the fire, but no' too close."

She nodded and spread out the first of the blankets. "'Tis chilly tonight," she said.

"Aye. The weather was warmer earlier today once the mist cleared and though it appeared it would rain, the clouds are disbursing some, so the night shouldna be too bad."

She looked up. A sprinkle of stars could be seen lighting a patch of cleared sky. "Aye. But..." She glanced at Niall who was already resting on his blanket. He quickly closed his eyes. "'Tis chilly tonight," she repeated to Angus.

As much as Angus told himself he should not tuck the bonny lass in his arms this eve again, he also reminded himself she could become chilled. "Aye," Angus said, mind made up. He would serve as a good Samaritan.

He retrieved his blankets, setting his next to hers.

She gave him a small smile. Sweet, innocent, lovely and that one smile heated his blood. Why was it that her hint of gratitude could make him want so much more?

He waited until she was lying down, facing the fire before he reclined on his blanket. His cousin gave him an evil smile that said Angus was headed for a darkling journey.

Attempting to ignore Niall, Angus had barely lain down, pondering wrapping his arms around the lass or just getting close enough to her without touching, when she scooted backward a bit until her soft warm body planted against his torso. He gritted his teeth to keep from groaning out loud as she seated that sweet arse against his growing arousal.

She squirmed again against him, trying to settle herself. He quickly wrapped his arms around her to keep her from moving about and causing him any more discomfort—as damned pleasurable as it was. Could she not feel how her body inflamed his?

Nay, she was a sweet innocent, unaware of the way of men. Which meant he had to ensure he kept his thoughts pure, even though he wrapped her more securely in his arms. She sighed and he smiled. He'd never had a better way to keep warm on a chilly night and the notion Niall would serve on guard duty next worked well for him.

When Gunnolf woke Angus later, he peered at the pinks and oranges as the sun began to rise. "Niall didna wake me for guard duty," Angus said, rising to his feet.

"The lass needed your warmth," Gunnolf said. "We suspected you wished neither of us to take your place."

Gunnolf assumed correctly, though Angus would not admit to the truth.

***

For two days, they traveled to Lockton Castle, home of Dunbarton, and when they caught sight of the keep, the gray castle walls ringed by four tours, Gunnolf headed for the caves where he and Dougald had once found shelter. Feeling unsure as to what to expect, Angus nodded to his companions to continue on their way.

"Let us see what we shall see." Angus prayed he would be worthy of Edana's father's faith in him in bringing his daughter home safely and in Edana's that he could help her free her brothers from whatever dungeon that they now resided.

The morning sun bathed the stone walls in warm light as the portcullis rose, creaking and groaning like an old man grumbling about his aches and pains. Guards on the wall walk above eyed the three riders. He had to admit having Edana with them made them appear to be less of a threat. No man in his right mind would take a woman into battle.

An older man was driving an empty cart out of the inner bailey and greeted them as he continued on his way.

Another approached, this one wearing a sword and dirk, his dark eyes wary. "How now," he said in greeting, his eyes quickly looking over the lass, but shifting again to the men who could give him trouble. "Who are ye and what do ye seek here?"

"We wish to speak with your laird," Angus said.

"Keary Dunbarton, Laird of Lockton, isna here at the moment."

So Keary had taken his father's place and since he had helped James to free Gunnolf and Dougald the last time they had been incarcerated, it seemed a good omen.

"Lady Allison? Is she here?" Angus asked quickly, before they lost the opportunity to learn what they could about Edana's brothers. Allison had rescued Gunnolf and Dougald the first time they had landed in the dungeon, and he hoped mayhap she would tell him what he needed to know. Though with Keary being in charge and his half-brother, Finbar, no longer able to vie for the position, his sister—who favored their brother Finbar for the position—and he might both be gone.

"She is inside. Does she know ye?"

Angus had never met Lady Allison that he could recall. He was trying to think of a way to gain an audience without making Keary's staff suspicious.

"Aye, we are friends. Tell her Lady Eilis wishes to speak with her," Edana quickly said, evidently recalling the rest of the story he had told her. "This is her...my brother, Angus MacNeill, by marriage."

Angus stared at her. What was she doing? It was true James's wife and Lady Allison had come to rescue Dougald and Gunnolf, but the lass didn't look anything like Eilis. And wasn't he supposed to be pretending to be Edana's husband? He knew he should have returned her home first.

The man nodded. "Come with me." He glanced at Niall, as if recalling he should know who he was also.

"Cousin to the MacNeills," Niall said.

"We have heard tell James fished you from the briny deep," the guard said to Edana.

Niall quickly jumped in to tell the tale as neither Angus nor Edana had witnessed it and he wasn't certain if Edana had ever heard it. "Her ship was wrecked and aye, I helped rescue the wee lass clinging to a mossy rock."

"She was supposed to be married to Keary's father when he was laird," the man said, looking her over. "'Tis too bad she is no longer available. Our current laird likes the fiery-headed lasses as well."

Edana cast a glance in Angus's direction. She looked a little bit like a rabbit—realizing the wolves were upon her. He imagined she'd never gotten herself in this kind of a predicament before.

The man escorted them to a small chamber inside the keep, then left.

"I was supposed to be your husband," Angus whispered to her as Niall kept a lookout, knowing they would have trouble once Lady Allison made her appearance and saw the woman pretending to be Eilis.

"I didna think they would admit us without one of us knowing the lady. And even if you had known her, I didna believe the guard would have wanted to bring you here to see her without her brother's approval," Edana said, arms folded across her breasts, chin up, eyes flashing with indignation.

He admired her tenacity and had never expected her to come up with a plan in the blink of an eye to make this work. If it worked.

Footsteps hastened in their direction. Angus tensed, hoping he, Niall, and Edana would not alarm Lady Allison when she discovered Edana was not who she claimed to be.

A woman rushed into the room, her hair and eyes dark brown, her expression turning from excitement to alarm as soon as she saw the woman who pretended to be Eilis. She didn't know Angus either, and she hadn't seen Niall standing slightly to the right of the door. Before she screamed, Niall clamped his hand over her mouth and shut the door to the room.

Edana finally found her tongue and quickly said, "'Tis all right. We have just come to speak with you. We would have talked to Keary, but they said he is no' here."

Angus said, "We wish you no harm, Lady Allison. Lady Eilis would have come to see you if she could, but she is unable to travel."

Niall removed his hand from the lady's mouth, her eyes still wild. "She is ill?" Allison asked.

"With child," Angus said.

Allison's eyes still huge, her apprehension didn't appear to abate. "What do you want?"

"I am James's youngest brother, Angus. You remember Niall?"

"Aye. He is the only one I knew. Why did you lie to say you are Eilis?" she asked Edana.

"I am Edana, daughter of the chief of the Clan Chattan."

"We have word that her brothers might have...had some trouble," Angus said, not about to tell how they had come of the news, and he didn't want to accuse her half-brother of locking the Chattan brothers in the dungeon.

"What has that to do with me?"

"We would have spoken to Keary, but he isna here," Angus said, repeating Edana's words, trying not to sound vexed.

"You...you think...what?" Allison asked. "I dinna understand."

"Is there a woman here by the name of Oppida?" Edana asked.

Allison's jaw dropped.

Angus did not take that as a good sign.

The door suddenly opened and everyone turned to see Keary standing there with two of his men, his bright expression changing to surprise, then anger. He looked at Edana. His brows rose, and then he scowled at Angus and Niall. "Arrest the men."

"Nay," Edana said, grabbing Angus's arm as if she could protect him. "We are here seeking my brothers."

"And you are?" Keary's eyes traveled over her body in a salacious manner.

Angus already had his hand on the hilt of his sword. He didn't like the way Keary looked at Edana—as if she was available when she was *supposed* to be Angus's wife.

"The daughter of the chief of the Chattan clan," she said.

Her scowl seemed to amuse Keary as his mouth curved up. "Why the ruse?" he asked.

"We wished only to speak with you," Angus said, repeating once again the same sentiment, "but you were no' here."

"About?"

"Her brothers," Allison quickly said, and Angus feared that meant Oppida was Keary's mistress.

"Come, 'tis time for the nooning meal. Let us eat," Allison said, taking hold of Edana's arm. "Tell me all about your brothers."

Angus watched the two ladies leave the chamber and hoped Edana didn't say anything that could get them all thrown into the dungeon.

# Chapter 7

Edana didn't know what to think. Was Oppida Keary's mistress? And had he locked Edana's brothers in the dungeon? But what bothered her most was the way Keary had looked at her as though he'd love to make *her* his new mistress.

She noted Angus scowling and though he'd kept his hand on his sword hilt when Keary first entered the chamber, his men had quickly disarmed both Niall and Angus before they went to eat.

Now in the great hall, intent on her words as the servants served food from thick fish soup to dove stew, Keary listened to Edana speaking to Allison about her brothers. The lady seemed quite interested in meeting them. Which meant Allison was very good about keeping a secret. Or she didn't know what her half-brother had been up to. Or Edana's brothers weren't here.

Edana wanted desperately to ask about Oppida, but after Allison had changed the subject so quickly, Edana had assumed the topic was too sensitive to discuss.

Angus had unsuccessfully attempted to engage Keary in conversation, also trying to learn what he could. But Keary seemed way too interested in what Edana had to say.

"Lady Eilis is married to James," Keary said, using his knife to spear a chunk of white meaty halibut floating in his soup. "Which means that you are not married to him. So…what *of* you?"

"She is married to me," Angus quickly spoke up.

Keary offered Edana a calculating smile, not glancing in Angus's direction. "Truly?"

Her cheeks burned and had to have flushed a brilliant red. She knew he was reading her expression, realizing she was not married to Angus as he had said.

"I venture to say your father would be surprised to hear it," Keary continued when Edana didn't respond. She was afraid to give herself—and Angus—away.

What did Keary know?

"Why would you say that?" Edana asked, trying to sound as indignant as she could.

Keary buttered his brown bread.

She barely breathed.

Keary looked up at her and gave her another smug smile, his dark eyes glittering with amusement. "Because the two guards and a maid who came here searching for you said you were alone."

Her escort. Her heart pounded. He knew she had not been with Angus.

"Naturally, I myself and several others have been looking for you ever since. I had just returned home to see if you might have reached my castle and was informed Lady Eilis was here. You canna imagine my surprise to learn you were no' she. And here you are the lady I have been searching for. Only you were no' alone. Your da wouldna be pleased to learn—"

"My da," she quickly informed him, "sent Angus to come for me. We agreed to the marriage. Both of us. We even had witnesses."

"Witnesses?"

Her heart did a little skip as she realized her mistake in including Gunnolf. "Well, Niall, and so 'tis done."

Keary glanced at Niall who appeared as though he'd rather be anywhere but here right now. He looked in Angus's direction who nodded just once.

"Aye," Niall said weakly.

"Under the moon and stars?" Keary asked.

He knew the answer to that question. He was playing with her to see if she would spill the truth. But she had told the truth. Even if she and Angus only meant it as a ruse.

"The weather hasna been agreeable always," she said.

"Forgive me if I dinna believe any of you, will you?" Keary said. "But I have been looking for a bonny lass to wed and I trust you should do nicely. I will send word to your da that you are safe with me and ask him for your hand in marriage. Your honor will remain intact that way."

He wanted her because she was a clan chief's daughter? Until he learned of her special ability. At least Angus was coming to believe in her. But she worried that if her father did get an offer for her hand in marriage, he would jump at the proposal. No one else was stepping forward to ask for it. And he was so angry with her for spying on him with Zenevieva in his bed, Edana had no doubt he no longer wished her to reside at home.

Angus rose from his seat. "The lass is mine," he growled. He looked like a dangerous wolf as determination and anger hardened his voice, his posture, his expression. But Keary had wisely disarmed both Angus and his cousin, so other than his fists, he had no way to protect her. Thankfully, she still had her dirk hidden under her skirts.

"You were alone with the lass," Keary said. "And I suspect her da has no knowledge of this union between you. So you have compromised her as well. I doubt you truly have, or I would kill you myself. Suffice it to say, I will do with you as James's did with me. When he took me prisoner—"

Angus's eyes widened.

"You didna know that? Aye, you had suffered a wound in battle and were staying with your older brother Malcolm. Niall knows the truth of it. James made me help repair the fortifications on his wall."

Niall contradicted the telling of the story. "James worked alongside you."

"Aye, true enough. But I willna make you work. Unless you wish it."

"Angus and I are married," Edana said vehemently, more than worried Keary would try to force the issue with her. "If you deny us our right to be together, both my clan and Angus's will be forced to deal with you—*harshly*."

Keary smiled, but the look was more self-satisfied rather than jovial. "Verra well. I will have you married in our kirk. Then you can tell your story to all who wish to attend the service. Allison, do you have something the lady can wear to her special ceremony?"

Allison looked on—horrified.

Angus did, too.

\*\*\*

If he wasn't in such a serious situation, Angus would have laughed. How in the blazes had he gotten himself into this? Gunnolf would have slapped him on the back and laughed. Niall looked as though he himself was condemned to marry the fae.

Not that Angus didn't care for the lass. He did. He was certain something about her faeness had captured him all those years ago and even now he had a devil of a time breaking free of her enchantment. He'd never thought about any woman so long or hard or often as he had the fae lass. He'd told himself his interest in her had only been due to curiosity concerning her odd abilities. Yet, when he had seen her fairly naked, and then slept with her the last three nights, his body awakening in a fevered pitch every time, he tried to tell himself he would have felt that way with any woman.

To an extent, aye, but with her, he wanted to go further. Now he had his chance. James would kill him. But he shouldn't have sent him on this mission. And her father would kill him. The lass herself didn't want this to be everlasting—not when she had agreed this arrangement was only a ruse.

They would have to do this and annul the marriage as quickly as possible.

They wouldn't share the same pallet again.

They'd be married according to spoken words only.

They would not consummate the marriage.

He couldn't read Edana's expression. Oh, aye, she was red-faced and embarrassed. He could see that plainly enough. But he didn't know if the whole idea of marriage horrified her or she was coming to agree with the notion. Mayhap she feared her father would say yes to a marriage between Keary and her. And Angus could be the lesser of two evils.

That's when Angus decided that he couldn't allow Keary to have her. He was certain she didn't wish to marry Keary—not with the way she had quickly explained again how she and Angus had already married. Threatened Keary even with her father's men and his in battle! Angus could see her da possibly agreeing to Keary's offer if no one else wished the lass's hand in marriage. Keary was now a laird of his clan.

But Angus couldn't see her belonging to the man.

"So when do we do this?" Angus asked, more demanding than asking as if *he* was going into battle.

Edana's lips parted and he thought about how kissable they looked, only now her cheeks had turned ice white.

***

It was all set then. Wearing his cleanest tunic and plaid, Angus stood in the small kirk with a gathering of Keary's clan members. Normally, Angus would have worn a dirk and his sword, but Keary had not returned his weapons to Niall or him.

He was anxious, waiting for Edana to arrive. Niall appeared just as nervous, his gaze shifting from Angus to the door and back to Angus again. Keary stood near the altar, arms folded across his chest, looking superior as he watched the entrance to the kirk.

Angus had the impression that Keary

expected either Edana or him to back out of the arrangement. Angus wouldn't, if it meant saving Edana from Keary. He thought Edana wouldn't, yet women were known to change their minds so he truly couldn't predict what she would do.

When she walked into the kirk with Lady Allison, Edana looked astonishing, wearing a lovely pale blue léine, her skin scrubbed clean, her hair plaited. Murmurs of approval rent the air. He wanted to take her in his arms and kiss her, release her hair, and make the faux marriage real. She looked apprehensive and he hated Keary for forcing them to do this in front of his people. He gave her a small encouraging smile, but then her gaze shifted to the left of him, and he turned to see Keary stalking toward her. He noted Allison was biting her lip, holding Edana's hand, her focus on her brother.

He thought Keary intended to escort Edana to stand with Angus, but instead, he took her arm and said, "A moment of your time." Then he escorted her promptly out of the kirk.

His clansmen began to whisper to each other, casting each other looks. Allison hurried after her brother and Edana.

Niall looked at Angus and Angus didn't know what to think. Not until he saw four armed clansmen enter the kirk headed straight for Angus and his cousin. "He has changed his mind about my marrying the lass," Angus warned Niall.

"Edana!" Angus yelled, as he and Niall readied themselves for a fight. Keary wasn't having his way this easily.

***

"I have changed my mind, Edana," Keary said, escorting her back to his sister's chamber. "The MacNeill brothers canna always have their way. I will send a messenger to your father, asking permission for your hand."

"But I am already married…," Edana said, trying to jerk her arm free from Keary's steel grip, her heart drumming with a mixture of anger and anxiety.

"Nay, you are no'. You wouldna have been riding with an escort in search of your brothers. They said you were alone and made no mention that you were married. Concerned for your safety, your husband, had he been Angus, wouldna have allowed you to travel with your wee escort." Keary left her in Allison's room and said, "Allison will stay here with you to provide companionship. But a guard will also be posted outside her door, so dinna think of leaving the chamber."

"Where would I go? You must be daft to think I would do anything but abide by your wishes."

His mouth curved up into a sinister grin. "I am glad to hear it. Dinna think ill of me if I dinna believe it." He turned to Allison. "Sister."

Then he stalked out of the chamber where a guard already stood and closed the door.

"What will he do to Angus and Niall?" Edana asked, wringing her hands. She had not considered anything like this would happen.

"Here," Allison said, handing her the léine she had traveled in. "I will help you to change clothes." As she helped her remove the garment, Allison asked, "Why were you looking for your brothers here?"

"One of my brothers said a woman by the name of Oppida had caused him trouble. Gunnolf—"

"Gunnolf?"

"Aye. He said that Dunbarton kept the woman as his mistress."

"Aye, my father's mistress. But she no longer resides here. As soon as Keary took charge of the clan, he threw her beyond the walls of the keep. I dinna know where she is now, but I suspect she has found another man to warm her bed and protect her. She is verra beautiful. But Keary hates the woman and forbids anyone to speak of her."

"Then...then my brothers were no' here when they saw this woman."

"No' unless it was months ago when my father was still alive."

"It wasna." Edana crossed the floor to the small arrow-slit of a window. At least it confirmed her fear that they might not be here. "Och. What will he do with Angus and Niall?"

"Free them. Eventually. Mayhap no' until your father agrees to your marriage to Keary. He may do so only on the contingency that you go through with the marriage arrangement."

"James took Keary prisoner once, but he said James gave him a chamber to stay in. Will he allow Angus and Niall the same luxury?"

Allison shook her head, but she was busy gathering items and stuffing them in a bag. "I fear not."

Edana paced across the floor. "If I tell him I will marry him, will your brother let them go?"

"I doubt it. He will be afraid you would say no to the marriage as soon as the men are gone. You said Gunnolf told you about Oppida..."

Edana had said too much already. If they did not leave the castle, Gunnolf would go to her father and mayhap her father's men could make Keary see the error of his ways. If she could help it, she would not marry the dreadful man. But if Allison thought Gunnolf waited for them beyond the castle walls, would she tell her brother? And the men would then search for the Viking and take him hostage as well? Then again, would her father be glad to be rid of her and just agree to marry her to Keary?

"If he is out there, 'tis good," Allison said. "You are all packed and ready for a journey. Aye?"

"We canna just walk out of here."

"Watch us." Allison went to the door and opened it. "Can you have a tray of food brought up for us? Edana looks pale and she believes if she has something to eat, she will feel better."

"Aye, Lady Allison."

She shut the door and smiled at Edana.

"He will still be guarding the door," Edana said.

"Oh, aye. But I have a plan."

# Chapter 8

Angus took measure of his cuts and bruises, not bad—all in all. Minor, compared to fighting in a real battle where he'd managed to incur sword wounds also. He glanced at Niall. "How did you fare, Cousin?"

"Better than Keary's men did," Niall said, sitting in the dark cell, the only light, a torch against one wall. "But I am certain it was only because the men were told to hold their punches. James wouldna have liked it if we had been hurt too badly. I guess Gunnolf had the right of it when he said all of you were just as likely to get us locked in a dungeon."

"How many times have you been in one?" Angus asked, sitting down on the pallet, wrapping the raggedy blanket around his shoulders.

"Two."

"This is my first stay in one, so mayhap *you* are the reason."

"Edana is the reason," Niall scoffed. "Would you have really gone through with it?

Married her?"

"Aye, I would have." She had an unswerving loyalty and love for her brothers, a fierce warrior's determination to protect herself from villains if what she said about the two ruffians who had attacked her was true, and even sought to safeguard her beloved horse, when she moved her inside the shieling. She was sweetness and light and innocence. Yet she was quick-witted, too. When he closed his eyes, he could feel her soft body pressed against his chest and yearned to be with her in marital bliss.

He couldn't help but worry about her with Keary and clenched the thin blanket tighter in his hands, the iron manacles around his wrists, jangling with the slightest of motions. If he could, he would wring the man's neck for what he had done.

"What if you had married Edana and Keary had insisted that he and others served as witnesses to the consummation. Would you have taken it that far?"

His blood hot with annoyance, Angus didn't want to envision that—him buried in the sweet lass for all to see. He wouldn't have allowed Keary or anyone of his staff to watch. "There is no sense in predicting what might have happened. We just have to come up with a plan to get out of here."

"Before Keary gets her father's agreement to marry her," Niall said.

Angus scowled at his predicament, glad James couldn't see him now.

It had been a couple of hours since they'd been incarcerated and the small window high above showed the sky was dark, the night upon them. The door creaked open to the cells below. Angus thought it odd that the door was not pulled roughly aside by some burly man, but slowly, cautiously.

Angus whispered, "Get ready."

Niall whispered back, "You have got a plan?"

"Aye, if someone else doesna already have one for us."

Footsteps tapped on the slippery, circular stone steps leading into the dungeon—tiny footsteps, not hulking booted man-sized footsteps.

"A woman," Niall whispered.

"Aye." Angus thought his brother Dougald would be the only one to have such luck with the ladies. He could barely make out the candlelight in the distance, heard the jingling of a ring of keys, and was ready to act if the maid was intent on freeing him and Niall.

As the figure drew closer, he could see the faint light cast on the most beautiful face in the world—Edana's, though her eyes were narrowed and her mouth pinched with worry. But he feared for her at the same time. She had changed back into her green léine, no longer wearing the blue one she'd worn for the wedding.

Overwhelmed with joy to see her, he wrapped the blanket around his waist to hide his nakedness. "Here," he whispered.

"And here," Niall said, as if worried she would forget to free him, too.

She had a devil of a time inserting the big keys into the steel lock of the door, and silently he prayed no one would catch her, wishing he could aid her. She entered the cell quickly and worked the key on Angus's manacles, her hands shaking terribly, and finally managed to set him free. He kissed her quickly on the cheek, took the keys from her, and hurried to unlock his cousin.

"Oh, Angus," she said, and placed the bone handle of a dirk in his hand.

He wrapped his arm around her to give her a brief, encouraging embrace. She trembled from the cold in the cell and from fear. "Bonny lass, follow behind us."

He and Niall led the way, intent on fighting for their freedom and not wanting the lass harmed. He would confront any danger they had to face, though he might have to ditch the thin, worn blanket to fight better. He hoped his cousin had covered himself also.

When they reached the top of the stairs, Allison was waiting for them, wearing a brown brat and léine. Three packed leather bags, a few blankets, and a sleeping guard rested at her feet. A tray of half-eaten bread and stew sat nearby.

Angus was surprised, then again—*not*—as Allison was the one who had rescued Dougald and Gunnolf the first time they had been incarcerated.

"Quickly," Allison whispered, giving Niall a dirk, then carrying one of the bags, she hurried down a corridor leading into another stairwell.

Niall seized one of the bags, and Edana carried the other, the rolled blankets tucked under her other arm. Angus stayed close to Allison, Niall following Edana.

None of them dared speak as Allison took them up more narrow winding stairs, then she stopped. "I must blow out the candle. This is

Keary's chamber. We canna make a sound. I know my way in the dark. Edana, hold the back of my brat. Angus and Niall, you will have to follow us. If he wakes, I dinna wish to be any of us."

Angus would not kill him if he could avoid it, though God's truth, he wanted to because of Keary's attempt to take Edana from him and force a marriage on her when she had already agreed she was Angus's wife.

"Aye, proceed," Angus said, praying Keary slept like the dead.

When they moved into the chamber, the place was dark as pitch. He held onto Edana's shoulder as Niall held onto his, stepping on his bare heel twice. It seemed to take forever before they made their way across the rushes on the cold stone floor and entered into another hidden passage, leaving Keary's chamber behind.

They continued down more stairs, and when they finally reached an outer door and he felt the chilly breeze and fresh air on his face, he breathed a tentative sigh of relief.

But they weren't out of danger yet.

"Thank you for rescuing us," Angus whispered as they moved quickly across the uneven terrain, a mixture of soft grasses and hard stones. He wanted to ask if Allison had clothes for them, their horses, swords, anything. Rocks cut into his feet and he shivered from the cold.

"My chamber was guarded," Allison quickly explained, her voice hushed. "We only came away with the clothes that belonged to Edana and some of my own."

That explained why she had no rags for them to wear.

As cold as it was this late spring night, he and Niall wouldn't last long wearing only thin, holey blankets.

But then he worried about her words. "Return to the keep, lass. You dinna need to concern yourself further about us," Angus said. He didn't want to have to fret over Lady Allison's safety as well.

"Are you mad, Angus? You are stuck with me. I helped you to escape. This time they will know of it. The last time, no one knew 'twas me who freed Dougald and Gunnolf. When Keary learns Edana and the two of you are gone, who would he blame?"

Angus heard Niall chuckle softly under his breath. He could laugh all he wanted but they were in a worse mess than before.

Praying no one would learn any of them had left the keep until morn, he continued with the others to make their way to the cave where Gunnolf should be staying. Without horses and as slow as he and Niall stumbled along, it could take a couple of hours.

"Stop," Angus said, his feet hurting too much to take another step. He pulled off his blanket, then stripped some pieces from it to tie around his feet. They could still see the torches lighting the castle, way off in the distance, but the light didn't stretch much further than a few feet from the massive stone walls. The night was so dark, the ladies would not see him or Niall in the shape they were in—naked, beaten, shoeless. "Strip off some of your blanket to use to protect your feet or you will never make it," he said to Niall.

"No one said we would need to be rescued from a dungeon, and that we would have to run away in the dark naked," Niall complained, though Angus knew his cousin was grateful to be free.

"There is a first time for everything." Angus stood and wrapped the remaining blanket around his waist.

Edana placed her hand on Angus's chest.

"Take our blankets. Between Allison and me, we have four. You and Niall can wear them and mayhap they will help keep you warm."

Angus quickly fashioned the cell blanket like a belt around the blankets Edana offered him as Niall did the same with the others.

"I am ready," Niall whispered, and they all headed out again with Angus in the lead, winding his way through wet woods, leaves, moss, and pine needles cushioning their path now. The rags covering his feet soaked up the dampness.

The air smelled like wet grass and moldy leaves and of pinesap—fresh and invigorating. They startled a resting male capercaillie, the slate-colored grouse, making a racket until it soared high above the treetops in silence.

When Angus was certain a small candle's flame could not be seen from the castle, he lit it. With Edana's hand in his, her hand on Allison, and Niall holding Allison's free hand, they continued on their way.

Even if they could reach Gunnolf in time, Angus didn't have any idea what they were going to do without horses or much in the line of weapons. Gunnolf had a spare tunic and brat and a couple of blankets that were warm. Edana would have her blankets, mayhap Allison also.

The biggest trouble was that they had no mounts. Though they could fashion a brat from the wool blankets, they had no shoes to wear. He wanted the women to ride Gunnolf's horse. But Niall and Angus could not travel far without shoes.

When he saw the caves, he hoped Gunnolf was still there. He feared Keary might suspect they'd come here for shelter since Dougald and Gunnolf had been found here before, and they'd need to leave at once.

Angus bade the ladies and Niall wait and he went inside, whispering, "Gunnolf."

He heard only the slightest movement, and then saw Gunnolf with his sword readied. His gaze quickly took in Angus's lack of clothing. "God's wounds, what has happened?"

"We are in trouble," Angus said. "We must leave at once."

"You have no clothes."

"Nay. We are lucky we managed to get free at all." Angus called out to Niall and the lasses, "'Tis safe to come in."

They hurried inside and made their way to the inner most cave where Gunnolf's bags and blankets were spread out on the gray rock. He quickly lit another candle. Gunnolf gaped at Allison. "What is *she* doing here?"

"Saving your friends," Allison said, sounding annoyed. "And before you suggest I return to the keep, what do you think my half-brother would do to me when he learns I have not only freed Edana so he canna marry her, but that I also released Angus and Niall, who he planned to use to get her concession? Eh?"

Gunnolf shook his head, then jerked his thumb at a couple of dark lumps lying near the back of the cavern, mostly immersed in the dark. Two hefty men from the looks of it. "Mayhap they will offer something that you can wear."

Angus frowned as he and Niall headed for the men. "Who are they?"

"They were on their way to see the chief of the Clan Chattan," Gunnolf said, "with news Keary intended to take the chief's daughter to wife. I quickly took care of them, figuring you had gotten yourselves into a quagmire. But I was waiting until first light to leave for Edana's castle. 'Tis good I did, too."

"Aye," Angus said, quickly stripping the one man of his clothes and dropped the dungeon blanket over him.

Niall did the same with the other.

"Keary will be furious," Allison whispered, sounding even more worried.

Served Keary right. Angus felt really hopeful they might get away. "They had mounts?"

"Aye, that they did. We are still short a couple, but that will give us three. So which direction will we head now?" Gunnolf said, packing up his blankets.

"Lady Allison said Oppida served as her father's mistress, but that Keary forced her to leave the clan's holdings. So she must be with some other laird," Edana said, sounding expectant that they would continue to search for her brothers.

Angus shook his head. "The only place we are going now is to your father's keep. As well as I know him, Keary will likely try to recapture us. He willna wish to lose you if he thinks he still has a chance to have you for his wife."

"He doesna even know me," Edana said, sounding annoyed.

"'Tis your charming ways and he couldna help seeing how bonny you are." Angus helped Edana onto the horse he would ride as Niall pulled Lady Allison onto his.

"Nana," Edana said, with regret.

"Your horse?" Angus asked, wrapping his arm around Edana as they headed out across the glen, more than glad to have her close again and under his protection, though he wished he had his own sword.

"Aye."

"I am sorry, Edana. If we could have taken our mounts, we would have."

"Aye," she said, leaning her back against him, and he was thankful to have her tucked in his arms again. "I understand. Mayhap my da can bargain with Keary to release her."

"Aye, and my horse and Niall's also. As long as you are no' part of the bargain." Angus smelled the lavender fragrance in Edana's hair and was at once reminded of where the night might have taken him—marriage and consummating the relationship with her later that very eve. He closed his arm tighter around her. Whatever would happen, would happen. If her father insisted he wed her, he would do so, if she wished the same.

He could do worse, he supposed, if he were his brother, Dougald, and sharing a bed with a wife whose ghostly brother bothered them at night.

Or one who saw visions of the future. He thought he'd end up with a wife like Eilis, who hadn't any special abilities, but he rather liked the idea of having a wife who was gifted. If it didn't land him in any more dungeons.

"Have you heard anything more from your brothers?" Angus asked.

She shook her head. "I fear for them."

"Aye, I know, lass. I would continue on our way to locate them, if it had not been for the trouble we are bound to face with Keary and his men, the fact we are not heavily enough armed, and we have two women with us."

She nodded.

"Your da willna permit you to leave with us should we reach your castle before Keary catches up to us."

"What if we were to see James instead? You could get another horse and—"

"Nay, lass. Concerned for your safety and with keeping clan peace, my brother willna permit you to leave with us either."

She slumped against him.

He ran his hand over her belly and kissed her hair. He hated disappointing her, but he couldn't allow her to believe she would go with him when he was certain she wouldn't have that option no matter where she went. "You were indeed bonny when I thought to have you as my bride, Edana," he said quietly.

"You wouldna have minded too awfully much?"

"To keep you from Keary, I would have married you in a heartbeat."

"But if it were no' for him…"

"I am surprised you have had no offers, lass."

"Many times over," she said, so quickly, he wondered if she was fibbing, not wishing any man to think no one wanted her hand in marriage.

If that was the case, he could understand the lass's feelings. He pondered that for a time. He couldn't imagine why anyone would not wed the lass, unless it had to do with her odd gift. It did not bother him, now that he understood more of what she could do. But other men with a weaker constitution could be unduly concerned. On the other hand, if she'd truly had so many offers, why was she still unwed?

"But you didna accept any of them. Or your da didna approve?" he asked.

She shook her head.

He opened his mouth to ask which. Then he

sighed heavily and asked about another matter still bothering him. "Why did you no' tell your da why you were leaving? You said you couldna speak to him."

She let out her breath. "Some things are no' meant to be discussed between a man and a woman."

He contemplated that, but couldn't come up with anything she could mean. "He will be angry that you left."

"Aye."

"What will he do with you?"

"Lock me in my chamber until my brothers come home. When they dinna, mayhap he will believe me. By then, it could be too late."

Angus was torn. If the lass could help him find her brothers, he still wished to take her with them. But they couldn't travel past Keary's keep without having more of an escort. "I will ask your da if you can continue to ride with us, if he will send some more of his men to safeguard you and a maid to ride with you."

"I thank you, Angus."

"Aye, lass. I wish your brothers safe." But he was certain her father would not permit her to go with him.

After spending even a few hours in the

cold, musty cell with naught more than a worn blanket, he knew how sick men could become. He planned to ride out from her home again as soon as they could and search for her brothers.

They traveled all night in the direction of Edana's castle, taking infrequent breaks to rest the horses and water them at a stream when the sun began to rise. At first, the only sounds they heard were the water trickling in the stream and birds singing in the trees. But then they heard the sound of horse's hooves striking the ground, coming from a northerly direction, they all turned to look and see who approached. Angus feared the worst. Keary's castle was north, and Edana's south.

"Keary's men," Allison said in a panic, as the sky grew lighter, a small yellow glow in the distance as the sun began to rise, though gray clouds hung in the sky and it appeared the sun would soon disappear behind them.

They quickly mounted, Allison riding again with Niall, Edana with Angus and headed at a gallop for Edana's castle. They were still too far from the safety of the curtain walls to ride at a full gallop with riders doubled up on two of the horses.

Angus was concentrating on what lay ahead

when he saw two men riding toward them from the south. At first, he feared further trouble, thinking Keary's men had circled around them.

"My father's guards," Edana said, sounding vastly relieved.

"We have more help headed our way," Angus called out to Gunnolf, who was following them, acting as a rear guard.

"Good, though the odds were still in our favor," Gunnolf said.

On a good day, aye, but having the women with them, nay.

"Where is Una?" Edana called out to her father's guards.

"We saw you from afar, and it appeared you were in trouble, lass," the older of the two men said, eying Angus. "We left her behind in the woods yonder. She is safe."

"This is Angus MacNeill," she offered. "And his cousin, Niall, and friend Gunnolf. My father asked for them to find me."

"And those men?" the man asked, pointing in Keary's direction.

"Keary Dunbarton, Laird of Lockton and his men. They are trouble, Kipper."

Six men rode with Keary and he probably had thought he could overtake them and reclaim

Edana and return his half-sister Allison home when he had only two naked, unarmed men to fight. But now that Keary and his men were facing five men instead of three, Keary motioned for his men to stop. They were still a goodly distance away, and Angus could barely make out that they were Keary and his men if it hadn't been for the direction they had come in and that Allison knew them so well.

"Your father has had men searching for you when we couldna find you, lass," Kipper said, riding beside them. "We came across them earlier yesterday morn and told them we had lost you during a storm."

Edana stiffened in Angus's arms, and he assumed she was worried what her father would say about her leaving her home as she did. Angus noted Keary and his men continued to follow them, keeping their distance.

"Where is your horse?" her father's guard asked.

"Oh, Kipper, the Laird of Lockton has got her."

"Mayhap your father can bargain for her and have her returned to you."

"Keary wishes me for a bride," she said.

The man's brows rose. "Does he now?"

"She already has a husband," Angus said, not liking how the man sounded. As if it was a good thing Keary wished her for his wife.

Kipper glanced at Angus and smiled. "Two offers at once? Things are looking up for you, lass. Your da will no' have much to say in what you do now. Your husband will."

Edana glanced up at Angus. "Do you hear him, Angus?" She wasn't smiling, but the eagerness in her voice said she was much intrigued with the notion.

He wondered then if she thought he would easily do her bidding without his objection. Much more so than her da. "Aye, lass."

It seemed he had a wife, and he still hoped neither her father nor James would want to kill him over it.

They soon came upon a green-eyed lass waiting in the woods who smiled with obvious relief. "Edana, oh thank the Lord you are safe."

"It seems the lass had two offers of marriage since we lost her during the storm," Kipper said, "and she has accepted one of them."

"Two offers? When you have never been offered for before?" Una said, grinning. "Who is the lucky man?"

No offers ever? Angus banked his expression, but Edana's face had flushed as if she'd taken in too much of the sun. He thought again about her unusual abilities and how a husband could be a danger to her if he had known of them too late and feared her and wished to get rid of her—expediently. Maybe she had offers, but concerned for her welfare, her father had said no to them.

"I am Angus MacNeill," he said to Una.

Una's face brightened. "He is the one you talked about. The one..." She paused as she studied Edana's face—her furrowed brow that said drop the subject—at once.

Angus was more than intrigued. What had Edana said about him?

Then Una smiled again. "You will have to tell me all about it later, Edana."

# Chapter 9

Edana wished she hadn't looked back at Angus to see how he had reacted to learning about her little white lie—and now he had seen how red faced she was. In truth, though she had tried to tell herself it didn't matter that not one man had offered for her hand, it bothered her more than she'd like to admit.

Did Una have to tell on her? Next, she'd tell Angus that Edana had never even been kissed! Another flush of heat invaded her as she thought about lying nearly naked with Angus that first night. And sleeping two more nights wrapped in his arms, though she had worn all her clothes. She had still felt his manhood pressed against her backside, suggesting her body forced his to react in such a manner. Gratified she could make a man feel something for her, she would treasure those nights forever—no matter how scandalous such behavior had been if anybody, not of their small party, had learned of it.

Gunnolf warned them, "Keary and his men are following us."

Her heart gave a little skip and Edana glanced back.

They were trailing them at a distance. "What do you think they mean to do?" Edana asked, her heart rate speeding up. She thought Keary would have given her up when he realized she had somewhat of an escort and that she didn't intend to wed him no matter what.

Before anyone could answer, she said, "Nay, he canna believe he can convince my da I would still marry him." She paused, then added, "He canna think to steal me away when we take a rest, can he?"

Angus tightened his hold on her, comforting her to an extent, but she still worried. What if Keary and his men planned to kill her escort?

He couldn't. Both James and her da would want Keary and his men's heads.

A worse notion came to her. What if her da believed he would have a greater advantage if he wed her to Keary? Angus was but James's younger brother. He didn't own a title or properties.

She rubbed her arms as the ghostly chilling mist descended upon them.

Lady Allison glanced over Niall's shoulder

to see her half-brother Keary riding after them. Allison appeared anxious. Her brother had to be furious with her for helping them all steal away from Lockton Castle.

Angus didn't know what to say to allay Edana's fears. He knew Keary's doggedly following them was not a good sign. But if Keary took her by force, Angus imagined her father would not be pleased with Keary. Even if he did make a better husband as far as alliances went. Truth was, the Clan MacNeill had many more men they could call upon and James would do it, too, if Angus asked it of him.

He wished her maid had not let on in front of everyone that Edana had never received an offer of marriage. He had felt her stiffen a little at the maid's words and immediately, without thinking even, he had leaned over and kissed Edana's cheek. He was fairly certain why she had not been asked and it all had to do with her fae-like abilities. If she had ended up with the wrong man, he might have her drowned as a witch.

He was curious about what Edana had thought of him that the maid let slip. More than curious. "Is it true what your maid said?"

"Una? She is mistaken," Edana said. "Many

suitors have approached my da for my hand in marriage."

"Aye," he said, not sure he believed her. "But that isna what I meant."

She glanced over her shoulder at him. "What then?"

She knew what he was intrigued about. She couldn't give him that wide-eyed innocent look and pretend she didn't know. "What Una said about you thinking of me?"

Edana's face blossomed anew with color, and she quickly turned away from him. He chuckled. She could not deny it.

"Was it about when we saw each other in our youth?" It must have been. They had not seen each other until now.

She remained quiet. He pressed her back against his chest, encouraging her to relax. "Tell me."

"There is naught to tell."

"You thought me a handsome lad? Wished I would kiss you?"

He shouldn't have mentioned such. With her settled against him, he knew she had to be well aware of how much her soft body incited his. Any talk of kissing or anything further than that was getting him worked up all the more.

When she didn't respond, Angus said, "I wanted to kiss you."

She was so still, he thought she wasn't breathing.

"Oh, aye," he said. "My brothers all gave me the devil when we returned home, saying I was bewitched by the fair maiden and so speechless, I could only stare dumbly and not say a word on my behalf."

She chuckled. "I...thought you believed me...odd."

"Beautiful. Different from the other lassies, aye. But that was some of why I was so drawn to you. The smiles you bestowed on your loved ones I wish you had bestowed on me."

She frowned at him. "I thought you believed me a foolish young girl."

"Nay. You made me smile."

"I made you laugh at me."

"Never. Your smiles rendered every day inside and outside the castle bright and sunny. Then when you saw me watching, you hid that beautiful smile away."

"You were afraid of me."

"Nay, no' afraid."

"You were," she insisted.

He chuckled. "A mon doesna tell a lass he

is interested in that he fears she might reject him."

"Reject you?" she asked, her tone disbelieving.

"Aye. What if I had tried to speak with you and you dismissed me, or…ran away."

She didn't say anything but he needed to know what she would have done.

"Aye, lass?"

"I dinna know. I might…I might have kissed you."

He grinned. "My brothers were right then," he said on a heavy sigh. "I should have spoken with you."

"I am no' saying I would have kissed you, but…"

"You wanted to. My brothers said it would be my loss if I didna speak to you. And then I was off with my brothers to fight and there was never any time to return there."

"Or any desire," Edana said, sounding a little disappointed.

"Nay, 'tis no' true." But what was true—he feared she'd truly bewitched him. And she had. Only now he believed it was not due to her fae abilities, but what he saw in her—the kindness and sweetness that was Edana. Not all wild

Highlander as he had thought.

When they stopped for the night, Keary and his men camped also in the distance. Angus halfway expected Keary to attempt to seek an audience with her father before Angus had a chance to return her home. But it appeared that wasn't his ploy.

Angus watched as she laid her blankets on the ground next to Una's, when he desired to be the one warming Edana tonight instead. He took first watch, observing Keary's camp, the men either sitting or huddled near the fire, sleeping, while his own companions rested. Footsteps approached from behind and he turned.

*Edana.* He smiled at her as he rose from the log he'd been sitting on. "Can you no' sleep, lass?"

She joined him and shook her head. "I worry about what Keary will try to pull."

"I am certain he intends to ride in with us and ask for your hand in marriage. Does he know about your ability?"

"Nay, no' that I believe."

That would be the point Angus would make with Edana's father if he even considered marrying her off to Keary. "Would you like to sit with me a spell?"

"Aye. I will be right back."

He worried she had some business she needed to take care of and he would have to have one of the men guard while he watched over her, but she stalked back to Una.

Gunnolf raised his head off his blanket to see the matter, then looked back at Angus when the lass carried her blankets to where he stood. Gunnolf shook his head as if to say Angus had lost his heart to the lass.

Angus smiled at him.

Before she could spread out her blankets next to him, he was doing the honors. "So you are going to guard with me tonight?" he asked, smiling.

"Nay. But if I am close to you, I know you will be better able to protect me."

"Aye, but you told me you had fought off two men as big as me, so I may need your help as well."

She patted her leg. "I have my dirk now that you have that man's sword. I will protect you if need be."

His eyes shifted from her leg and met her gaze. "Did you still want that kiss?" He did. Ever since he'd laid eyes on her at the shieling, her damp chemise clinging to her breasts and hips and legs, when he'd awakened to find her resting heavily against his staff, when he thought he was about to be married to her in the kirk, when he rode with her, and when he slept with her the last two nights. Aye, the thought of kissing her was ever present in his thoughts.

"We are married," she said, sounding hopeful that he would kiss her, mayhap agree that they were truly married and the notion was no longer a ruse.

He leaned down then, cupping her chilled cheeks in his hands and brushed his lips over hers. She took in a deep breath as if he'd startled her. He meant to pull back, knowing he'd have to go slow with an innocent maid who had never had one offer of marriage—he didn't believe— when she clasped her arms around his back, lifted her face to his, and licked his mouth.

He was stunned. But her reaction to his chaste kiss was all that it took to press his mouth more firmly on hers. She melted against him, all soft feminine curves, and he was reminded just how well the lass fit with his body. And how much he would like to take this further.

She pressed her lips against his, her body tight to him, stirring his loins.

He was lost to her now if he hadn't been

already.

She kissed him harder, her arms tightening around his waist, wanting more. Mayhap she wasn't as innocent as he thought. That had him wanting to kill the man who had kissed her before. Then she parted her lips. She could not want him to kiss her in the way he'd like to. They would have to work up to it. Be in a bedchamber at the very least. The lass could not know about such tawdry kisses.

He looked at her. Her eyes were closed as she licked at his mouth again. And then to his shock, she touched her tongue to the seam of his mouth and tried to gain entrance!

His body burned with desire and his staff pressed against her belly. He wanted her. But damn, he was supposed to be guarding the camp! He'd only meant to give her the briefest of kisses.

He parted his lips to see just what the lass had in mind to do. She slipped her tongue into his mouth, tentatively—which gladdened him because it again caused him to believe she was truly unsullied—and she caressed his tongue. That had him groaning. She was unraveling him one woolen thread at a time.

He could not hold back any longer and

stroked her tongue with mayhap too much gusto because the lass's eyes opened and widened. He smiled a little, relieved to see she was still very much an innocent in the way of kissing, and then continued to teach her just how powerful that form of tongue play could be.

This time she moaned a little and clung more to him. He thought if he had not held her up, she would have melted into the soft green grasses at their feet.

He heard movement behind him and turned to see Gunnolf with his blanket wrapped around his shoulders. "'Tis my turn to guard."

It wasn't. But when Gunnolf glanced down at Edana, who was now looking at her feet, Angus knew Gunnolf meant to allow them more time together alone.

Bowing his head a little to Gunnolf in gratitude, Angus scooped up his and Edana's blankets and moved her back toward the campfire. He was well married to the lass, no matter what anyone else said, unless the lass did not wish it.

Even though, he would have liked to have kissed her longer, they needed to sleep, and he worried with them sleeping together, he would take this further than prudent.

This time when they reclined on the ground together, she rested her head against his chest and for a while they were quiet. But then she said, "I...like the way you kiss."

He wasn't sure what to say. He wanted to ask where she got the notion a lass kissed a man with her tongue. He stroked her soft cheek with his fingers. "We are married, are we no'?"

She stared up at him and didn't say. Then she took a deep breath and cuddled against him again. "If you wish it."

"Do you *wish* to be married to me, Edana?"

"You dinna mind that I am different?"

"Och, lass. I love that you are different."

She offered a sweet and grateful smile.

"Your da willna object, will he?"

She shook her head and looked away from Angus.

That made him suspicious. "Did you have a quarrel with him?"

She didn't say.

"Edana?"

"He isna happy with me. He would like naught better for me than if I left and didna return."

That had Angus frowning. Tibold, chief of the Clan Chattan, loved his only daughter.

Angus couldn't imagine why they were at odds or why she would think he wanted her gone, when in truth, he wanted her returned at all haste.

Unless it was as his companions had said. Her da had hoped Angus would find her and then marry her and indeed would take her off his hands.

"Is your da upset with you concerning what you heard? From your brothers?" Angus asked. She had said her father had not listened to her. So what had happened?

She shook her head.

"What then?"

"I canna speak of it."

Angus thought about that for some time, but couldn't come up with anything.

"We are married," he said, matter-of-factly. "A husband and wife must share everything with each other. Because...they are married. So tell me, what was the quarrel between you and your father?"

She looked up at him, her eyes swimming with tears. And her sadness undid him. He stroked her hair soothingly. "Och, lass, dinna fret. We will work whatever it is out."

"Nay. He...he..." She turned her face away

again.

He let out his breath and caressed her arm, loving the feel of her body warming his, but wanting to clear up this matter between his...wife—he smiled at the notion—and her father. He didn't want them to be estranged.

"I can guess all night long what it might be about. I can imagine all kinds of things you might not wish me to conclude. Can you no' tell me, your husband?"

"You will think me silly."

"Your da didna, I take it."

"Nay, he was angry with me. Wished me to leave."

"He wanted you back. He sent a messenger all the way to Craigly Castle to have you returned at once. He worried about you, lass. He loves you."

"He doesna," she said softly, and brushed at her cheek.

He touched her face and felt tears there. "Ah, lass, dinna cry."

"He...he...I..." She shook her head.

"Does your maid know?" He thought mayhap her maid could speak of the trouble when Edana could not.

"Nay. I mean, aye, but you canna ask her."

He waited a heartbeat, about to tell her that he longed to hear what had distressed her so, but then she blurted out, "He was in bed with a scullery maid!"

So taken aback, Angus didn't know what to say. Had she seen her father and the maid kissing—and that's how Edana had learned the intimate role the tongue could play between a man and woman?

"I...am sorry, Edana." He didn't know what else he could tell her to lessen her upset. She had to have been shocked to the marrow of her bones.

"She doesna even like my da!"

Then the realization dawned. Her father must have seen Edana witness the debacle, was horrified, and lashed out at her.

"So he knew you had witnessed them together."

"Nay. The maid did, and she must have told him."

He knew he shouldn't ask. But he still wanted to learn how she knew to use her tongue to elicit such a response in Angus. "Were they kissing?"

"Nay, they were no'."

Then where the devil had Edana learned

about kissing?

She continued to explain that she had always visited her da's chamber if some matter was most urgent, any day or night. Even after her mother was gone. She had never expected to find him...

Her words abruptly stopped.

He rubbed her arm soothingly. "This is why you believe he doesna want you home any longer?"

She nodded.

"'Tis no' why you have agreed to marry me? Because you believe your da doesna wish to see you any longer?" He hoped it was not, because he could think of nothing else but being with the lass as husband and wife.

"Nay," she said softly against his chest.

"Are you certain?"

"Aye." She released her breath. "I dinna wish to see him."

"Do you wish for me to speak with him on your behalf?"

She finally shook her head. Then she nodded.

"Sometimes unfortunate situations occur...," Angus said.

"Nay, despicable."

He paused. "Aye. But I fathom he was just as shocked to learn you had witnessed him with the woman."

"Naked," she said, nodding.

Another pause. Just how much had the lass witnessed? He began rubbing her arm again. "So when I speak with him—"

"No' about that," she quickly said.

"About what you heard from your brothers and that we could use some men to help locate them and have them released?"

"Aye."

Good. He didn't wish to speak to her father about what Edana had witnessed. But then he wanted to make it clear that he understood how she was feeling. To a point. The feelings would be different for a man beholding such a thing. Yet, he still had been angered with his own father because he knew how much he hurt his mother by tupping other women.

He kissed the top of Edana's head. "My own father had a number of...indiscretions. He was deep in his cups more often than no'. I chanced upon him once with a maid in the stable. Being the youngest of my brothers, I was mayhap more appalled than they might have been."

"Oh, Angus. I am sorry. But your mother still lives, so it was worse for you."

"Nay, lass. The hurt is still there. You lost your mother no' so long ago. 'Tis understandable to see how you would feel. No' that I mean to excuse him in any manner, but sometimes a man like that who has been with a woman for a very long time, may need a woman's…comfort."

"You…think they were only sleeping together? Naked?"

No, he knew that wasn't what they had been doing. Not the whole time. That meant she had not witnessed her father tupping the wench. That was good. Now how to get himself out of this. He knew she'd be upset with her father all over again, but if she believed he only needed to be comforted after his wife had died…

Edana shook her head against his chest. "Nay. They would not have been naked."

He smiled at her insight and loved her. "Would you wish to reside with me at Craigly Castle?"

"Aye."

"Your father may wish you to remain at his keep."

"He doesna. If I see that woman as much as smirk at me, I will yank out her hair."

Angus again smiled, recalling the fiery lass who had fought the lass and lads taunting her. He'd much rather see her ready to fight, than sad. Though if her father had fallen for the wench, Edana could only make things worse.

While they stayed with her father, Angus would have to keep Edana in hand.

# Chapter 10

The next morning with the sun's appearance warming the windy day, Edana noticed at once that Keary's men had left before her own party could continue on their way to her home. Her heart stuttered. "Keary is gone," she said to Angus. "We must hurry and catch up to him before...before he convinces my da that I want to be with him and conveniently leaves out the fact that you and I are already married."

"Aye, lass, but he will have a time explaining why he is asking for your hand and you are nowhere in sight."

They quickly ate a piece of brown bread to break their fast and Angus helped her to mount his horse—borrowed horse.

It was nightfall when they reached Rondover Castle, the torches casting light on the gray stone walls, the portcullis shut. Which meant Keary had not told her father that she was on her way here with Angus.

When they reached the portcullis, a man on the wall walk shouted, "Is that you, Edana?"

"Aye, Pwyll," she said.

"'Tis Angus MacNeill, my cousin, friend, Gunnolf, and Edana's escort," Angus shouted, "bringing the lass home."

"Good," the guard said, hurrying to get two more men to open the portcullis to admit them. He gave Seumas and Kipper a disparaging look. "The chief wishes to speak with the two of you. But his daughter first. And, Una, your father wishes to speak with you as soon as you returned home as well."

"What of Keary?" Edana asked, as Angus helped her to dismount, then she held onto his hand as Una stood on the other side of her, not making a move to see her own father. Allison was nearby, ringing her hands.

A couple of lads ran out to take the horses' reins and lead them to the stable.

"The Laird of Lockton is supping with your father," Pwyll said, motioning to the other guards to close the iron grate. "He has offered for your hand in marriage and your da has accepted."

"Nay!" Edana shouted, yanking her hand free of Angus's and ran with all haste for the keep.

Una raced after her, but Angus caught up with Edana and took hold of her arm. "'Tis all right, lass. We are married. We had witnesses. He canna have you."

Allison joined them. "I would prefer no' to see my half-brother," she said in a small voice.

"Una, can you take Allison up to my chamber? I will be there forthwith," Edana said, half expecting that if her da was angry with Edana before, he'd be twice as mad when she said she had married another man when he had arranged for her to wed Keary in her absence.

"Aye," Una said, and hastened to take Allison up the stairs.

To Seumas and Kipper, Edana said, "You dinna have to go with us. Mayhap it would be better if you didna see my da just yet."

Casting each other a look and appearing relieved, they nodded to her and headed for the barracks.

With her back stiff, she stalked toward the great hall, her heart pounding, her face hot with anger as Angus stayed close by her side—which she appreciated more than she could say. When she entered the large hall, everyone was talking and eating until a few at one of the low tables saw her and Angus. Then the voices died down, first at one table, then at another as heads turned to look in their direction.

Her father rose from his table, a leg of squab in one hand, his knife in the other. "Edana," he said, his voice a whisper.

She swore he had a few gray hairs mixed with his dark brown locks since the last time she'd seen him, his blue eyes widening to see her. She couldn't read his expression. Shocked to see her, aye. He didn't appear to be angry, and for that she was glad.

Keary quickly jumped to his feet, all smiles. "My bride to be."

Was that why her da wasn't upset with her? He'd already offered her hand in marriage to Keary? And he thought she'd accept?

She narrowed her eyes at her father. "I am married to Angus. We both pledged ourselves to each other," Edana said, stalking toward the high table. "As soon as I have packed my things, we will leave for Craigly Castle and you will never have to see me—"

"A word with the two of you—Angus, Edana," her father said, cutting her off. "In private." His face and eyes darkened, but Angus's hold on her hand gave her strength.

"I wish to join you," Keary said.

"Nay," Edana said, knowing full well her father would not like her deciding who he would speak with, but she didn't want Keary in on the discussion.

Keary directed his comment to her father, but he still kept his eyes on her. "The lass will be my wife. I will speak in this matter."

Angus shook his head. "We have well consummated the marriage. The lass is my wife. Keary, we told you this already, before you imprisoned my cousin and me in your dungeon."

Her father looked from Angus to Keary.

"'Twas a slight misunderstanding. You were freed."

"No' by your orders. If we hadna found a way to escape, we would still be there. And Edana would have been forced to take you as her husband."

"In…private," her father said.

"I am a laird. You have naught to give the lass," Kearly said. "You are the youngest brother to James and have no land, no title, naught at all."

Her father suddenly motioned to four of his guards. Afraid they were going to take Angus and lock him away in the dungeon, Edana stood in front of him.

"If we dinna move this discussion to my private quarters, I will have you, Edana, locked in your chamber, and Angus and Keary locked away elsewhere."

She ground her teeth, glowering at her father. She saw Zenevieva smirking at her from a lower table, licking her fingers and though Edana would like very much to pull her hair out, she wanted more to ensure Angus remained her husband.

Edana turned and tugged Angus with her, her father and that impossible Keary following behind. Keary said, "She is young and impressionable but you shouldna trust in her—"

"Enough," her da said. "We speak in… private."

When they reached her father's solar, he motioned to a wooden bench where Edana took a seat. Angus stood beside her, arms folded, looking like he was ready to do battle with Keary.

Her father sat on his chair while Keary stood nearby, glowering at Angus.

Tibold said, "Now, first—"

"My brothers are locked in a dungeon somewhere and Angus and I need more men to accompany us because *he*," she said and motioned to Keary, "stole our horses, Angus's and Niall's clothes and weapons, and we had to return here first."

"You left your horses behind, rather," Keary said. "I didna make you run off like that."

"His sister, Lady Allison, helped me to free Angus and his cousin, Niall, who were locked in his dungeon. Da, you asked Angus to find me. He did. We agreed to marry one another. You canna undo what has been done."

"Have you truly consummated the marriage?" her father asked Edana.

Her whole body warmed with embarrassment. She would not have told him such a thing except in the most dire of circumstances. That being that it was the only way her father would allow her to remain with Angus.

"We need a word in private with you," Angus said to her father.

Her father nodded. "Keary, wait outside, if you will."

"They havena consummated the marriage,"

Keary argued.

"Outside," her father said, his voice darkening.

Keary stalked out of the solar and slammed the door.

"Does your husband know why you left here without my permission?" her father asked, his tone gentled.

Tears filled her eyes and she nodded.

Angus swallowed hard and put his hand on her shoulder.

Her father observed them for a moment. "How do you know your brothers are in a dungeon?"

"They have told me…in that special way," Edana said.

"Angus knows of this?" her father asked.

"Aye, and Keary doesna," Angus said quickly. "'Tis dangerous to force her to wed such a man. Besides, she is well and good married to me."

"But the marriage hasna been consummated," her father said.

"It doesna have to be for it to be legitimate," Angus insisted.

"I wish it to be. And to have the wedding. About that night…," Tibold said, his stern face softening.

"I am sorry I walked in on you," Edana said, her eyes downcast. She could not look at her father. "I...I was worried about my brothers. I wanted to give you word. I...I tried to wake you from the doorway of your chamber. I called to you before I reached the bed."

"Aye, Edana. I am sorry I snapped at you when we broke our fast." He reached his hand out to her.

She hesitated. He was offering a truce and she wanted things between them the same as they had been before. But there was no going back.

"Edana," he said softly.

She rose to her feet and walked across her father's solar. He stood and gathered her in his arms and hugged her tight. "You are your mother's daughter, my one and only sweet young lassie. 'Twas a mistake I made, but I willna make it again. I feared I would never see you alive again."

She sobbed and hugged him back.

"Shh, dinna cry, lass. Your husband doesna wish to see your tears."

"Why did you betroth me to Keary without my say?" she asked, wiping her wet cheeks.

"I thought you wanted to leave me for good. He has a title and was enthusiastic about making you his wife. I thought you would be pleased." He shook his head. "But I wished Angus to take you for a wife."

"Why?"

"Edana, I saw the way he watched you when you were younger. The way you had enchanted him. He and his brothers had gone to your aid that day, and Angus had pestered the maids continually about how you fared after that until he and his brothers left. You dinna know how much that meant to me. I hoped if the two of you saw each other again now that you are both mature enough, you might discover you still felt something for each other. When we had no word of you…" He wiped away some of her tears. "I am sorry for what you saw. It was a mistake, no' one I am willing to make again. You may live wherever your husband wishes, but I hope that you will both spend some time here with me."

"Aye, if Edana wishes it," Angus agreed wholeheartedly.

She nodded.

"The truth is I have turned down five offers of marriage for you over the years and I…" He smiled a little when she snapped her gaping mouth shut. "I dinna tell you because I feared the men would mistake your abilities for something evil. I couldna allow you to come to harm."

"Why Keary?"

"I must admit when he said he had fallen in love with you from the moment he had met you, that I wanted to believe he would be the right man for you. His title helped, but I believe Angus is the one for you, lass. He has proven he cares for you."

"Thank you, Da. He is the only one for me. Can you convince Keary to give back our things, my horse?" she asked.

"Aye."

"And can we have men to help us rescue my brothers?" she asked.

"Have you any idea where they could be?" her father asked.

"Oppida is the only name they shared that might give a clue."

"Dunbarton's mistress," her father said.

Angus explained more about what had happened as far as they knew.

"I will make inquiries and go with you," her father said to Angus. To Edana, he said, "Wash up and make yourself presentable, lass. You will marry Angus in the kirk this eve if that is what you both wish. Keary can witness it for himself."

She gave her father a warm embrace.

"Quit your crying, daughter," her father said, running his hand over her hair. "Angus may change his mind."

"I willna change my mind," Angus said, smiling at her, giving her a heartfelt embrace also and a quick kiss on the lips before she left her father's solar. "She only cries happy tears now and they are most welcome."

She loved Angus for being so supportive all along. And she loved her father just as she had before. Now if only they could free her brothers. She had to admit she still wanted to pay Zenevieva back as well.

*** 

Angus, Niall, and Gunnolf quickly washed. The whole time, Angus thought about his own wife bathing in a tub and helping to scrub every bit of her before they shared a bed. He had to get his mind on wedding her in the kirk first before he embarrassed himself in front of his companions.

Dressed in cleaner garments, Gunnolf said,

"Didna I tell you so?"

Angus shook his head. "'Twas the lass and my doing and no' her da's. He was right about one thing, getting us together again made all the difference in the world."

Niall said, "Do you think James will have assumed such? Or will this be a surprise to him?"

"James is hard to figure sometimes. He was the one who, after we left for home that time so many years ago, chided me the most for not having spoken to the lass. He might have come to the conclusion that I would see her, grown, a bonny lass indeed, and want her for my own."

"If you hadna offered, I would have. She would make a fine warrior wife," Gunnolf said, and they headed out of the chamber and down the corridor to the stairs.

"Aye, which is another reason she would be mine. You would make her help fight your battles. I wish to keep her safe and love her every chance I get," Angus said.

Gunnolf and Niall laughed. Niall let out his breath as they headed down the stairs. "Looks to me like 'tis only you and me now, Gunnolf, who will be ready for more adventures."

\*\*\*

Once again, Angus stood in a kirk waiting for Edana to join with him and say the vows to make them husband and wife. Only this time, her father was there, and as many of the Chattan clansmen and women also who could pack themselves into the kirk. Gunnolf was able to witness it, too, this time. Niall was nearby, smiling and shaking his head. Angus wished Edana's mother and the rest of his family could have been there also.

Keary had left with his men, demanding his sister come home with him. But Lady Allison stayed with the Chattan clan, interested in meeting Edana's brothers and not wishing to incur her brother's wrath for having freed the MacNeills and Edana and run away with them.

When Angus saw Edana dressed in green this time, the bodice of her léine trimmed in gold threads, the gown showing off her soft curves, he smiled. She was beautiful. Every bit of her from her dark reddish brown hair shiny and curling about her shoulders, her rosy lips smiling at him, her blue eyes wide with expectation, to her cheeks turning rosy with his perusal.

He loved her with all his heart. Truth was he would prefer to leave her home in the safety of the keep, but she might be able to help them locate her brothers. He didn't trust she'd stay at home if he left her behind while he searched for them with her father and his men.

This time he said his vows with Edana, kissed her as chastely as he could, considering how much farther he wished to go, and even then, she blushed beautifully. Everyone, her people and his cousin and Gunnolf smiled broadly at them as they made their way out of the kirk and headed for the great hall where the feasting would begin.

He hoped as late as it was getting and knowing the early start they'd have to make in the morn, that everyone would leave them in peace before long.

But it was not to happen that way. After much drinking and celebrating and finally Allison and Una hauling Edana off to her chamber, Gunnolf and Niall gave Angus a difficult time.

"I was never more surprised than to see Gunnolf taking your place to guard because the lovely lass distracted you so much," Niall said, lifting another tankard of ale.

"We had others to guard, unlike the previous nights that we travelled," Angus said, defending himself. Truth be told, he had felt guilty for ignoring his duties.

"Och," Gunnolf said, "Angus *was* guarding."

Niall laughed. "Aye, one bonny lass."

"All night long," Gunnolf said.

Angus shook his head at them, amused by all the good-natured ribbing and looked at the doorway to the great hall again. What was taking the ladies so long in fetching him to join his wife? He rose from the bench.

Much of the conversation died as everyone waited expectantly for Angus to say something.

"He is just like Dougald. Impatient," Gunnolf said. "Go to her, mon. We have a long journey tomorrow, and I doubt you will get much sleep this eve."

Both Gunnolf and Niall stood then, and gave him a brotherly slap on the back and a shove toward the door.

Edana's father raised his tankard to Angus, "Take care with my precious daughter."

"Aye," Angus said, bowing his head a little. "It will be my pleasure." He strode toward the doorway with purpose while everyone cheered him from the great hall, many of the men adding their coarse comments concerning keeping the lass well satisfied the whole night through.

Amused at their good-hearted cheer, he was still a little apprehensive. He prayed he would not alarm or hurt the lass when he made love to her.

When he approached the bedchamber door, he heard giggling inside and smiled. He hoped that the ladies had helped to allay Edana's concerns about his bedding her. He knocked at the door. Silence.

Then hurried feminine footsteps. The door opened. Una grinned at Angus, then quickly stepped out of his way. Allison hastened across the floor, grabbed Una's hand, and rushed her out the door. As he shut it, he listened to their giggles as they continued down the corridor.

His new wife was hidden by the drapes surrounding the bed. But as he went to her, hoping he would not find a frightened rabbit, she tossed aside the covers and hurried out of the bed dressed in only a chemise, and threw herself at him.

"The anticipation is killing me," she said, hugging him tightly against her soft body. "Is it no' you?"

"Aye," he said smiling down at her, more than he, a braw Highland warrior, wished to admit.

# Chapter 11

To put Edana at ease, Una and Allison had shared with her scanty details of dalliances between men and women they had witnessed or gossip they'd overheard as servants had revealed their experiences. Edana had been so nervous—particularly when she heard the knock on her chamber door and knew Angus stood on the other side of it—that she thought she'd die from expectation.

The ladies told her the first time would be... sore. After a couple of days, she would feel more comfortable and could stand to do it again. She would do her duty, though she couldn't wait for more of Angus's kisses. They had to hurry, though, because the sooner they got this over, the faster she would heal and then be ready for him again.

Angus entered Edana's bedchamber and shut the door. Sitting on the bed, half hidden by the curtains draped around it, she couldn't see him. And she couldn't fight the anticipation any longer as he walked toward the bed.

She threw the curtains aside, fairly leapt off the bed, and rushed to embrace him. His eyes widened a bit to see her flying across the room to join him. She hoped he didn't mind that she threw herself at him right after he entered her chamber.

Smiling, he enveloped her in his arms at once. "Bonny lass."

She tugged at his belt, eager to get this over with. But he cupped her face and looked down at her, his dark brown eyes swimming with desire, his mouth seeking hers. At first his kisses were gentle, unassuming, loving. She adored this part of the sharing between a man and a woman. Wanting to touch every bit of him, she ran her hands over his waist and down his hips. His kisses became more urgent and she enjoyed knowing her caresses made him crave her even more.

She used her tongue on him again, just as she had seen Una doing with Seumas. The technique had worked wonders with Angus the last time. Except this time, he growled or mayhap groaned, she could not say for certain.

But his kisses grew more intense, capturing her mouth, his tongue sliding into *her* mouth this time. She nearly collapsed as he thrust his tongue between her parted lips, and she realized just what this was like. A man tupping a woman. The experience was most pleasurable. And wickedly decadent.

She sucked on his tongue, enjoying the sweet honeyed mead. He groaned, a growly, sensuous sound that she delighted in. His hands shifted down her shoulders to her waist, and then her arse. She felt lost in his touch as he ran his fingers over her body until he pulled her tight against his manhood. Hard, huge, he was ready for her, thrilling her.

That her hands or tongue on him could arouse him that quickly fascinated her. She loved the way his big hands caressed her, stroked her, making her hot and wet for him. Every bit of her tingled with eagerness and need. She wanted his hands touching every part of her, felt the tension pool in her belly, a restlessness to experience more.

Again, she tried to remove his belt when he jerked her chemise down and exposed her breasts. The room was cool and her breasts felt heavy and hot. Her nipples puckered and then

Angus did the most extraordinary thing. He kissed her breast, while one hand cupped the other. She thought she would die and go to heaven as his thumb stroked over the nipple and his mouth captured the other. This time he suckled and she groaned.

The ladies had not said one thing about a man touching a woman's breasts and just how pleasurable that could be.

Her fingers attempted to work on his belt, but he quickly removed his sword and *sgian dubh*, belt, and boots. Then he dispensed with his plaid, wearing only his tunic now. The neckline of her chemise was resting at her hips, and she wanted his chest bared to her also so she could run her hands over his muscles and skin. But if she pulled his tunic down over his shoulders, it would slip to the floor, and he would be completely naked. She didn't believe she was quite ready for that.

As quick as it was for him to remove his plaid, she didn't have time to breathe before he was kissing her again, his mouth on hers, his hands on her breasts. Her insides turned into heated wax as she felt every bit of her melting deep within.

Yearning to touch him, she lifted his tunic

to run her hands underneath the fabric so she could stroke his chest. Being so close, she wouldn't see all of him—not unless she stepped away from him. She hadn't expected him to stop everything he was undertaking with her while he concentrated on her touching him.

She didn't want him to quit caressing her. "Continue what you were doing," she said.

He only gave her a pained smile. She barely noticed as she swept her hands up his torso, felt the rigid muscles tightening, skimmed her fingers over his smooth chest except for streaks of raised skin where she knew he'd fought and been cut. Her father had them as well, so she was well aware of what that meant. She praised God that the injuries had not proved fatal.

He still held her so close she couldn't see what he actually looked like, though running her hands along his lightly haired chest felt pleasurable indeed. She tried to lift his tunic higher, to remove it so she could see him—his broad chest, his muscled shoulders. Mayhap she was not ready to witness the lower part of him yet, but it could not be helped.

"In a hurry, lass?" he asked, his hushed words strained as he kissed her forehead, a smile in his voice.

"I want to see you," she said, quite plainly.

As if she had said the magic words, he quickly shucked his tunic and then yanked at her chemise so that it puddled around her ankles.

He stepped back to observe her and the cool air in the bedchamber swept around her. Taking a deep breath, she took in his nakedness, her skin hot from his touching her. For a moment, they studied each other. Her skin felt flushed with his perusal. She tried not to think of how he regarded her as she relished viewing his magnificent body from this hardened muscles and scars, to the dark hair that trailed down to his manhood, that part of him that stood firm and proud.

She gawked at his staff, realizing now why the women said it would hurt the first time because it was so much bigger than she had imagined. She reached out and touched the weeping top and slid the moisture over him.

He sucked in his breath, rested his hands on her shoulders, and watched what she did. He held very still as she ran her fingers lightly down the rigid male appendage that responded instantly to her touch. Now, she knew just what *that* part of his body looked like that had pressed so very indecently against her back on the ride to her castle and when she had tried to sleep next to him. Now, every time he held her close, she would no longer have to guess.

"Harder," he said, his voice ragged.

She looked up at him, not comprehending. His eyes were dark and heavily lidded.

He took her hand and placed it on his staff, squeezed her fingers around him until she was holding him firmly, and then he guided her up and down.

He looked like he was ready to die—with pleasure. And she loved that her touching him proved just as pleasurable for him.

Then as if he couldn't take any more, he moved her hand to his hip, renewed his deliciously decadent kisses on her mouth, and touched his fingers to the place between her legs that had never been explored before. His remarkable fingers swept all over that very sensitive part of her, skipping, and teasing and slipping inside her as her heart pounded and her knees weakened. She couldn't describe the feelings—nothing that she'd ever experienced before—of pleasure and lightness and a heavenly uplifting, though she held on tight to him so that she wouldn't fall. She pressed her body wantonly against his fingers, his assault on her senses making her crave having him finish her off in a hurry. She had to appear as though *she* was ready to die—with pleasure.

Then the most amazing feelings rushed through her. She cried out at the sense of joy and enlightenment washing over her. She hardly noticed when he swept her off her feet in the next instant and deposited her on the bed.

She tensed a little, apprehensive again about the part of their lovemaking that would hurt. For all the rest, she'd eagerly do it over and over again.

His mouth covered hers now, his tongue stroking hers again, his body rubbing against her as if waiting for her to give permission to come inside. She loved every bit of the way he brought her to another pleasure pitch, and she cried out, "Oh aye, aye."

As if she had signaled him to enter her, he thrust that massive part of him into her feminine heat him that fascinated her so. A pinch of pain resulted, and she tensed. But he was inside her, warming her very core. Her husband, her lover, her Highlander.

"Relax, bonny Edana," he said, kissing her mouth.

She tried to relax, but the anticipation was

killing her. She stroked his backside, encouraging him to continue, but when he still didn't move deeper inside her, she said, "Are you hurting?"

He smiled then and kissed her cheek and deepened his thrust. She welcomed him with urgent kisses, caressing his arms and back and even his arse, loving every bit of him.

Edana was Angus's, the sweetest, most impulsive—for being such an innocent—lass he'd ever known. When she'd thrown herself into his arms, he'd loved it. No quivering rabbit waiting for him in bed. Though he'd had every intention of showing her he would give her as much pleasure as he could and change her opinion about sex if she had been afraid of the intimacy shared between a man and woman. She proved to be a dream in the flesh.

Twice, he'd brought her to pleasure, and twice she had looked ravishing and ravished all at once. He couldn't believe she'd touch his staff, and he nearly groaned out loud. He had assumed it might be weeks—if ever—before she had the courage.

Her hands on his face, his tongue enjoying hers, her teeth nipping at his lip, he continued to kiss her. And to thrust into her, enveloped in her tight, hot heat, unable to hold off. Then he came deep inside her, bathing her in his love.

He prayed his lovemaking hadn't made her too sore or anxious about joining with him again. With traveling the next day and for several more, they would probably not get another chance for some time, which would give her time to heal.

He finished and eased out of her. Saw her smiling up at him, full of wonder, and he kissed her again. She was everything he needed in a woman and a wife.

"Was it all right?" he asked, leaving her to get a towel, wet it, and wash her.

"Aye," she said, watching him. "Can we do it again?"

He grinned. He *loved* her.

\*\*\*

The next morning in the great hall, Edana couldn't help but feel a little shy when she broke her fast among her clansmen. Many of her people offered her smiles when they had never done so before. Had they accepted her just because Angus had taken her for his wife? Annoyance filled her, yet, making up with her father had meant the world to her. Her father had smiled at her and whispered in her ear that he hoped she would soon have wee grandchildren for him to spoil, especially if she had daughters.

That made her face heat and she knew she had to be blushing to high heaven.

Now, if only she could help Angus and her father to locate her brothers, all would be well.

Lady Allison practically bounced around on her toes she appeared so eager to see Edana off after they ate, so Edana and the others could bring her brothers home. Una would accompany her as before, and she seemed just as eager to get on their way.

Niall and Gunnolf kept smiling at Edana and Angus, knowing just what had happened all last night. Mayhap not all that had happened. She had walked slower than she normally did this morning, and she feared riding a horse might be a wee bit taxing. Yet she wouldn't have had it any other way. She believed she and Angus wouldn't have much of a chance to share carnal pleasures during the journey. The memories had to be lasting so she could reflect on them and smile all over again.

Twice during the night, Angus had been rather reluctant to make love to her. But only because he'd worried how she might feel today, especially with having to ride for who knew how long. Half in the haze of lovemaking, she thought he had murmured she was his wild Highlander, which had pleased her all the more. She adored the way he had treasured her for waking him to make love with her again and hadn't been annoyed that she had disturbed his sleep so.

Before he helped her to mount the horse, he whispered into her ear, his warmth sweet breath making her tingly all over again, and she wished they were in her bed still, "Edana, are you sure you can manage?"

"Aye." She would suffer any discomfort to search for her brothers.

Looking anxious, his brow furrowed and his dark eyes on her, Angus helped her onto the horse. And then they rode through the gates and headed for Lockton Castle.

When they reached there, they intended to stop and would request her horse and Niall's and Angus's belongings be returned to them, as they had allowed Keary to take the horses, clothes, and weapons of the men Gunnolf had knocked out and left unconscious in the cave.

With a force of twenty-five men and two women, she was glad the journey was uneventful this time.

She slept with Una both nights, but only after Edana had shared kisses with Angus in the dark, felt his mouth on her breasts, stroked his staff through his plaid, and then still feeling wet and needy, retired to the tent she shared with her maid.

The days were sunny, the nights cool and breezy, and clouds dusted the heavens. She was grateful the rain had let them be.

When they reached Lockton Castle, they had not expected to receive such a warm welcome. Keary made amends by offering to serve them a meal that eve, giving Edana and Angus a bedchamber for them to use when they retired for the night. He had noted his sister was not among them, but had not made any issue of the fact.

Edana didn't know what to think of Keary's change of heart. He smiled at her, but was careful not to show too much interest. And he was just as friendly toward Angus, who appeared as wary of his intentions as she felt. Keary joked with her father and with Niall, both of whom shared in the jests, but with a reserve that showed they were just as suspicious. Gunnolf remained aloof, arms folded, guarded.

While everyone else enjoyed the food, she and Angus had been anxious to leave the great hall and retire to the bedchamber. He ran his hand over her thigh again, and she smiled knowingly up at him.

"Think you anyone would notice if we slipped away to the chamber?" she asked Angus.

He smiled wickedly down at her. "All of your men, Keary, his people, and my own friends. Aye. Nary an eye would be anywhere except on us."

She poked at her bread. "Doing it would almost be worth it. Except I would be embarrassed to hear all the comments when we left the hall. Was it verra bad when you left to join me in my bed?"

Angus grinned at her and sipped from his mead. "You would have blushed furiously, lass."

She sighed. No one had said anything when she had left with Lady Allison and Una to retire to her bedchamber. "Mayhap if we left together, they would say naught."

"I am game to try it if you are," Angus said, his hand sliding up and down her thigh, making her blood heat.

Before she could agree to take their leave, her brother Kayne warned her—*Drummond ill. Fitz...burn.*

Her heart skipped. "I have heard from Kayne," she whispered to Angus. "Drummond is sick. Do you know of a Fitzburn?"

Frowning deeply, Angus shook his head.

She turned to her father seated on the other side of her and repeated what she'd heard.

Her father's face paled a little. "Drummond ill? That isna good to hear." His voice hard with concern, he asked, "What is this Fitzburn? A person? Place?"

"I dinna know what significance it has. The name doesna mean anything to you?" she asked.

"Mayhap a tavern by that name?" Angus asked.

Keary must have gotten the gist of their conversation, though she'd noticed he'd been watching her during nearly the whole of the meal—despite that she had been trying to ignore him—and said, "There is a tavern by that name a day's ride from here. Due north."

"We must go," Edana said anxiously, glad Keary had proved helpful. "If we leave tonight, we would reach the place by morn or a little later. If we wait, it would be nighttime again.

My youngest brother, Drummond is ill. We canna delay."

"What is it you seek?" Keary asked.

Edana stiffened, recalling Allison's reluctance to mention the woman in front of Keary, but mayhap he knew which chief kept her as his mistress. "Oppida. Do you know of her?"

Keary's eyes narrowed. "Aye. What of her?"

"My brothers must have…" She had to have blushed with embarrassment as hot as her face felt. "Done something that caused someone to take offense, and the man serving as her protector has placed them in his dungeon."

Keary slammed his fist on the table.

Edana jumped a little. Angus took her hand in his and squeezed it with reassurance.

"I should have killed the witch instead of allowing her to run away. No' that I thought a whole lot of the matter while my brothers fought me to rule the clan," Keary growled and Edana had no doubt the woman had angered him.

"What did she do to earn your ire?" Edana asked, worrying the woman might cause her brothers further pain and suffering.

"'Tis too delicate a subject for you to hear,

lass." Keary said to her father, "I dinna know where the wench is, but if a powerful chief is keeping her and he willna let the slight go and release your sons, mayhap a few more men and another clan to back yours might be in order."

Edana clamped her mouth shut. She couldn't believe how much Keary's attitude had changed with regard to her.

She suspected he was up to no good.

# Chapter 12

Instead of getting a good night's rest, and for Edana and Angus that meant no lovemaking as they had both hoped, the much larger group of men rode out from Lockton Castle, this time with Keary leading a force that amounted to thirty-strong of his own. As much as Angus was disappointed he could not spend the night with Edana in marital bliss, he was just as motivated to free Edana's brothers, and concerned about Drummond's health.

He remembered Drummond for being the most impetuous of Edana's brothers when Angus had last seen him. Drummond had been so angry over the girl's drowning and so upset that Edana had locked herself in her chambers for the final three days of the MacNeills' visit, that Angus had been quite impressed with him. He'd felt as Drummond had about Edana, concerned for her peace of mind.

Angus glanced at her, her brat covering her

head like a hood to protect her from the chilly breeze. He wished he could be with her in a big bed making love to her, keeping her warm, pleasuring her. Not believing his fortune in marrying the lass, he was glad Keary had not had the chance. Angus wished he had gone to see her at Rondover Castle way before now and...

He shook his head. What was done was done, and now he had every intention of always being there for her.

The winds shifted, whipping out of the north, and he knew they were in for another storm.

"Drummond canna die on us," Edana said, sounding anxious.

"Aye, lass. He is a strong man—a fighter. He will come through." Angus believed that with all his heart, though he still prayed fervently that it would come to pass.

That day so long ago, he had observed Drummond take the lads to task who had been involved in the tragic drowning—using his fists on the lads because he was so angry. Drummond hadn't cared that their father had already punished the boys with making them do extra work.

Their pranks had hurt Edana deeply, not to mention they had contributed to the older lass's drowning. Edana's eldest brothers had overseen the lads' work, making certain their duties were even more onerous. But Angus had admired Drummond for taking it to a more physical level. He truly believed if Drummond had not, the lads could very well have done the extra menial labor and smirked about it the whole time. They had needed some other form of punishment to serve as a deterrent from treating Edana so horribly. They had to know if they did anything further to her like that, their actions would earn them more of the same kind of rough treatment.

If any had tried to stop Drummond in meting out his own form of punishment, Angus would have stepped in to help Drummond. Or if any of the boys had looked to be getting the better of him, Angus would have fought on his behalf. He truly liked him and all his brothers.

"When we free your brothers, think you they will approve of my marrying you?" Angus asked, trying to get her mind off worrying about them.

She gave him a small smile. "They will want to know why we wed so hastily when you have no' seen me in years. Once we free them, and that is no longer a concern, they may be troubled. After the initial shock, will they be happy for me? Oh, aye, husband, because they will see how contented I am."

Angus smiled at her. "'Tis good. I like your brothers."

"They will treat you as one of their own," Edana said.

Amused, he raised a brow. "As long as *you* dinna treat me like your brother, we will do well."

She chuckled and gave him another smile. He swore she blushed a little.

Angus considered Keary's men spread out among Tibold's. He didn't like that Keary's men outnumbered theirs—even by just a few. Angus shared Edana's whispered sentiment—he didn't trust Keary completely. He suspected he wanted something out of the deal. Though what, the man wouldn't say.

As Angus had predicted, the weather that had started out so beautifully turned into a deluge—drenching man, woman, and beast. The cold rain and wind whipped about them that could chill the stoutest of men.

Huddling over their horses, the women put

on a good face, Edana cheering Una on and Una doing the same with Edana when one or the other appeared to falter. He wished he hadn't had to take Edana with him, but after she'd heard from her brother, he suspected they needed her help to steer them in the right direction. He was glad to see the women making the most of the bad weather.

He just prayed they'd find her brothers soon before Edana became ill.

***

Keary had made a concerted effort to avoid coveting Angus's wife while they had been dining in his great hall, but he couldn't help it. He kept thinking how he should have been the one seated next to her, whispering sweet sentiments in her ear, slipping his hand onto her thigh, giving it a squeeze, and watching her smile—at him, not at Angus.

Keary had suffered for years at the hand of an abusive father for being an illegitimate son like the rest of his half-brothers. Now that Keary had the title and lands, he deserved having a loving woman at his side. Edana should be that woman. Just as she deserved him—and all that he could give her. What could Angus provide her? Nothing but bed sport, and Keary could best him there as well. He was certain.

He had trailed Angus and Edana to keep an eye on the lass, but observing Angus watching her as if he was a besotted lad had proved more than Keary could bear. So he rode up ahead with Edana's father.

"'Tis said my aim with a bow is as good as the Welshmen who are so admired for their skill," Keary said, attempting to explain to the Chattan chief how worthy he was in fighting. "I have never been wounded in combat, save a small cut here or there, which attests to my skill in sword play also."

Tibold glanced in Keary's direction.

Keary smiled. He hoped he was winning favor with Edana's father. What if Angus was killed in battle at some point or another? Tibold had already agreed Keary could wed the lass, so Keary would hold him to the agreement when Angus was no longer in his way.

As to Edana, he had to tread lightly, show her how much he cared about her brothers, help her to locate and free them. It was another reason he had given her a bedchamber at Lockton Castle so that she could spend the night with her husband—to show friendship, as much as it had killed him to do so. He couldn't praise

God enough that Angus and she had not used that bed after all.

Not that going with Tibold and the others had all to do with currying favor with her father and with Edana though. Keary had to stop Oppida from ruining any more lives with her maliciousness. This was personal.

When he returned to Lockton Castle before he had to witness the wedding between Edana and Angus, he'd stewed about the situation the whole way back and come to the conclusion that even if it took more work to obtain his final goal—having Edana for his wife—it would be worth just about any sacrifice.

He was having a devil of a time not looking back over his shoulder to see how Edana fared in the torrent of rain pummeling them now. And to see if Angus was still watching her like an infatuated fool.

Then he laughed to himself because that's just what *he* was with regard to Edana. Why had he not visited Tibold once he had gained his title and lands?

He let out his breath in exasperation. Frankly, he hadn't given her a thought because he had only seen Edana when she was a young lass, and though he had loved her dark red hair and her fetching blue eyes, he had been more interested in *older* lasses at the time. As he recalled, she hadn't shown any interest in the lads, which for now was a good thing as she was unspoiled. Or had been until Angus got hold of her.

She had grown into a veritable beauty. And now that he had seen her, spoken with her, saw how much his sister liked her even, he wanted Edana for his own.

Tibold seemed lost in his own thoughts, probably worrying about his sons, while Keary kept puzzling over Edana and how she knew where her brothers had been. How *had* she known?

He stared straight ahead, rode maybe another mile before he couldn't stand not knowing. But he couldn't ask her or alert Angus he was still interested in the lass. He would have to speak with Angus on the matter and learn what he could from him. If Keary continued to be as friendly as he could toward Angus, mayhap Edana would see Keary as a friend also. And Angus would not suspect Keary had designs on his wife.

*** 

To Angus's surprise, Keary rode from a

place alongside Tibold near the front to join Angus and indicated he wanted to speak in private, saying only, "May I have a word?"

Angus dropped back behind the women and rode alongside Keary, wondering what he was up to.

"I would never have thought to take the lass on a journey like this," Keary said, his tone filled with haughty disapproval.

Angus didn't say anything as the rain poured down from the heavens even worse than before. They were barely able to see the riders in front of Edana and her maid now. He wanted the lass out of this weather as soon as possible. And to that end, he could barely think of anything else.

"She appears hardy enough. It just doesna seem to be the place for a woman," Keary persisted.

Angus suspected Keary was trying to learn why she rode with them. Their reasoning was none of his business.

Every breath Angus took and released, just like his horse's and Keary's, came out in a cold white mist. He prayed Edana and Una would not get sick.

"How does the lass know where her

brothers are?" Keary asked, poking into the matter again with another pointed question. "When she didna even know the place. She hadna seen her brothers there. How did she know they met with the wench?"

"Why did you come with us?" Angus asked, wondering if he would get the truth or a lie or something halfway in between. He was not about to discuss Edana's gift with him.

Keary took a deep breath, yanked at his plaid covering his head, attempting to keep it in place as a hood, the wind tugging it back again. "Everyone knows how much animosity I have for the whore."

"Oppida? I didna know." This was news to Angus. And he worried that Keary could cause more trouble than good when they arrived at the keep in question if the man wanted vengeance.

"She rallied our father against me and my brothers. Aye, not one of us was legitimate, and my da was always killing off a new wife who couldna manage childbirth. Or so we thought. Oppida canna have a child. But she is young and beautiful, and she greatly influenced him. I came to believe she actually murdered his two wives during childbirth because she feared if he had a legitimate son, my da would force Oppida to leave. Then he tried to marry another woman—the woman your brother wed—and when that didna come to pass, Oppida murdered my own da, knowing he would find yet another wife."

Angus glanced at Keary and saw he was serious, his face dark and grim.

"Someone poisoned him. 'Twas thought one of my brothers had done the deed so he could take his place. But I never believed it. Poison is a woman's method of murder. As soon as da was dead, Oppida tried to pit brother against brother. I saw right through her. She convinced one of my youngest half-brothers that she loved him and tried to get him to fight me. She wanted a younger man. One she thought to control. She knew she couldna wield any power over me. But he would never have an heir by her."

"I understand," Angus said, more than a little shocked over the matter. He understood the woman's wish to eliminate those who their father had loved—his wives and future legitimate heirs. But Angus couldn't comprehend the other matter. Certainly, not all families were close like he and his brothers or Edana and her brothers were. But to allow a conniving woman to lead them into battling each other? He couldn't imagine what was wrong with Keary's brothers.

Keary patted his horse's neck. "Thankfully, Finbar liked me well enough not to attempt to kill me and left our lands instead, ashamed, beaten. I would have eliminated the wench for everything she had done. Before I could locate her in all the turmoil, she escaped. Her meddling at Lockton had come to an end. Think you I would show the woman any mercy if I got hold of her? Nay."

"Some believe you forced her to leave."

"Aye, and I left it at that. I truly believed she wouldna make it on her own. In a roundabout way, 'tis my fault Edana's brothers are incarcerated. 'Twill be the last time that whore causes trouble in the Highlands."

Angus pondered the notion. He feared Keary still harbored a plan to somehow take Edana for his wife. The thought did occur that if Angus was conveniently killed in a skirmish, Keary could step in and offer to marry the grieving widow. So mayhap Keary still did have such a design in mind. But Angus also grew concerned Keary could cause more trouble between the clans should he attempt to kill Oppida for her past murderous deeds. Whoever the chief was who currently gave her a place in his home would not like that.

*\*\*\**

A stabbing pain struck Kayne in the arse, and he came off the pallet swinging his manacled wrists, clanging and clanking. A gray rat scurried off, squeaking, and disappeared through a small hole in the rock wall near the stone floor. Kayne cursed the bloody beast. Then he guessed where it had bitten him was better than some other place he might have suffered a bite, if he was willing to see this in a more positive light. Which he wasn't.

His brothers eyed him warily.

"Rat." Kayne glanced at Drummond, who was still shivering. Kayne had already piled his own threadbare blanket on top of his youngest brother to warm him.

Kayne thought he heard a noise near the cell door and turned and suddenly realized why he could see somewhat in the dark cell. A boy of eight or nine, thin, small of stature, round green eyes set in an owlish face, and wild red hair, stood with candle in hand, staring at him, his mouth gaping.

"How now?" Kayne eased to a sitting position so as not to alarm the boy, surprised to see the lad at whatever ungodly hour it was in this place. He had to be a guard's son, or...the chief's to gain entrance?

The boy didn't say anything as Gildas wiped the sleep from his eyes and sat up. Drummond shook with fever, mumbling something incoherent. Despite not wanting Edana to search for them on her own, Kayne had to get word to her that Drummond was ill and could die. He'd tried to alert her several times, praying she had received his message.

"What is your name, son?" Kayne asked.

"Pol," the lad said, his voice so quiet that Kayne had to strain to hear it.

"Why, you are a strapping young lad, Pol. To what do we owe the pleasure of your company?" Maybe if he could garner a friendship with the wee lad, he might help them win their freedom one way or another.

"They...they say you were with Oppida," Pol said, hesitantly at first, then blurting the rest out.

"Aye, but no' mayhap in the way you have heard. Drummond is very ill and could die," Kayne said, motioning to his brother. Kayne himself was sick with worry that his youngest brother might not make it. And then who would be the next to succumb to the hardships of life in a dank dungeon?

The boy studied Drummond.

"He made the mistake of kissing…Oppida. She has a way of enticing a man to do such that he should not do. Drummond is the youngest of my brothers, so he doesna think about the consequences as much as he should," Kayne said.

Tying his long dark hair back in a tail, Halwn sat up now, watching the exchange.

Pol turned to look at Halwn briefly, then his eyes riveted back to Kayne. "They said he did more. That all of you did."

Kayne and Halwn snorted in unison. The boy's eyes widened again.

Halwn tugged his blanket around his bare shoulders and leaned close to the moss-covered wall. "We dinna kiss that kind of woman or avail ourselves of anything further."

"What do you mean?" Pol asked, curious.

"Ah, lad, 'tis no' for us to say about such a matter. Only to say we didna touch the woman in any manner. We only defended our brother when he was attacked, as any brother would another. Do you have brothers?" Kayne asked.

Pol shook his head. "I…I wish I did. Like

you." He again surveyed the men.

Kayne's eldest brother, Egan, opened his eyes, but he didn't sit up and Kayne believed Egan didn't wish to spook the lad. If Kayne or Halwn could gain the lad's trust, all the better.

"You have lost your mother?" Kayne asked, assuming he must have and that was the reason Oppida was here.

Pol nodded, his eyes bright with tears.

"Och, lass, we lost ours only last winter. 'Tis a terrible thing to lose your mother." It wasn't the same—as they were grown men, but the lad seemed to believe it was because as a young boy he could only think of it from his standpoint.

"Can you get Drummond another blanket?" Halwn asked. "He shakes something awful from the chills."

"Aye," Pol said, his voice again soft. He raced to an empty cell, the candle flame flickering wildly.

Kayne exchanged a hopeful look with his brothers. Mayhap the lad could truly help them.

Pol dashed back with a blanket and shoved it through the cell bars. When Kayne took it, Pol quickly stepped away from the cell as if he knew he should not get so close to the dangerous men.

"Our da and sister will be fairly worried about us when we dinna return. I can imagine our sister in tears."

"You have a sister, too?" Pol marveled.

"Aye. She is verra bonny indeed. She has red hair, mayhap darker than yours and blue eyes instead of green like yours. If people didna know, they might think she was your sister," Kayne said.

"Is she my age?"

"Nay, but she is the youngest of us."

"Will she come for you?"

"We fear she might and then what would your..." Kayne almost said chief. The boy might be just a guard's son, allowed to see what it was like for the prisoners kept down here because one day he would be a guard. But what if he was the chief's son? "What would your da do then if she came looking for us? Put her in here with us?"

Pol licked his lips with nervousness.

"Would he strip her of her clothes?" Halwn asked, his voice hard with anger.

"Would...would she look for you...here?" Pol asked, his voice wilting.

"Aye. We fear for her safety. She, who is a

sweet innocent, unlike Oppida," Kayne said.

Pol stiffened, his red brows furrowing.

Kayne feared he'd said the wrong thing and forced the lad to side with the witch.

"She...she is no innocent," Pol said, his words bitter.

Halwn was about to make exception to the boy's comment, but Kayne put his hand on his chest, willing him to silence his tongue. "Oppida?" Kayne asked.

"Aye. She is the devil," Pol said.

Kayne smiled, albeit a wee bit evilly. "Aye, lad. The witch blinds a man to do her bidding. She is no innocent."

"She scowls at me when she thinks I dinna see. She tries to make me drink things that I dinna want to drink. She pretends to love me when my da watches. I dinna like her," Pol said.

"What of the other men in your da's castle?" Kayne asked, still attempting to verify that the lad was the chief's son.

Pol said nothing, just stared at him solemnly.

"They like her?" Kayne prompted.

"They...want her...like my da does. I hear the men talk. She...smiles at them. Teases them. But at least no' that I have ever seen, she doesna allow the men to touch her. Mayhap they are afraid they will end up down here. Or mayhap she is afraid *she* will." Pol let out his breath and the candle flame flickered. "I wish he would send her away and find me a real mother."

Kayne didn't want to suggest it as he was afraid of where this might lead, but he didn't know what else to say that might encourage the lad to help them. "Our sister, Edana, is sweetness and light. She loves children and we had hoped she would find a husband soon as she needs one to keep her safe."

Halwn jumped in and added, "She wishes wee bairns of her own, but she could use a good stout lad such as yourself who would help her and protect her when your da is away."

"She would look as though she were your mother as red haired as she is, and she would treat you as her own son, mark my word," Kayne said.

"Is...she bonny? My da wouldna look at her if she was no'."

"Oh, aye," Kayne said. "Once her eyes capture a mon's gaze, he finds himself looking into those pools of blue, entranced. Her hair catches the sunlight and fairly sparkles. Her cheeks blush the most beautiful red when she is embarrassed," Kayne said, Halwn nodding.

"Alas, we are but her brothers, meant to protect her, and now we are here," Halwn said, spreading his hand out to emphasize just where that meant.

"How...how will she know to come to the MacRae keep?"

Kayne felt the anvil pressed against his chest lighten a wee bit. Now they knew where they were. "She loves us so dearly, Pol, as she does anyone she grows close to, that she will do everything in her power to find us. But we fear your da will do to her what he has done to us."

Pol shook his head. "He canna."

"But what if he does if she comes here? Or what if Oppida does something evil to her? Tells your da something that makes him believe our sweet dear sister isna an innocent?"

Pol chewed on his bottom lip, then swallowed hard. He reached inside his tunic and pulled out a bannock and slipped it through the cell door. "I will come back. I...I dinna know what to do. Where are you from?"

"Like you, our father is a chief."

The boy's eyes rounded.

"Aye. Our sister is the daughter of a chief. A suitable wife for a chief." Kayne wanted the lad to know they were of the same rank as him so that he could see their plight better, if he envisioned himself in Kayne's place. Yet he feared the boy might believe the Clan Chattan would wage war on the MacRaes if they learned of this and so no word would be leaked of their imprisonment.

"I...I canna unlock the door or your manacles. The guard let me come down here to talk to you. But he wouldna let me have the keys to free you." Pol slipped his hand underneath his tunic again, and this time he pulled out a flask. "Drink of the honey mead. I will fill it back up and return again later. But I canna let my da know I came to see you."

"Thank you, lad. When we see Edana, we will tell her of your kindness to us."

The boy waited while Kayne took the flask and tried to get Drummond to drink of the mead. He had already tossed the extra worn blanket off, his skin flushed, his eyes wild. "Drink, Drummond. The lad, Pol, has brought you something to help with your fever," Kayne said, reminding the boy that their brother was ill and could die.

"I...I will see if our healer can give me something to give to him...or...mayhap I can

ask how to go about ridding a body of fever."
Pol seemed contemplative.

"Can you trust her?" Halwn asked. "If she gave you something to give Drummond?"

"Oh, aye, she wouldna harm him."

"Nay, I am meaning, would she tell your da you had spoken to her about such?"

"Nay," Pol said with conviction. "We are friends. I aid her in finding the herbs she needs. She says I am a great help to her. She has even been closer to me since my mother died."

"Good," Kayne said. "We thank you for your kindness, Pol. You will make a fine chief someday."

A shadow of a smile ghosted across Pol's small face.

The brothers quickly finished off the mead, then Kayne handed the empty flask back to Pol. "No' that she intends you any harm, lad, but if Oppida attempts to force you to eat or drink that which you dinna want, tell your da, and dinna allow her to make you succumb to her wishes."

"Aye." Pol jammed his flask back inside his tunic and said, "Later." Then he hurried off, leaving them behind in darkness.

# Chapter 13

Angus, Edana, her maid, and all the men who had traveled with them arrived at the Fitzburn Tavern later than they intended because the weather held them back. Angus had hoped they would arrive earlier so they could learn where Oppida lived and continue on their way. He didn't want Edana out in this weather further. He had hoped to leave her at the tavern with a guard posted while he and her father and his men continued to the place where Edana's brothers were being held prisoner.

The two-story tavern's gray stone walls and thatched roof blended with the gray sky and day. It was late afternoon, the rain slackening off, and no one in the village was out in the dreary weather. The men and women were all drenched and exhausted. Several had taken refuge in the tavern while Angus and Tibold hastened to pay for rooms, taking six of the eight rooms that were available. Some of the men would bed down in the stables. Others found owners of crofts who would take them in. Gunnolf and Niall shared a room with Tibold and Keary.

Since Tibold was the father of the men who were incarcerated, he kept four of his guards with him as they questioned everyone already eating or drinking in the common room of the tavern, concerning the whereabouts of Oppida. Did any of them know where she lived? Hopefully, answers would soon be forthcoming.

A peat fire burned in the hearth on one wall, the smell of leather, horse, man, wet wool, and peat permeating the air. Ale and fish stew added to the smells while voices grew more boisterous as men gathered at the tables, glad to be out of the bad weather, and having food and drink to bolster their spirits.

Angus intended to retire to one of the rooms with Edana for a brief time. But she wished to learn if anyone had word about her brothers. She was shivering so hard, he feared if he didn't get her out of her wet clothes, she would grow ill. Still, she proved reluctant to leave her da's side. Undeterred, Angus scooped her into his arms without warning. Her expression revealed shock, eyes wide, her lips parted as she let out a small squeal.

Not waiting for her to object, Angus carried her up the wooden steps to the second floor of the tavern. A few laughs and ribald comments punctuated their exodus—about a man being in charge, a woman knowing her place, and other such things that had him smiling and her frowning.

Una followed close behind, just as wet and bedraggled and tired looking.

Angus set Edana on her feet inside the room, unsure what to do with Una. He didn't wish her to join them, but they couldn't afford to give her a room to herself as few rooms as there were, nor could they safely foist her off on the men. Angus had no intention of sleeping with the men, but Una needed to divest herself of her wet clothing as well.

Fully intending to help Edana out of her wet garments and then leave so that Una could do the same with hers, he shut the door to the room. He started across the floor to help Edana as her chilled fingers worked to unfasten her brooch. Before he reached her, a knock at the door stopped him. He stalked back to it and opened the door.

Una's father, one of Tibold's head guards, black-bearded and black-eyed, stood in the doorway and said, "I have found a crofter who will take Una and me and two of my men in. My chief says that they still have no word of where his sons are, but he will continue to question newcomers to the pub to see if any know of the woman and where she may be. Then he will make further plans. He says to sleep and food will be sent up in a few hours." Una's da bowed his head a little to Angus. "Sleep well." Then he smiled at Angus and hurried his very wet daughter down the corridor to the stairs.

Vastly relieved that the maid's father took her off Angus's hands, he quickly shut and barred the door and turned to see Edana struggling to get out of her wet brat, her fingers icy cold.

He strode forth, unfastened her brooch, and helped her out of her damp léine, chemise, hose, and shoes. Before he could remove his own clothes, she buried her naked body under furs in the big bed. He smiled at the sight, ready to warm her better than even the furs could.

He laid his clothes out to dry beside hers. Then he pulled the covers aside, glimpsed her arousing nakedness—light unmarred skin, dusky rose nipples peaked, the red curly hair at the juncture of her thighs. Her blue eyes and rosy lips smiled at him. And he wanted to bury himself in her—make love to her, and then sleep with her tucked in his arms.

He quickly climbed onto her and yanked the furs back over them.

"You are so cold." Her teeth chattered as she ran her hands over his back.

"Aye, you as well, wife. But we shall soon remedy that," he said, already seeking her mouth with his.

Even kissing her and pressing his body against the length of her soft skin brought his to life. His body burned hot with desire, and before he knew it, she was no longer shivering.

She parted her legs for him, and he rubbed her in that feminine place that made her arch against him, pushing for more. The days they had not been able to love each other made this one even more special.

She seemed to be holding her breath, her heart pounding wildly as he continued to stroke her need. Her expression was taut with concentration. He loved how responsive she was to him, but as soon as she looked ready to come and took a breath, he covered her cry of pleasure—not wanting the whole tavern full of men to hear just what was going on above stairs.

Not that they wouldn't have a good idea.

He slid his cock inside her warm, welcoming sheath and kissed her again. Her tongue wickedly teased his mouth, gaining entrance, taking charge, dominating him. He loved every new experience they shared. Her hands caressed his skin, her fingertips soft and kneading, encouraging him to thrust deeper, over and over again.

The stolen kisses at night before she had retired to her tent with Una were nothing like this. He had only imagined what it would be like to see her naked again, to feel her body all around his, to enjoy her lips and tongue on his. He loved cupping her breasts in his hands and feeling the taut nipples underneath his thumbs, in his mouth, his tongue tantalizing them.

She came again, only this time, he concentrated on his own raw need and missed capturing her cry with a kiss. A shock of heat speared him as he spilled his seed inside her. Hot and satiated and satisfied, he sank down on her and kissed her now thawed cheeks.

"Are you warm enough now, lass?"

She cast him a mischievous grin. "You have warmed me up just fine, husband."

"I was a fool no' to see you sooner," he

said, truly regretting looking for a wife anywhere else such as when he, Malcolm, and Dougald had searched in England for a woman, when the one for him had been so close at hand.

She smiled as he moved to her side, and she turned to rest half her body on his, her head on his chest. "Aye."

He chuckled, stroking her naked back, the furs still burying them, and he felt relaxed after the long night's ride and pummeling from the rain. This was how he wished to spend all his nights, and if he could get away with it, half his days.

But he knew she would not like the next part of his plan. Once he learned just where her brothers were, he wished to leave her safe somewhere. Even here, mayhap. He didn't want her with him, should they have to do battle to free her brothers.

***

Dunbarton, the old fool had lost his chance at happiness, MacRae thought as he watched Oppida enter the great hall. She looked as bonny as ever, her black hair plaited against her head, her dark sultry eyes on him and only on him. He loved that about her. She didn't flirt with other men. And that's what infuriated him—that some men would attempt to take advantage of her anytime she left the keep without him. But she loved so to visit with the people in nearby villages, spreading her cheer and seeing to their welfare. How could he not allow her to continue to do so?

Why Dunbarton only kept the woman as his mistress while he was alive and didn't make her the lady of Lockton Castle, taking some other woman as his wife instead, MacRae couldn't fathom. He rubbed his bearded chin. Though he had to admit he'd been reluctant to make her his wife as well. Devil take it, he couldn't say why, either.

She offered him a radiant smile and practically glided across the stone floor to where he was seated at the high table. His eyes weren't the only ones on her, however. He could never be certain if that bothered him that his men lusted after her as much as he did, or appealed that the woman was his and not theirs. And he alone had garnered such a prize.

She joined him at the table, wrapping her arms around him as if she hadn't had enough of him, though only a short time ago they had been naked in his bedchamber making love. Again, he noted the rabid interest from some of his men, the amusement from others. She took her seat next to him and plucked some of the goat cheese off his trencher. His gaze caught sight of his son of nine summers who looked on with disgust, his mouth turned down, his green eyes narrowed.

Mayhap that was why he had not taken Oppida for his wife. She seemed kind and loving toward Pol when MacRae was in their company, but the lad would not warm up to her. Was it that he had lost his mother and did not wish Oppida to take her place? He had talked to the boy about it over and over again. But not once had Pol told him why he didn't like her.

He would grow up and learn the way of men soon enough. One thing MacRae would not allow was for the boy to talk to the men in his dungeon again. How many times had he visited them before MacRae learned of it? What was the lad thinking?

Thankfully, his advisor had seen Pol leaving the corridor that led into the dungeon and had brought the difficulty to MacRae at once. But no matter how much MacRae had questioned his son, he remained adamant the men said nothing. And that he worried the one man was ill and dying.

Pol had much too kind a heart. Let the men who had molested his Oppida rot the rest of their days in his dungeon, for all he cared.

Shifting his attention from his son, MacRae gazed upon his adoring Oppida. He enjoyed loving her naked body in his chambers. The most extraordinary creature, she'd convinced him to pleasure her by the lake, in the woods, in the kitchen while the servants slept—any number of places—making him feel as he did in his youth. Spontaneous, lighthearted, young again.

He would not give her up for anything.

***

Angus and Edana slept for some time, then he woke and wished to see if Tibold or any of the other men had word about her brothers. "I am going downstairs to fetch us a meal and see if anyone has learned where your brothers might be, lass," Angus said, brushing his lips against her cheek as he leaned over her.

Edana opened her eyes and looked up at him. "I will go with you."

"Nay. Sleep, lass. I will have one of the men posted as a guard until I return."

"You will no' leave me behind?" she asked, her eyes rounding.

"We will talk about it when we have a clearer idea where they may be. Sleep, lass. I will return with our food in a bit."

Thankfully, she nodded and closed her eyes. He had quickly learned that when he suggested something she didn't agree with, she would attempt to change his mind. Which had to mean that the trip here had wearied the lass too much. And that again made him want to leave her behind to rest up further.

He left the bed and hurried to dress, then with one last kiss on her warm cheek, he left the room. Seeing Gunnolf headed up the stairs, Angus asked, "What news?"

"None."

"Will you watch Edana's room while I get us some food?"

"*Ja.*"

"Did you sleep?"

"For a while. Niall is still asleep. I am no' sure he can handle our adventures."

Agnes smiled, thinking that Niall had missed out all this time as he had helped James manage the MacNeill clan and their holdings.

The wooden steps creaking with his weight, Angus headed down them to the main floor. Every table was filled with men drinking and eating, laughing, and talking, the clinking of tankards adding to the noise in the room. A fire helped warm the place, though some travelers sat close to it, attempting to dry their wet clothes.

The smoky smell of peat mixed with wet wool, leather, the baking of bread, and fish stew.

Tibold motioned to Angus. His faced looked drawn. "We have spoken to everyone that has passed through here while you slept. No one knows of the woman."

"The pub owner?"

"He recalls naught of it," Tibold said, rubbing his eyes.

"Mayhap she met your sons outside the tavern and her benefactor saw the situation and had his men take them hostage."

"Aye. Could very well be. Others are asking the villagers if anyone had seen or heard anything," Tibold said.

"Have you rested at all?" Angus asked. It would not do if Edana's father grew ill.

He shook his head.

"Go, rest. I will continue to query newcomers."

"What of Edana?"

"Gunnolf is guarding the room. She is

sleeping. I will take food up to her later."

Tibold clapped his hand on Angus's shoulder. "I am pleased to call you son. Should you learn anything of my sons' whereabouts, come get me."

"Aye."

Tibold headed for the stairs, looking weary and beat, his stride shortened and his footsteps more of a shuffle than his usual brusque manner of stomping about.

Angus turned his attention to the crowd. Was Keary sleeping as well? He saw no sign of him.

Angus went to speak to the owner, a large beefy man with a red face, who was pouring ale into tankards. "I already know what you are going to ask and I will tell you the same as I told Tibold. I know of no incident where men hauled others out of here by force."

"And the woman? Oppida? Has she been here of late?"

"Aye...once...or twice."

"Who keeps the woman?" Angus asked.

The tavern owner shrugged.

Angus watched the man's gaze slide to the other side of the room. Angus was certain the man knew. "This has happened before, has it no'?"

The man's gaze returned to Angus's. "Like I said—"

"You fear retribution. The chief lives nearby and he and his men frequent the tavern. Is that no' so? You worry if you tell us, the chief will return and want revenge? But *we* are *here* now. And all I have to do is tell Tibold you know where his sons are, and that you are protecting this woman or the man who keeps her as his mistress. Do you know how many combined forces we have? How Tibold himself would do anything to learn the truth? Need I say more?"

"MacRae," the man spit out. "We have no quarrel with you or him either. 'Tis the woman who has caused all the grief of late."

"How many times has she done so?"

"Three, that I know of. She is the devil, that one. I dinna know how Chief MacRae canna see it. The woman is beautiful, but she tempts the men into losing their senses. Aye, they want her, but if she didna offer herself to them, naught would come of it."

"Where is his keep?"

"Three hour's ride due north of here. She comes with an escort while the chief is away on business. If he catches her with a mon, the wretch is done for. Why MacRae doesna kill the woman..." He shook his head. "Och, she claims the men took advantage of her and the chief always believes her when anybody else could see the right of it."

"But the brothers...they are still alive?" Angus asked, fearing the worst.

"The men fought hard and wouldna give up their brother. MacRae took the whole lot of them. I suspect he willna want to kill them, fearing who he might offend this time." The tavern owner leaned closer. "I dinna believe he knows just whose sons he has though or he wouldna have hauled them all away like he did."

That worried Angus. What if MacRae feared repercussions and killed Tibold's sons and attempted to bury the bodies and say they had never been at his castle? Any one of the men who had visited the tavern who they'd questioned might have gone to speak with the chief and warn him about what would come to pass if Angus or anyone in his party learned the truth.

"I thank you for your honesty." Angus stalked off and ran up the stairs to Tibold's shared quarters.

"News?" Gunnolf asked, straightening next to the door leading to Edana and his room, his blue eyes widening.

"Aye, 'tis MacRae who has the Chattan brothers." Angus knocked on Tibold's door.

Niall answered it, dressed and looking as though he was on his way out of the room. "Have you any word?"

"Aye, 'tis MacRae who has the men," Angus said, loud enough for Tibold to hear.

Tibold quickly came off the bed and began to dress. "Where is MacRae's keep?"

Angus told him. "I must speak with Edana."

"You dinna plan to take her with us, do you?" her father asked, his face dark with concern.

"I will talk to her." Angus hoped to leave her here, but he was torn between worrying for her safety if she remained behind and taking her into a potential battle if that's what they were bound for. He entered their room, then shut the door.

Her eyes remained closed, her hair spilling over the furs, her face angelic in sleep. He sighed. He did not want to move her from here. But he suspected if he left her behind, she might just try to follow him. He sat down beside her on the bed and caressed her hair. "Lass, we have word of where the woman resides."

Edana eyes popped open and she quickly sat up. "MacRae! Kayne just told me. We must go at once."

"Aye, but wouldna it be better if you stayed here with a few of your father's men?"

"Nay," she said, and tried to get out of bed, but he was sitting on the furs, pinning her down and blocking her path.

He leaned over and kissed her forehead. "All right. Dress. I will get us some food and then we will be on our way."

Before he could leave the room, a knock on the door sounded. He answered it and found the tavern keeper's daughter standing there with a tray of two bowls of fish soup, bannocks, and chunks of goat cheese.

"Thank you." He took the tray from her, then shut the door with his foot.

"How long will it take us to get there?" Edana asked, slipping the chemise over her head.

Fascinated, he watched the fabric catch on her breasts. He didn't offer to help her with her garment, not believing how lucky he was that he could feast on such beauty. She quickly tugged the chemise down and rushed to pull the léine over her head next.

He took a deep breath. "Mayhap about three hours. Depending on the weather."

"Is it raining again?" she asked, sitting down to eat her food.

"Nay. You canna see the stars tonight, though." He wolfed down his food, like he often did, but noticed she was trying to eat hers just as fast so they could be on their way. "Are you certain you dinna want to wait here for us with your maid? 'Tis late. And I dinna want you in the middle of a skirmish if it comes to that."

"Nay. I want to see my brothers as soon as possible."

A knock on the door sounded. "Come!" Angus said.

The door opened and Niall said, "We are ready to go."

Edana hurried to pull on her hose and slipped on her shoes, finished the last of her soup, seized her bread, and said, "We are also."

Angus prayed to God he wasn't making a mistake with allowing Edana to come with them this time.

# Chapter 14

Oppida whispered in MacRae's ear, "I will be waiting for you in bed. Dinna delay."

Then she gave him another one of her come-hither smiles and hurried off. Just her whispered breath on his ear made his cock twitch with eagerness. He watched her hips sway as she left the great hall, most of his men's eyes on her. Eager to join her, he rose from his seat and brought an end to the meal.

Fairly racing up the narrow stairs like an over-exuberant lad, he soon reached his chambers. She would be in the bed, the curtains drawn around it. He never knew what kind of sex play she would be interested in, and the anticipation made him all the more randy. He stripped down to his tunic when a knock sounded on his door. Unless a battle raged in the outer bailey, he had made it clear no one was to disturb him here. He headed for the door and yanked it open, his face hot with annoyance.

Scully, black-bearded and eyed, his indomitable advisor, who never looked worried, stood before him, wearing a prominent crease of concern over his brows and said quickly, "One of our men was at Fitzburn Tavern. The chief of the Clan Chattan is looking for his son. From what our man learned, he thought it had to be one of the men manacled in our dungeon. The sick one."

MacRae cursed about the folly of the situation. "How many men does he have?"

"He wasna certain. Several were staying at various crofters' homes. Some in the tavern. Others in the stable. With everyone split up so much, he couldna say."

Damnation. "Aye, let me get dressed. I will meet you below stairs shortly. Wait."

MacRae did *not* want to give up the men in his dungeon. Worse, he hated the notion anyone would attempt to intimidate him into doing what he didn't wish, particularly when he was within his rights to punish the men. He'd had every intention of letting them rot in hell for the rest of their short lives in the foul place of their making.

"Send men to the tavern and learn as much

as you can about Chattan's numbers." MacRae paused. "He doesna know I have them here, does he?"

"Nay. Before our man left, he had witnessed the Chattan chief speaking to the tavern owner. He didna tell him anything."

"Good. Send a man to learn what he can and return here at once with the news." MacRae closed the door and stared at the bed. Even if anyone did learn of the men being held here, it would take time for them to reach the keep.

But he couldn't think of anything else. Making love to Oppida was out of the question for the moment. Cursing aloud, he redressed. He left the room and slammed the door. As he stormed down the corridor, he vowed that the next time some man bothered his woman, MacRae would learn who sired the whelp first. God's wounds, if all the men were brothers? No wonder the chief of the Chattan clan would be looking for them. MacRae would tear down any castle's fortifications himself if he knew his own son was imprisoned inside.

Mayhap they were only the man's friends or some of the chief's men sent to protect him. Even so, if one of the men was his son, that meant trouble.

MacRae ran down the stairs. He had to know the truth.

\*\*\*

"We are moving much too slowly," Edana said to Angus, wishing they could gallop the whole way to the MacRae keep. "What if he learns we are coming? What if he wishes to get rid of them before we arrive?" She couldn't stop worrying about her brothers.

"Lass, no good will come of stewing about what may happen. We must have faith that all will be settled peaceably."

She eyed Keary then, riding with Tibold ahead of the pack. She was forced to canter in the middle with Angus and Gunnolf and Niall, serving as her dutiful personal bodyguards. They had made Una stay behind in the village— despite her maid's objections. But Tibold hadn't wanted either woman to come along for the journey. Since Edana was Angus's responsibility now, he'd left the decision about taking her with them up to him.

She realized then just how much she appreciated Angus as a husband. Her da would have left her behind. Angus had wanted to keep her safe, but knew how much of a stake she had in being with them, and he had agreed to take her with him based on what she'd wanted. She loved him for it.

"I worry about Keary," she said.

"Aye."

She glanced at Angus. "Do you think it will be enough that we get my brothers back? Do you think Keary will want Oppida's head?"

"Aye, lass. I do believe if he could, he would kill the woman."

"Does my da know?"

"I spoke to him in private about Keary's interest in all of this."

"Good. Mayhap he can stop Keary if he attempts to involve us in a battle." She pondered the chief, MacRae. "Do you know this mon?"

"Nay. I have never met him."

"My da?"

"Once, he said. But he had been busy speaking with others and didna truly get a sense of the man. He said he had a small son, and he seemed devoted to him. But that was it."

"If he is devoted..." She paused. "What if Keary was right in believing that Oppida poisoned his da's two wives? And poisoned his da? What if the woman wants to rid the chief of his son?"

"'Tis possible," Angus said. "I suspect

Keary intends to reveal all he knows of the matter to MacRae. Whether the man is blinded by the woman's beauty and will do naught about it is another matter."

Edana gave a soft ladylike snort. "I canna imagine a woman having such an effect on any man to that degree."

Angus smiled warmly at her. "You have that effect on me, my bonny wife. You could tell me anything, and I would believe you."

She smiled at him. "I doubt it."

He chuckled.

The men of their party had spread out across the glen, only tightening their ranks when they encountered woodlands. Again, they did so when they had to ford a river that narrowed at one location and widened in either direction from there.

Once they crossed the river, some commotion ahead of them made her perk up in her saddle. "What is the difficulty? Can you tell?" she asked Angus, as she strained to see around the men riding in front of her.

"I will investigate." He rode up ahead, but when she tried to follow, Niall and Gunnolf cut her off and smiled to see her scowl at them.

She sighed deeply. Maybe a fight was about

to ensue and they were right to keep her safe in the center.

Angus quickly returned to her and said, "'Tis one of MacRae's guards. He was told to learn how many of us there are. Now he knows. Only he isna returning to tell MacRae of it."

"Was he the only man sent to scout for us?"

"That he knows of. But all of the men are so spread out, if they come across anymore of MacRae's men, they will apprehend them and bring them to Tibold. The scout was told we didna know that your brothers had been imprisoned at the MacRae holdings, nor did they know how many there are of us. I am certain MacRae will quickly concede, once he realizes he is up against three forces, no' just one clan."

She smiled a little at Angus. He raised his brows. "Aye, though the MacNeills only number two, and Gunnolf is as much a brother to my cousin and me, we call him a MacNeill— but we are powerful, despite our small force. I only have to call on James to strengthen our numbers in short order."

"Have I told you how much I love you?" she asked.

Gunnolf and Niall glanced in their

direction.

"Aye, lass, in every way that it counts and then some," Angus said, smiling.

Her cheeks heated, chasing away the chill.

Carrying torches to light their way, they finally reached the MacRae fortifications in the dark. Six towers sat at equal points along the curtain wall, torches lighting a couple of places on the wall walk where only a handful of men appeared to be guarding on top of the walls.

A shout went out as guards quickly assembled to see the number of men on horseback heading for the keep. Tibold and Keary kept their men well out of range of arrowshot.

A man shouted down to someone else and the shouts continued as MacRae men were rallied from their beds.

Between the chilly night air, the brisk breeze, and the impending danger, Edana felt the cold seep into her bones. She was glad Una was not with them, but also relieved they had not had to face another bout of rain.

"What are they waiting for?" she asked Angus, whispering as if the men on the wall walk could hear her from this distance.

"Your da is waiting for all of our combined

forces to line up, to show MacRae that he isna dealing with a mere matter of a couple of handfuls of men."

She watched then to see the others lighting torches to show how many men stretched across the dark landscape. She had no knowledge of battle tactics, though she knew they remained this far away to avoid an archer's arrows.

She wished someone would do something. She wanted her brothers released now. She wanted to care for Drummond at once. Despite believing the men knew what they were doing, if she had been in charge, she would have gone straight to the gate and demanded her brothers' freedom.

Then her father rode forth with two of his men. She was surprised Keary didn't accompany him.

"I am here to demand my sons be released at once. I am Tibold, chief of the Clan Chattan. But I am no' the only one here. Two other clans have pledged their men to me in this matter. Tell that to MacRae."

A man disappeared from the wall walk.

"What will he do? This MacRae?" Edana asked Angus.

"If he is smart, he will release your

brothers."

She chewed on her bottom lip and squirmed in her saddle. The men had much more patience than she.

Finally, someone joined the others at the wall walk and shouted down, "MacRae said he will speak to Chattan upon the morrow."

"Now!" Tibold shouted. "My son, Drummond, is sick with fever. If he dies, it will be on MacRae's head."

The men on top of the wall walk exchanged looks. Then the one disappeared again.

Edana assumed they wondered how her father would know that.

"Why would he make my da wait until the morrow? Can he no' realize how infuriating that is?" Edana asked.

Angus said, "I am wondering if he is having your brothers fed and clothed. Mayhap attempting to improve their condition before your da sees them."

She ground her teeth, furious with this MacRae chief.

*"Edana,"* her brother, Kayne, whispered across her thoughts.

Tell me, she wanted to say back to him. Tell me what is going on inside MacRae's keep.

"My brother, Kayne, called out my name, or thought of it."

"Anything else?" Angus asked.

She shook her head. "If I could ask him to tell us all we wanted to know, I would."

The same man as before finally reappeared on the wall walk. "He said to let you in, and two of your men. No others."

Not about to be left out, Edana bolted for her father. She would accompany him no matter what.

"Edana!" Angus shouted, commanding, yet concerned as he galloped after her.

Along the wall walk, the guards crowded around to watch.

Tibold turned to see her riding toward him, his face tight with anger. "Edana, return at once to your place behind the men."

"Nay," she said. "I wish to see my brothers."

Angus caught up to her. "Devil have it, Edana. I dinna want you entering this place."

"I must see my brothers," she said. She implored her da, "Kayne called to me. I must see them."

Another rider's approach made them turn to learn who else would join them. *Keary.*

"I must speak with MacRae as well. I have learned he has a young son who could be in the gravest danger," Keary said.

From Oppida. Edana agreed. Though she hoped that he would not cause them trouble when they were attempting to free her brothers.

The gates were opened and instead of Tibold and his two guards accompanying him, his daughter, Angus, and Keary did.

As soon as they rode inside the bailey, they were disarmed, except for Edana who had her dirk hidden under her skirts. The men dismounted and Angus hurried to help Edana from her horse.

The portcullis ground shut and guards escorted them to the keep.

Her father's face grew hard with anger. Angus's expression appeared just as dark. Keary hid his expression under a mask of indifference. Her heart pounded as they entered the keep and were led to benches placed next to the fire in the hearth.

"Sit here. MacRae will join you in a moment," the guard said.

None of them sat. All stood rigid, her da and Angus's arms folded over their chests. Then Keary copied their stance.

259

A couple of servants moved through the great hall, not saying a word, eyes downcast, afraid of the fierce-looking men of three clans standing there, watching any movement.

Then a man strode toward them, red haired and bearded, his blue eyes hard, his face flushed with annoyance. He was accompanied by two other men, one whose hair was a light red gold. The other had a head full of brown hair, both wearing scowls just as dark. "I am MacRae," the man said, his voice hardened steel.

"Let me see my sons," Tibold growled, his voice low with threat.

"They are being awakened as we speak," MacRae said. "The one was caught forcing himself on my woman. He deserves to be punished. The others fought my men and had to be taken in hand as well. If the woman had been your wife and the roles had been reversed—"

"My wife is dead, MacRae, and she wouldna have been selling herself off to the highest bidder at some tavern."

"Now wait just a minute," MacRae said, his face turning purple with rage.

"He has the right of it," Keary spoke out, his voice just as dark. "I am Laird Lockton. My da was the laird before me, and Oppida served as his mistress. Ask her how she poisoned my da. Ask her how she murdered both his wives before that. 'Twas easy enough to do as she waited until the women were in childbirth, and she made it appear they died because of that. She didna want the competition. But my da wouldna marry her because she canna have children. Ask her of these things. Did she throw herself willingly at other men? Aye. My youngest brother also, after she murdered my father, thinking Finbar would become laird and she would be his wife. Think you she has a loyal bone in her body? Nay, only to serve her own dark purposes. Once that is accomplished, she is done with you."

"You lie," MacRae growled, his face a deadly scowl. "You lost her to me. You envy what I have."

Keary gave a scornful bark of laughter. "She is the devil, I say. I would have killed her for murdering my da and the women he had called his wives, though neither were my mother. Oppida slipped out of the castle during the fighting when she realized my youngest brother could not beat me. Would you risk your own son's life on such a woman? Ask him if she has ever tried to force some food or drink on him. My half-brothers and sister didna matter to her because we were not his legitimate sons and daughter. My da didna treat us with any respect. But your son still garners your affection, does he no'? She is evil. Anyone who gets in her way can easily be disposed of."

MacRae stared at Keary, the vein in his neck pulsing with anger, but he did not say anything.

"You want proof? I found the herbs she used to poison my da in her chamber. A man doesna resort to poisoning. A woman does," Keary said. "For your own son's sake, listen to what I have to say. Dinna allow her to blind you like she did my da."

"Fetch my son," MacRae said to one of his men. To the other, he commanded, "Bring Oppida down here."

With relief, Edana thought MacRae would be reasonable and learn the truth. But what of her brothers?

He turned his attention to Edana. "Who are you?"

"Edana, sister to the men you hold in your dungeon. And this is Angus MacNeill, my husband."

"MacNeill?" MacRae said, then swore

under his breath.

"Aye," Angus said. "Laird James is my brother."

But she suspected MacRae had already guessed that and was concerned the MacNeills would back the Chattan clan in this venture.

Both of the men MacRae sent to retrieve his son and mistress rushed back into the great hall. "They are missing," the one said, short of breath. "Oppida and your son."

# Chapter 15

MacRae stared at his men in disbelief. Edana felt sick to her stomach that Oppida could be holding the chief's son hostage, hiding somewhere.

"Their chambers are empty. Both of them," the man elaborated.

"Have everyone search for them. Now!" MacRae ordered.

"Aye."

The two men hurried off to wake the staff.

"Since you seemed to know so much about her, would Oppida have taken my son somewhere?" MacRae asked Keary.

"Mayhap to buy her time. If she thought you might turn her over to me to mete out her punishment, possibly. Mayhap to silence him if he should be able to corroborate that she has been trying to poison him."

"I have been blind," MacRae said under his breath.

"My brothers," Edana said. She wished she

could help MacRae search for the boy, but she had to see to her sick brother.

"Take them to see the Chattan brothers," MacRae said to one of the two guards.

"Nay, lass," Angus said. "I dinna want you to see the filth down there."

"They have been moved to a chamber near mine," MacRae said, verging on apologetic.

"If you wish it, I will help you look for the woman. I know what she looks like," Keary said, his voice dark with threat.

"Leave the woman to me," MacRae said, his voice stern. "But, aye, you may help with the search."

Keary bowed his head a little, but Edana thought if Keary got hold of her, he would dispense with Oppida himself. Edana hoped he would not and would allow MacRae to deal with her instead to keep some semblance of peace between the clans.

The man led Edana, Angus, and her father up a flight of narrow curved stairs, then down a long corridor. When they reached a chamber where a guard stood, the man with them said, "Let them pass."

"Wait here," Edana's da said, and she felt her eyes fill with tears. Angus wrapped his arms around her shoulders and held her close.

Tibold quickly returned from the bedchamber and said, "Come, daughter, Angus."

They joined him inside the chamber and found Drummond shivering in a bed, buried in furs, his face pale, sweaty. Her other brothers sat on the mattress, looking thinner than she remembered.

But when they saw her, their expressions brightened and they all hurried to greet her.

She expected them to smell badly, but they'd all been scrubbed clean, though it didn't matter. Too glad to see them all alive and as well as could be expected given the circumstances, she quickly hugged each of them. Then, as if she was their mother, she made them return to their seats on the bed. She quickly went to see Drummond.

"Was he injured? Has a healer seen to him?" she asked the man who had escorted them to the room.

"Nay, he wasna wounded. No' by a weapon. A healer has seen to him."

"Then the fever is due to the conditions of the dungeon."

"Aye," the guard said.

Glad that her youngest brother hadn't suffered an infection from a wound, she ran her hand over Drummond's hot brow. He stared at her, appearing not to comprehend who she was, and she felt sick at heart. She placed his hot hand against her cheek. "Drummond, I have come all this way to rescue you. You must come home with me now."

"Did you hear us, lass? Calling for you?" Kayne asked, as if trying to ease the tension in the chamber.

She nodded. "Aye, I heard you. And you said for me to stay away." She couldn't help sounding annoyed with him.

"For your own safety," Gildas said.

She humpfed. "I have brought men from three clans with me, willing to fight for your release. Did you think I would come alone?"

Her brothers looked at their da for confirmation. Angus quirked a brow as if telling on her in a silent way.

"Well, I didna. I lost my escort in a storm. How could I know that would happen?" she said.

Gildas groaned. Kayne shook his head and folded his arms.

"Dinna fret, Gildas, Kayne. I ended up with

a husband. Isna that good news?"

Her brothers, all but Drummond, looked at Angus.

"Angus MacNeill, youngest brother to Laird James MacNeill of Craigly Castle," Angus said, bowing his head slightly.

Most likely wondering how in the world that had happened, her brothers all stared at him, except for Drummond. He just gazed upon her. She couldn't tell if he really saw her or was in a world of his own.

She took a deep breath and held his hand, caressing it with her free hand. "Drummond, you must get well. We have a long way to travel before we are able to return home."

"He canna travel like this until he is well," her father said. "Taking him into the cold chilly weather could kill him."

Drummond could die even if he stayed here. But she couldn't think of that. He would get well. She would see to it.

"How do the rest of you feel?" she asked, hoping that none of them would become ill also.

"We are fine," Kayne said, "though we could use more food and mead to improve our strength before we leave. They did feed us some before you arrived."

Halwn shook his head. "I am ready to quit this place. What if this MacRae changes his mind and decides to toss us back in the cell again?"

"I believe he may understand the situation better. Laird Lockton is here, and he has explained something of Oppida's nature. I trust MacRae may see that you were all innocent of any wrongdoing where Oppida is concerned," Edana said.

"Edana," Drummond croaked out.

Relieved beyond measure that her youngest brother finally recognized her, she looked down at him. "Oh, aye, 'tis me. You must get better and we will take you home. Da is here. And our brothers are all well. Hungry, but they shall live. And my husband, Angus MacNeill." She motioned to Angus, who nodded to Drummond in greeting.

Drummond stared at him, then a small smile appeared. "The lad who was interested in our sister."

The others looked back at him as if they hadn't realized just who Angus was. They all rose from the bed and clapped him on the shoulders as if he was their long lost brother or friend.

"I will be damned," Kayne said. "You were the one my sister spoke of in a cryptic way, though we all knew who she meant."

She felt her face flush. She hadn't remembered speaking to her brothers about Angus in any manner, cryptic or otherwise.

Halwn grinned. "Took you long enough, mon."

"Aye, I canna agree more," Angus said, running his hand over her hair, his eyes on hers, looking concerned.

"But we are free to go?" Drummond asked, glancing around at the chamber as if realizing he was no longer manacled in a dungeon.

"Aye, but you canna. You are too ill," Edana said.

The movement of people outside the door caused them to glance in that direction.

"What is happening?" Kayne asked, his voice anxious.

"Keary told MacRae that Oppida poisoned his da's wives and his da. He warned she might wish to do the same to—" their da explained.

"The boy," Kayne exclaimed. "God's wounds. Pol told us she tried to force him to drink something he didna wish."

"He is missing. Both the boy and Oppida,"

their da said.

"We will help them search for the boy." Kayne glanced at his brothers, seeking their agreement. They all nodded their affirmation.

"Nay." Their da shook his head. "You have already found yourself in the dungeon—"

"The boy may have saved our lives," Kayne insisted. "He brought us bread and cheese and mead. He brought a drink laced with herbs for Drummond to help bring down his fever. He secured a blanket from another cell to keep Drummond warm. We owe the boy our lives."

"You are too weak." Their da frowned at them.

"Nay, we must do this, Da," Halwn agreed. "We will stay together. The boy liked us. He trusted us."

The brothers all looked at Edana, brows furrowed. "What?" she asked.

Kayne cleared his throat. "We said you were innocence and light. That you liked children."

"Aye, so?" She might not be all innocence or light, but if they thought so, she would not disagree with them.

Kayne blushed furiously.

Suddenly getting the gist of his concern,

she scowled at him. "You dinna tell him I would be his mother, did you, Kayne?"

"No' in so many words, nay," Kayne said.

Halwn quickly jumped in to defend him. "We were worried you would come here seeking us out and MacRae would take you in. We wanted Pol to warn you about the woman."

"What?" Edana asked.

"You should come with us," Halwn said.

"You want me to go with you to look for the boy? I must stay with Drummond." Edana soaked a cloth in a bowl of water and wrung it out.

"I will go with you," her da said to her brothers. "To keep you out of further trouble."

"'Twas Drummond who got us into trouble," Kayne said, and she thought he sounded like a lad of ten, instead of a grown man. Kayne glanced at Angus. "You will watch over Edana and Drummond?"

"Aye. The guard is still at the door also," Angus said.

Not that they needed a guard, she didn't believe.

The brothers left with their father, a little unsteady on their feet. The man who had shown Edana, Angus, and her father to the chamber met up with them just outside the door. "Can I help you?"

"We wish to help search for the boy," Kayne said.

"He spoke with you when you were down below?" the man asked the brothers.

"Aye, he is a kind-hearted lad," Kayne said. "We wish to help find him."

"Come with me then."

Edana continued to cool Drummond's brow. He seemed tired, but more alert now. "Do you remember the time I was running a fever and you helped to cool me with a wet cloth when the healer was too tired to do it any longer? You sat beside me and even when our brothers tried to relieve you, you wouldna go?" she asked.

"Aye," Drummond said.

"You didna call for me this time."

"You...would search for us...alone. I worried." Drummond looked at Angus. "Should I have...worried?"

Angus frowned. "Aye. We found the lass alone in an abandoned shieling. She was sharing it with her horse."

Drummond smiled at her. "Only you would take a horse...into a shieling."

She smiled back at him, guardedly relieved

he felt somewhat better.

*"Edana,"* a lad's voice called to her, in her usual strange way.

She looked at the doorway. No one but the guard stood there.

"Edana," Angus said, rubbing her arm. "What is the matter? You look as though you have seen a ghost."

"I...I heard a lad's voice speaking to me."

"Pol's?" Drummond said, trying to sit up.

"Nay, lie still," she said, and didn't like that she could push him back on the bed as he had no reserve strength.

She concentrated. And she tried to contact the boy through her thoughts, knowing it wouldn't work. It never had before. *"Are you with Oppida?"* she urgently asked the lad.

*"Aye,"* the small voice in her head said, and she was so shocked, she nearly collapsed on the floor.

Angus grabbed her arm and made her sit on the bed beside Drummond. "Edana, your face lost every bit of color. What is wrong?"

"He heard my thoughts and answered my question," she whispered to Angus and Drummond, not wanting the guard standing in the corridor outside the open door to overhear.

"How? That has never happened before, has it?" Drummond asked.

"Nay."

"Where is he? Can you ask him?" Angus asked.

"He said he is with Oppida." Edana concentrated again and asked the lad this time, *"Where has she taken you?"*

*"The woods past the postern gate where the servants enter."*

She quickly repeated what the lad had told her to Drummond and Angus. "This is bad. How can we tell his da where he is and how we know of it?"

"He wouldna believe you," Drummond said.

"We must tell him," Edana said. "If no one has gone beyond the castle walls to search for the lad, he is in imminent danger."

In a hushed tone, men spoke in the corridor. Edana swung around just in time to see MacRae and two of his guards stalk into the chamber.

"How do you know any of this?" MacRae asked.

Her heart beat rapidly, her skin chilling. He had to have overheard her speaking to Angus and Drummond.

"You were in on this. In with Oppida," MacRae charged.

"What?" She could not grasp what he was accusing of her exactly. She was so used to people not believing in her abilities, but to think she was...in on a plot to harm his son? How could he think such a thing?

"'Tis the only way you would know where the two of them are. I canna fathom how or why you would be working with the woman against me, but know this, if the woman kills my son, you and your kin will be dead," MacRae said. "Keep them here." He advanced on Edana and Angus moved to stop him, but the two guards seized his arms and slammed him up against a stone wall.

He fought to free himself, cursing at them in Gaelic.

Another couple of guards had gathered outside the chamber door. Drummond attempted to get out of bed, but Edana clasped his shoulder. "Stay, Drummond. You must get well."

And then MacRae, seized her arm and her heart stuttered. She gave out a shocked squeak.

Angus shouted, "God's wounds, release Edana at once!"

Ignoring Angus, MacRae yanked her out of the chamber.

# Chapter 16

Edana's heart pumped wildly as she feared what MacRae would do to her. He jerked her into a large chamber that she suspected was his, a dark bed sitting in the center of it, men's tunics hanging from pegs on the wall, and a chest sitting next to another wall. He released her, then slammed the solid oak door.

"Tell me where my son is and what part you have in this," MacRae growled, his face filled with fury.

*"Pol, does your da know you have the gift?"* she quickly asked him.

*"He doesna believe me."*

She straightened her back and gave MacRae her fiercest look. "Your son is in grave danger and it has naught to do with me. If you wish to save him, he told me where the woman has taken him."

"Told you?" he said skeptically.

"Aye, aye, just as he has told you that he

can hear others speaking to him in his thoughts."

The man's eyes rounded and he looked like he wanted to strangle her. "You know him. You have spoken with him."

"I have never seen your son. I have the same abilities as he has. 'Tis why I knew you had locked my brothers in your dungeon. And that my brother, Drummond, was ill."

MacRae's mouth gaped for a minute. "You canna do such a thing."

"I will try to learn more from your son. Ask what you will of me and I will ask him. But every moment we wait, Oppida is taking your son farther away from the castle."

"I sent men that way as soon as I heard your conspiratorial words. Ask Pol what name he gave his pony."

*"Pol, what did you name your pony?"*

*"She is taking me to the river, threatening to drown me."*

"The river. The woman is taking him to it and threatens to drown him," Edana hastened to tell his father.

"The name of his pony," MacRae grit out.

The man was a tyrant! *"The name of your pony, Pol. Your da doesna believe I can hear you speaking to me."*

*"Argent. He is gray. I call him Argent for silver."*

"Argent," she quickly told MacRae, "for silver. His pony is gray."

MacRae stared at her in disbelief.

"Let me return to my sick brother," Edana urged. "Free Angus. We are no' responsible for Oppida's evil doings."

*"Are you Edana? Is that why you knew where your brothers were? They wouldna tell me,"* Pol asked.

*"Aye."*

*"Help me."*

*"I have told your father. He has sent men to find you."*

"Your son asks for you to rescue him," Edana said to MacRae.

"Come with me." MacRae gave her no choice as he grabbed her arm and hauled her from the chamber. Two of his men waiting for him in the corridor hurried after them. "The river," MacRae said to his men.

She yanked her arm, trying to free herself from his steel grip, to no avail. She dug at his fingers, unable to loosen them from their stranglehold on her.

MacRae rushed her through the keep and

outside as if unaware of her struggles. Men quickly joined them with lighted torches. And he passed the word as to where his son and Oppida were.

Barely able to keep up with MacRae's long stride, she still attempted to pull free from his titan hold. His hand on her arm was bruising her skin. "What have you done to my brothers? My da?" she asked, her voice low with scorn.

"They still search within the keep. 'Twas my luck that I happened to pass by the chamber when I heard your words concerning where my son had been taken."

"We had naught to do with this." Edana understood how people would mistrust her words, but she had to make him understand.

"How did you learn your brothers were here?" MacRae asked, taking her to a horse, not her own. He helped her into the saddle.

He hadn't believed her.

"In the same manner I heard your son speaking to me. My brothers called to me."

MacRae mounted his horse and a dozen men soon followed them. "Someone must have talked in the village."

"Nay. I began searching for them days ago when one of my brothers called out to me."

"They were blindfolded. They didna know which castle they were being held in. Someone in the village had to have talked."

"My brothers didna know where they were being held at first. Aye. But…then they did. I dinna know how. I didna ask my brothers when I was reunited with them, but finally one of them said—in my thoughts—it was *your* castle."

MacRae snorted as he led her away from the castle at a gallop and into the woods, following a man with a torch. Several others carried them as well.

The sky had cleared, only a hint of cloud, but a full moon clung to the dark sky while stars twinkled like candles against the inkiness.

*"Pol, where are you?"* she asked.

*"She is taking me along the river to where it narrows."*

She told MacRae what his son had revealed.

"I dinna believe he is telling you these things. You must have known her plan," he growled at her.

"How would I know what the woman planned? I have never met her!" Stubborn, goat-headed, impossible man. "Ask me something that I canna know. Something that mayhap only you and your son know," Edana said, as she ducked beneath a low hanging oak branch.

MacRae didn't say anything for a while as they hurried as quickly as they could through the woods to reach the river. Then he finally said, "Ask him which girl he kissed yestereve."

"How old is he?" Edana asked, thinking he sounded young and the notion he wasna shocked her.

"He will be ten soon, but he is as precocious as I was at that age. *Ask him.*"

The lad reminded her of her brothers at that age. Had Angus been the same way? She took a deep breath and asked the question of Pol. He didn't answer her for the longest time, and she worried Oppida had injured him and he could not speak.

"Well?" MacRae asked.

"He isna saying anything."

"I knew you couldna do as you said you could," MacRae snapped at her.

*"Ingrid was the girl's name,"* Pol said. *"Hurry! Oppida is dragging me across the river."*

Edana quickly relayed the information to MacRae.

For a heartbeat, he stared at her as if he

couldn't believe she could know such things. Then he cursed up a storm, spurred his horse on, and they finally bolted out of the woods. Only a few feet away, a frothing river plunged down the hill. The woman attempted to drag the boy across the river south of them, but because of her long skirts and the swift flow of the water, she wasn't making much headway. The boy struggled to return to shore, a torch clutched in his hand as he lighted their way. He tugged and threw her off balance.

Redheaded like his father, he looked in their direction and saw them. His face was pale, but his eyes widened.

"Da!"

One of MacRae's men nocked an arrow. "Should I shoot her?"

"Nay, mon. She could take the lad down with her and drown him as far out as she is," MacRae warned and kicked his horse to a gallop to reach the two of them.

With his men, Edana rode after MacRae, not sure what she could do, wishing she could help in some way as she watched the frightened lad attempt to pull loose of the woman's tight grip.

The woman's black hair streamed down her

back, the strong breeze whipping some of it around her face. She turned and saw the men coming for her. She screamed. That's when Edana saw the *sgian dubh* in Oppida's free hand. That was why she wasn't carrying the torch. Her skin prickling, Edana feared she would use it on the boy, either to attempt to bargain with MacRae or to kill the lad if she thought she had no chance to live.

*"Fall into the water as if you have slipped,"* Edana told Pol. *"Oppida will either let go of you or fall with you and you can get free. Your da will save you."*

Without hesitation, Pol did as Edana told him, dropping into the water like a falling sapling. Only he doused the torch's flame and they could barely see him and Oppida in the black waters. Oppida nearly fell with him and lost her grip on his arm. She lunged forward to secure her hold on him to use him as a shield. But too late. MacRae struck with all his fury, sword slicing through the air, cutting her down. She screamed and sank into the water.

Edana quickly looked away as she tried to reach the boy. MacRae's men all gathered around, some dismounting and running into the water, others riding into it as Edana had done.

"Take my hand, Pol!" MacRae shouted.

The lad couldn't get to his feet and the water swept him down river. Edana and MacRae galloped after him, the other men soon joining them.

Her heart was beating so hard, she could hardly hear her shouts, "Pol! We are coming!"

MacRae reached him first and leapt off his horse. He landed in the water with a splash. He seized Pol by the arm and pulled him into his embrace. The boy coughed and spit out water. "How clever of you to think of falling and wrenching free of the woman in such a manner, Pol," his father said with pride.

"Edana told me to do it. She said you would save me."

MacRae turned slowly to see Edana sitting on her mount nearby. Relieved and glad for the lad's safety, she smiled at him, wishing to scowl at his father. "Thank you for aiding my brothers," she said to Pol with all the gratitude she felt in her heart. But she hadn't wished another clan to know of her gift.

"They were kind to me when Oppida wasna. *She* should have been in the dungeon and no' your brothers." Pol turned to look up at his da. "Will you marry Edana, Da? She is like me. She is bonny. Her brothers said she would be a good mother for me. And she would have bairns so I would have more brothers and sisters."

Her face feeling hot when the air proved so cold, Edana would kill her brothers.

MacRae lifted his son onto his horse, then joined him. "The lass is spoken for, son. Otherwise, I do believe I would have wed her." He cast a dark smile at her.

She frowned at MacRae. The lad was a charmer. The father was not. She would *not* have married the man. Anyone who would be so taken in with Oppida's charms was not the man for her.

"They said she has no husband," Pol insisted, as if he was ready to get this wedding between his father and her over and done with at once.

MacRae looked her over as if he finally saw her as a woman, and not an enemy of his clan.

"A man I knew in my youth came looking for me, Pol," Edana said, ignoring MacRae's sudden interest in her. "Before we discovered where my brothers were being held, I married him. So my brothers knew naught of the marriage." She didn't want the boy thinking her brothers had lied to him.

Wet and shivering, Pol leaned back against his father. His father wrapped his arm around Pol's waist as he cantered alongside Edana, the lad looking disheartened. She felt badly for him and wished he could find a mother who would be good for him.

"What about Oppida?" one of MacRae's men asked as they gathered about MacRae.

"Bury her somewhere out there," he said, motioning to the woods, not looking back at the woman he had killed. He maneuvered back through the woods to the keep.

She imagined MacRae had some soul searching to do of his own, concerning how his son could have died because MacRae had taken Oppida in.

Edana hoped when they arrived at the keep that all hell had not broken loose if her brothers and father learned Angus and Drummond were being held prisoner and she had been forcibly removed from the chamber.

A man carrying a torch rode into the woods to meet them, his brown eyes wide. "Fighting has broken out between our men and the Chattan and MacNeill."

"Damnation," MacRae said. "Ride ahead

and tell the men my son is safe and the other men had naught to do with Oppida's taking him. Edana is unharmed and will be returned shortly."

"Aye."

Not about to wait, Edana urged her mount to gallop after the man.

"Edana!" MacRae shouted, but she ignored the chief.

If his men killed any of her kin or her husband, she would not be responsible for her own actions.

*** 

As soon as MacRae took off with Edana, Angus had fought as if he was on the battlefield, protecting his brothers and his men. She was everything to him, and he wasn't about to lose her now.

"He willna hurt her," one of MacRae's guards said, but Angus didn't trust MacRae. Not as angry as he was over his son and not when he thought Edana had something to do with Oppida taking the lad hostage.

Angus hit one of the men in the head with his fist so hard, the guard stumbled and fell to his knees, turning his head back and forth, trying to shake off the blow.

Drummond was sitting on the bed, but as soon as he tried to stand, he collapsed on the floor among the rushes and swore out loud.

Angus didn't need his help, and the guards were leaving him alone. "Stay where you are, Drummond."

Angus had just slammed his fist into the other guard's jaw when a commotion outside the chamber told him Tibold and the rest of his sons had returned to find the guards fighting with Angus, and others not allowing them entrance into the chamber.

Fists flew as the Chattan family fought with the MacRae men until Kayne was able to knock out the man fighting Angus. Angus hurried to help Drummond back to bed.

"Where is Edana?" Kayne asked, winded and furious.

"MacRae took her, thinking we were in on the kidnapping of his son," Angus said.

"How the hell did he come to that conclusion?" Kayne asked, looking confused.

"She learned where the boy was—you know the way in which she does," Angus said.

Kayne swore under his breath. "Can you stay and watch over my brother?"

"God's knees, nay," Angus said, divesting

one of the knocked-out guards of his sword. "The chief has taken my wife."

Kayne looked back at Drummond. "Can you do without us?"

"Aye, find Edana. Make sure she is safe," Drummond said, his eyelids drooping, his face red with fever.

"Aye, we will return soon." Angus prayed they would be victorious in short order.

Kayne took the other guard's sword, and with his brothers and their da relieving the men in the hall of their weapons and now duly armed, they headed for the stairs that led to the great hall.

Keary, who was with some of MacRae's men, had not received word of what had happened concerning the boy either, as many continued to look for him inside the castle. He quickly joined Angus and the Chattan men.

Unlike them, he was still unarmed. "What has happened?"

Seeing the Chattan men and Angus with swords in hand, MacRae's men drew their own weapons, but none of them attacked.

"MacRae believes Edana had something to do with Oppida taking his son," Angus told Keary, as he and the others with him stalked toward the door that led into the bailey. "He took her with him and they have gone to the river."

"That is absurd!" Keary said, keeping pace with him.

"Aye, it is. The chief has gone mad," Angus agreed, though he knew differently. He could see now just how much trouble his wife could get into if she revealed what she knew to the wrong person. He would protect her always if he could save her before it was too late. He would run MacRae through with his guard's sword himself if the man had done any harm to the bonny lass.

Outside, he headed for the stables, intent on retrieving his horse and riding to the river. MacRae's men stood back, none of them engaging the fierce warriors who looked ready to kill anyone who stood in their way, since Angus and the others with him did not make a move to attack.

"So, Oppida has taken the lad beyond the castle walls," Keary said, sounding as if he was thinking aloud.

"Aye."

Angus wondered then if Edana could hear how furious he was, how worried for her.

Would she know he was coming to her rescue?

\*\*\*

The matter could only get worse, Edana thought, if she couldn't reach Angus before he, her brothers, and her da began killing MacRae's men. Or MacRae's men slaughtered her family. *I am all right,* she silently entreated. *All is well.* But she knew neither Angus nor any of the members of her family could know what had happened to her.

She had heard MacRae galloping after her and then his horse's hooves clomping on the ground in the dense forest faded away. The man with the torch, who was returning to the keep to tell everyone that all was well, who she had been following, disappeared into the woods far ahead of her, leaving her in the pitch blackness. It would be hours before the sun rose and she could not see far enough ahead of her to make her way through the woods. Which direction did she need to go?

She stopped and shouted, "MacRae!" When he did not return her call to tell her where he was, she tried to reach the boy. As much as she hated to speak of her folly, she had to let the lad know she must have gone the wrong way, thinking she was headed straight back to the castle. But the woods were unfamiliar to her and in the dark, she must have gotten turned around if MacRae no longer followed her.

*"Pol, tell your da I think I am lost."*

# Chapter 17

The portcullis was down, so Angus turned his horse toward the postern gate. The Chattan men and Keary thundered after him and they all raced outside. Keary shouted, "I will gather my men to hunt them down."

"I will get mine," Tibold said.

"We will stay with you," Kayne told Angus, chasing after him as he had not waited to see what would happen next.

He had barely reached the woods when he saw one of MacRae's guards, torch in hand, as he rode out of them. "MacNeill," he said, surprised. "They are all right. MacRae told me to come and let you know. The boy is safe. Oppida is dead at MacRae's hand."

"Edana!" That's who Angus cared about. Aye, the boy, but with him safe, his wife was more important than anything.

"She…she is with MacRae. She is safe."

"Where?"

"I rode ahead when we got word that you

295

were fighting our men. I...I was to tell you that all is well."

"Take me to MacRae."

"I need to tell everyone that Pol is safe," the man insisted.

Tibold, his men, and Keary's rode around the castle and headed for them like a stampede of cattle.

The guard's eyes widened.

"You may tell them. But then, I want you to take me to MacRae and my wife," Angus said, impatient, not believing anything that MacRae said until he saw she was safe with his own eyes.

"Aye." The guard kicked his horse to a gallop and went to head off Tibold and Keary. "The lad is safe! Oppida is dead!"

Angus shook his head. Tibold and his men wanted to know about *Edana's* safety! Fool.

"Where is Edana?" Tibold roared.

Angus witnessed more torchlights moving through the woods. Each time a man emerged from the trees, Angus spied no sign of his wife.

"Where is Edana?" Angus growled at each man.

"She is behind us with MacRae. The lad fell asleep in his da's arms. MacRae wanted us to hurry to ensure all was well with you and the rest of your men," a guard said.

Tibold waited with his men nearby, Edana's brothers sticking close to Angus.

Keary held his men back on the other side of Tibold and his clansmen.

When MacRae materialized from the woods, Angus thought Edana must have followed him, but there was no sign of her. "Where is Edana!" Angus shouted.

MacRae looked puzzled. "She was ahead of me. She should have arrived at the same time the first man was sent to give you word everything was well."

"She is not here! Wake the lad," Angus ordered.

MacRae scowled at Angus.

"She may have tried to reach him. If the lad has been sleeping all this time, she couldna. Wake your son!" Angus commanded again.

MacRae's face was red with anger. Angus was certain the man was not used to the brother of a laird giving him orders.

MacRae said, "Pol, wake up."

Pol stirred and rubbed his eyes.

"Pol," Angus said, "Edana is lost. Can you reach her?"

Pol stared at him as if he wasn't quite sure what the matter was.

"Edana. She is lost in the woods. Can you speak to her?"

"Aye, I will try." Pol scrunched up his small face as if concertedly attempting to contact Edana. But then he shook his head.

Tibold motioned to his men, "Spread out. We search for my daughter."

"My wife," Angus said to himself, furious with MacRae and more than anxious for Edana's safety. "The boy comes with us."

"I am returning him to the keep where he belongs," MacRae said.

"Nay, you dinna. You forced her to go with you against her will. Now you have lost her. The boy may be the only one who can help us now."

"She saved my life, Da," Pol said, looking up at his father's stern face. "I want to help."

Looking as though he'd eaten something particularly sour, MacRae finally nodded. "Come," he said to his men, "we search for the woman." He cast over his shoulder to Angus, "If she had stayed with me when I commanded it, she wouldna be lost."

"And why would she have run off?" Angus

asked, his voice hard. Had she been afraid of MacRae?

"She was worried about you and her kin. We had word that fighting had broken out. I suspect she wished to stop it. To show she was unharmed."

Edana. Always thinking of others. Wanting to rescue them.

Danger in the form of wolves, wild boar, but worse—man, made Angus clench his reins in his hand. She had nothing but a *sgian dubh* to keep her safe. At least she was on horseback.

"A rider-less horse!" someone shouted.

Angus cursed aloud.

\*\*\*

Edana cursed under her breath as she felt a cold wet substance on her forehead. Her spine and arse ached as she reclined on her back on the ground beneath the oaks. Ponderous trees still surrounded her on all sides. Her head pounded with pain, and she was so very cold! Where was she? What had happened?

Then she vaguely remembered.

Something had spooked the mare she'd been riding. She had reared up and Edana lost her hold and tumbled from her mount. She'd hit her head hard on a branch, then again on a nasty rock as she fell the rest of the way to the ground. And then... she guessed she had lost consciousness because she couldn't remember what happened next.

Where was the mare now?

Then she heard snorting nearby. Not a horse's snort. Something else.

She listened carefully. Her skin chilled. What was the sound she heard?

She tried to sit up and grew so dizzy, she lay her head back down, wanting to be swallowed up by a big bed and her husband's warm embrace.

Angus! Her father. Her brothers. She groaned. Surely MacRae's men had arrived back at the castle to give word the boy was...

She started to shake her head in annoyance, but the pain shredded the very thought.

They might have received the news the boy was all right, but then discovered *she* was missing.

She'd only wanted to ensure that her family and her husband had believed MacRae's men spoke the truth. That they had to cease fighting. She hadn't wanted her husband or family injured or killed. And now...

She gave a bitter half laugh. Now, she was

*not* all right.

The snuffling and snorting grew closer. And then she knew very well the sound she heard. Little piglets and a sow. Not good. She had to climb up off the ground. If the mother boar thought Edana wished to harm her little ones, the sow could gore Edana with her monstrous sharp tusks.

Being anywhere near the great wild beast while it protected its young could enrage it.

She'd heard of a man attempting to hide in the heather, no trees around for him to climb into, and he was gored terribly.

But every time she tried to lift her head, she felt it splinter with pain. She stifled the groan she nearly released, not wanting the boar to hear her. She must be downwind of it, thank the heavens.

With every slight movement a major painful effort, her whole body aching from the fall, but her head the worst, she sat up as slowly as she could. And nearly passed out again.

She gritted her teeth, attempting to keep her wits about her. Then turned her head slightly to consider the lowest branches of an old oak. It would have to do, if she could only get to her feet.

She tried to stand, but the sharp pain shrieking across the back of her skull made her stomach roil with upset.

She saw a little piglet, and then another, and her heart that was pounding as hard as if she were being chased by wolves, gave a stutter and nearly died. Four more of the little boars scurried after their brethren. Mother would be nearby and maybe even watching them now.

And then? She'd see Edana. Despite what some said about wild boar, they could see well, they proved smarter than her da's hunting dogs, and were extremely dangerous.

Attempting not to startle the wee ones that would cause them to let out a blood-curdling squeal that could bring the mother and any other boar in the area running to protect them, Edana again tried to stand.

Managing, she clutched her waist, wanting to bend over and release the meal she'd eaten earlier, and saw white stars across inky blackness form in front of her eyes. She realized she was falling, until her shoulder struck a branch, bringing her again to ragged consciousness.

She quickly—or at least she tried—to pull herself up into the lower limbs of the tree. Every effort made her head and stomach swim. She groaned, the wee pigs squealed, and the great beast of a sow charged out of the brush and headed for the tree. The one Edana was scrambling to climb higher in.

The boar struck the tree right below Edana's foot, the sow's razor sharp tusks gleaming in the early morning filtered light. The weight and the phenomenal strength of the beast shook the tree and with as much as Edana's head hurt, she feared being unsettled from her shuddering perch.

Worse, the wild boar and her piglets hung around at the base of the tree. She would not leave soon, Edana worried.

As she closed her eyes, trying to calm her wooziness and clung to the tree, she heard a small voice say in her head, *"'Tis me, Pol. Where are you?"*

A small trickle of hope wormed its way inside her, but when she tried to speak to him, the pain streaked through her head, shattering every thought, and she felt herself tumbling into a black abyss, and prayed she did not fall from the tree.

*** 

Keary couldn't help that he wanted Edana.

He loved fiery-headed lasses. Had he known the Chattan chief's daughter had grown to be so resourceful, kind-hearted, loyal, and bonny—he would have asked for her hand in marriage years ago. Not that he'd had any title at the time, and her father probably would have discounted his wish back then.

Keary had not believed Angus had wed the lass, but no matter how much Keary had plotted to wed her himself, he hated he had been unsuccessful.

Now, here he was looking for the lass—again—and wishing she could be his. *Again.* Aye, it was true he had had every intention of ensuring Oppida no longer bedeviled or murdered anyone else. That had been one of his main goals in accompanying the Chattan chief and his men. But in truth, he wished he could in some way rid himself of Edana's new husband. A perfectly timed accident. No witnesses. Just a quick drowning. Something that would not make *him* suspect.

Not that he hated the MacNeill. He just desired the lass for his own that much.

He would ask for the grieving widow's hand in marriage—and succeed in getting her into his bed.

If she were already carrying a MacNeill babe, no matter. He would call it his own. And provide her with more that would be spawned by *his* seed and not the MacNeill's.

The trouble was he wished to be the one who rescued her and returned her to MacRae's keep. The more he could do to show how chivalrous he was, the more she would be willing to agree to his marrying her.

He wanted a couple of his men to dispose of MacNeill in the most tragically accidental way possible. But the man was with MacRae and his lad, and Keary wasn't about to have them tragically disposed of as well. He truly liked children.

So he was in a quandary what to do.

He had the notion that somehow he and some of his men could follow the lass and MacNeill back to James's keep. Just MacNeill, his cousin, Niall, and the Viking would not prove a difficult number to deal with.

Not that Keary intended to kill them all. But he thought at some time or another, MacNeill would leave the others on personal business and some misfortune could befall him.

None would suspect Keary or his men, who at his word, had returned to Lockton Castle and were not even in the area at the time—or so their ruse would indicate. He would wait for a short time after the man's demise. Then he would make some excuse to visit James's castle and enquire within as to Angus and Edana's health. He would act his part to show shock at Angus's death, as if they had been best of friends. He would do his utmost to console the grieving widow. He'd already convinced her father he would be a suitable husband since he had a title and he desired to have the lass as his wife. James would have to see the benefit as well as he was also a laird.

Keary smiled to himself. Aye, one way or another, the lass would be his. Sooner than later, he hoped.

*** 

Beside himself with worry, Angus didn't know what to think. Edana's horse must have been spooked. By what though?

What bothered him just as much was that Pol could not reach her. That made Angus fear she'd been too injured to respond.

Men calling her name throughout the woods in every direction gave him hope they would soon find her. If she could but hear them and call out in return. He prayed she was all right.

"Edana!" he hollered again, his voice near hoarse with yelling for so long. "Edana!"

"We will find her," Kayne said, riding nearby.

"Aye," Hawln said. "She is a resourceful lass. She has taken spills before and has been all right."

"She is a hardy one that," Gildas agreed.

But Egan said not a word.

And Angus thought her brother Egan felt as he did. She was in trouble.

He looked over at Pol who appeared to be sleeping again. He hated to wake the boy, knowing the lad had been through one awful trauma already and now was forced to stay awake when he had been up all night.

"Pol, call her again," Angus insisted.

MacRae scowled at Angus. "Can you see 'tis no' working? Leave the lad be." The chief still sounded as though he didn't believe Pol and Edana could speak to each other in their unusual way.

"Pol, try again," Angus said, his voice angry, then turned his wrath on the lad's father. "If you hadna dragged her out here, MacRae, she wouldna be in trouble. And from what your son has said, she saved his life."

"I…I am trying," Pol said.

They all paused in the woods and waited to hear if Pol was able to reach Edana.

Then his face brightened. "She…she *spoke* to me."

"Where is she?" Angus asked in unison with two of her brothers.

Pol looked puzzled. "She…she says she is in a tree. I didna think girls climbed trees."

"Where?" Angus asked.

Pol shook his head. "She doesna know."

"Is she hurt?"

"Aye. Her head. She fell."

"Why is she in a tree?" Angus asked, concerned that someone or something had attempted to hurt her further.

Pol's eyes widened. "A wild boar."

"God's wounds. Is she safe where she is?"

"The sow is still below the tree with its piglets."

"But is she safe?" Angus asked.

"Aye, she says unless she falls from the tree."

"Is she unable to hold on?" Angus didn't wish to hear that she was too weak to do so when they had no idea where she was and the threat of a wild boar roaming around below her perch still existed.

Pol stared in the direction of the trees and Angus assumed he was listening to her talk to him. But then Pol shook his head. "She didna answer."

Kayne cursed.

"Does she hear men calling for her? Can she call out to let us know where she is?" Angus asked.

Again a lengthy pause, and then Pol shook his head. "She didna say anything."

They moved again, calling her name. It was all they could do until someone alerted them they had found the lass. He prayed she had not fallen from the tree and run afoul of the wild boar.

"Nay!" Angus heard a woman shriek. It was *his* woman.

"Edana!" Angus said, riding as fast as he could through the thick woods, her brothers keeping up with him. Niall and Gunnolf were somewhere nearby but he could not see them. "Edana!"

"Edana!" Kayne called out, the only one of the brothers whose voice hadn't given out.

"Nay!" she screamed again. "She has wee

ones!"

Angus's jaw dropped. Someone must have found her and intended to kill the sow so he could rescue Edana. In all her goodness, she hadn't wanted the mother of the piglets killed.

He came upon several of Keary's men attempting to draw off the mother while Keary tried to reach Edana.

It didn't matter who rescued her from the tree as long as she was taken from it before she fell and injured herself further. Yet the notion Keary would be the one to do so, and not one of her brothers, her da, or his own kin or good friend, Gunnolf—if it could not be Angus— forced the bile to rise in his gullet.

With a mighty roar, he galloped his horse into the fray, piglets squealing and running every which way, sow dashing after one rider, who attempted to draw her away from the tree, and then another.

Before Keary could offer Edana his mount, Angus rode in under the branch that she clung to, reached up his arms, and offered her protection and security. She slipped into his grasp, then he galloped out of the tusked boar's path before his horse was injured.

"Edana," Angus said, wishing his voice was

soothing when all that came out was an anxious croak.

"You have lost your voice," she said, then closed her eyes.

"Edana, dinna sleep, lass." He feared she would not wake up, like sometimes would happen when men suffered head injuries on the battlefield. "Pol told us you were in a tree. He didna think girls climbed trees." He hoped she would smile or react in some manner, but he couldn't get a word out of her and she didn't smile either.

When he saw MacRae staying out of the boar's path, Angus said, "Pol, can you reach her?"

"She is with you," Pol said, as if he thought it silly that Angus would not just talk to her when she was resting in his lap.

"She must no' sleep. She may no' wake up. Can you wake her? I canna."

They rode with all haste back to the keep, the word soon spreading that they had found the lass and all were to return to the castle.

"She is asleep," Pol said. "I canna wake her."

# Chapter 18

As soon as they reached the keep, several men began giving orders. Tibold told ten of his men to return to his castle. Keary ordered half of his own to return home as well.

Gildas pulled Edana from Angus's arms so Angus could dismount. Anxious about her head injury, Angus took her back, and he and her brothers, her father, Niall, and Gunnolf headed for the keep.

"I will have a chamber readied for her at once," MacRae said, then issued instructions to his people.

"I will get the healer," Pol said. "She will take care of her." The boy dashed off.

Edana stirred in Angus's arms. His heartbeat quickened to see her coming to. "Edana."

She moaned, then her eyes fluttered open. And in that instant, she gave him the sweetest smile, her blue eyes swimming with tears.

No matter how worried he was for her, he

smiled back, her expression cheering him to the center of his being. "How are you feeling?" he asked, his damnable voice nearly gone from all the yelling he had done while trying to locate her in the woods.

"My head hurts something awful."

"Pol is getting the healer. She will give you something for your pain." He wanted to scold Edana for trying to rescue him when she should have stayed safely with MacRae, but he couldn't do it. Her loyalty and caring nature was part of what he loved about her.

She glanced at someone and furrowed her brow. Angus looked to see who she was frowning at. *Keary.* But she didn't say a word, and Angus wouldn't either until he'd settled her in a chamber and Keary was no longer within earshot.

"What were you thinking, daughter?" Tibold asked, annoyed with her and when Angus hadn't scolded her, her father took up the reins.

"Of saving you, Da."

Angus shook his head.

"Then we had to rescue you," her father said, "and your husband near died over it."

As if her father and her brothers hadn't felt

the same panic.

"The same for me when the guard came and told us you were fighting MacRae's men. I had to stop it," Edana said softly.

"Dinna fret, lass," Angus said. "You need to rest and when you and Drummond are well again, you and I will travel to Craigly Castle where we will meet with my brother, his wife, and my clansmen." Angus still wondered if James knew what might have happened between Edana and him when he found her.

"Is everyone all right?" she asked.

"Aye," Angus said. "'Tis you who are no' well."

"Drummond?" she asked, ignoring his comment as if it didn't matter that *she* had been hurt.

Gildas spoke up then. "Kayne and Halwn have already headed inside to check on him."

"I want to see him for myself," Edana said.

"See the grief she gives us?" Gildas opened the door to the keep for them.

"I will rest better if I see Drummond."

"Aye, lass, you will get your wish." Angus would begrudge her nothing that would lift her spirits and make her injuries fade into the background.

MacRae met them at the narrow, curving stairs. "The lass has the chamber next to Drummond's."

"Thank you," Edana said.

Still angry that MacRae had forcibly taken Edana with him, believing that she had been in league with the devil named Oppida, Angus couldn't see the chief in a good light for now.

He climbed the stone steps and strode down the corridor toward Drummond's chamber, following her father. Her remaining brothers, Niall, and Gunnolf kept in step behind them. When they entered the chamber, Drummond scowled at her, though his face was again pale and not flushed with fever. Halwn and Kayne stood nearby, arms crossed over their chests, brows raised.

"What do you think you were doing?" Drummond asked, sounding highly agitated when he saw how pale Edana was, that she had to be carried into the chamber, and that blood streaked her temple. Bruising had already begun to turn her injured skin a soft purple, blue, and burgundy.

"Rescuing you," she said, her voice resolute.

That earned her several chuckles from her

brothers.

Drummond groaned. "And you see how well that turned out."

Her father shook his head, then directed a comment to Angus. "You have your work cut out for you." He sympathetically patted Angus on his shoulder.

"You have seen your brother is still going to live, Edana," Angus said, kissing her forehead, and headed for the doorway, anxious to get her settled.

"Aye, and Drummond is getting better. He is always a beastly grouch when he does." Edana snuggled closer to Angus, and he tightened his hold on her.

"Wait until you see how Edana acts when she is bed bound," Drummond hollered.

Thinking of Edana bound to the bed, Angus paused in the doorway and turned to smile at Drummond. Her brothers all laughed, and Edana flushed beautifully. Her father merely grinned. And so did Niall and Gunnolf. But Drummond's face flushed as bright a red as Edana's.

"Oh, do take me away from my brothers," Edana said, poking her finger into Angus's chest.

He smiled at her and carried her out of

Drummond's chamber and into the next one where a middle-aged woman waited for him to place Edana on the bed. He did and quickly divested Edana of her shoes and hose, though the maid raised her brows, and he suspected she believed she was to do the undressing.

"Are you the healer?" Angus asked.

"Nay. I am to make the lady comfortable."

"I will take care of her," he said, dismissing the maid.

When she looked at Edana as if she thought his wife may have some other notion, Edana squeezed his hand. "Angus will provide for me."

"Aye, if you need anything...," she said, curtseyed and hurried out of the chamber.

Another woman, older, her hair in gray curls, eyes as gray, her dress a light brown, the colors making her nearly fade into nothingness, entered, carrying a bowl of water, a leather bag slung over her shoulder. "I am Chantel, MacRae's healer. You have suffered an injury?"

"Her head," Angus said. "Anywhere else, lass?"

"Nay."

Chantel shut the door, set the bowl on a table, then the bag next to it. She joined them at the bed and examined Edana's head as Angus held his wife's hand, caressing it with the other as he watched Edana's expression. The healer poked and prodded gently and Edana's mouth pursed and her eyes slimmed as she let out wee moans.

"She has hit her head hard, it appears. She has a goose egg at the back of the head, some bleeding, and it will be sore for a while. The swelling will go down. I will need to wash her head."

"Have a bath brought up for her," Angus said.

The healer frowned at him.

"I will wash her," Angus said.

The healer looked at Edana as if she wished her to say yes or no about the matter.

Edana gave a dramatic sigh. "Do as my husband wishes, please, Chantel."

"Aye." The woman took her leave to ask the chief's permission.

"You didna really mean it, did you, Angus?" Edana looked shyly at him, her lashes lowered partway.

"Aye, lass. You gave me a scare. I want to see if you were injured anywhere else. I will be reassured if I bathe you."

Her cheeks flushed beautifully again. He sat

beside her on the bed, rested his hand on her thigh, and smiled at her. "We are wed. You have no need to be uncomfortable about it."

"Men dinna bathe their wives." Her blue eyes were wide now.

"How do you know?"

Her lips parted and he kissed her mouth, touched his tongue gently to hers, but worried about her injury paining her, he kept his kisses light and loving.

Her hands gripped his arms, and she sighed against his mouth. "You need to break your fast."

"I am certain MacRae will have food sent up to us."

"Dinna you have anything else you could spend your time on more wisely?"

Never imagining she would be so shy with him now, he grinned at her, touched her hair lightly, and shook his head. "With you is the only place I wish to be."

Someone finally knocked on the door and he called, "Come in."

"We brought the tub," a lady said, and then women began filling it with water heated over the fires in the hearth downstairs.

When they were done, they stood watching

as if Angus would change his mind about bathing his wife himself. "Thank you," he said, and dismissed them.

Eyes rounded, most of the six women hid smiles, then quickly left the chamber and closed the door. They giggled as they hurried down the corridor.

Edana's cheeks blushed anew. "They will tell everyone in the whole castle what you are about to do."

He smiled.

She slapped his arm in nothing more than a love pat. "They probably wished that you were about to bathe *them* and not me."

He laughed. "I wouldna have been interested in bathing any of them. You are the only treasure for me. Didna I mention this before, when I found you in the abandoned shieling?"

"You were probably talking about my mare."

He chuckled.

"You teased me."

"I told the truth." Though he thought her father would consider her a treasure, Angus had denied that he would see her in the same manner. He had quickly come to realize she truly was a gem.

Angus helped Edana to stand and began to remove her brat, then her léine, attempting not to hurt her. But she sucked in her breath several times, and he knew he wasn't succeeding. When she stood naked before him, he checked her all over. "Your arm is bruised. MacRae's fingerprints, I assume." Angus was ready to knock the teeth out of the chief's head.

"I struggled."

Angus kissed her arm lightly. "He gripped you too hard, the bastard. You shouldna have had to struggle against the tyrant." He helped her into the warm bathwater, and then he had her sit forward so he could run water over the back of her head and clean the wound. She barely breathed.

"Are you all right, Edana? Does this hurt too much?"

"It stings."

He cleaned her wound and washed the rest of her hair, then found strips of fabric the healer had left in her pouch to bind Edana's head. "Lean back now, lass."

"The wound is clean. Is it no'?" she asked, her eyes growing wide.

"Aye, lass. No sense in letting the

bathwater that the maids carried all the way up here go to waste."

"I can wash myself."

"Nay. You have been injured. Let me do this." And with tender care, he washed every inch of her skin, trying his darnedest not to be so tempted by the lass. It was of no use as her body reacted, her nipples hardening, her breasts appearing as if they had swollen in size, just as fast as his cock thickened and hardened. He was grateful she had closed her eyes and was resting as comfortably as she could, while he fantasized about making love to his bonny wife.

When he pushed her legs apart and dipped the wet cloth between them, her eyes popped open.

"I missed a spot." His voice was too husky as he tried for lighthearted, knowing his smile was too wicked by far. Then recalling the way she had looked at Keary outside, Angus asked, "Keary disturbed you in some manner. What was that about, lass?"

"I saw two of him," she said, sounding relaxed.

"Two...of...him."

"Aye."

"And how many of me, do you see?" he

asked, worried her head injury was worse than he had at first suspected.

She smiled. "One. But when he approached me, there were two of him. He wanted to help me down from the tree, but I didna wish to go to him. Even if I had, I couldna tell which of him to go to. Then you were there, and the matter was decided."

"There was more to it than that," Angus said, suspecting it was so.

"I...I was afraid to go with him after he had locked me in a chamber at Lockton Castle before. The fear was unfounded, I am certain, but...I didna see you or anyone I knew, only him and his men, and I feared going with him."

"Aye, lass, 'tis good you listened to your instincts." As she had said, her fears may have been unwarranted, but Keary had already proved untrustworthy.

Once Edana was clean, Angus helped her out of the tub and carefully dried her. She was nearly limp with relaxation—and he was glad for that—as he tended to her. Then he scooped her up in his arms and conveyed her to the curtained bed.

A knock at the door made him say, "Just a minute." He covered her in the furs and then said, "Come in."

"I apologize, but MacRae asked me to bring you porridge to break your fast." The maid held a tray in her hands and lowered her gaze to the rushes on the floor.

Angus was glad for it as he couldn't get his own rampant need for Edana that quickly under control. It took him a moment to reach the door, then he accepted the tray from her. "Our thanks."

The maid curtsied, then hurried off, and he shut the door.

"Are you ready to eat something, Edana?" He turned to look at her.

Her eyes were closed and she was already sound asleep.

*** 

Three days later, Drummond and Edana were well enough to travel. They planned on staying at the Fitzburn Tavern on their way to Craigly Castle. Keary and his men parted ways with them before they reached the village. Yet, the way Keary had continued to look at Edana as if he were a besotted lad, Angus hadn't trusted him. He was glad Keary and his men finally left for Lockton Castle.

Angus had thought he would be traveling

with his wife, his cousin, and Gunnolf as before when he headed home this time, but Tibold would not hear of it. He had ten men as escort and vowed to get them safely to Craigly Castle without further trouble.

When they arrived at Fitzburn Tavern that eve, Angus wanted to take Edana up to a room and eat with her there, not have strangers looking at her as if she was a commodity to be bought.

But Edana said, "Nay, Angus. You made me stay in the chamber at MacRae's keep the whole time we remained there until I felt well enough to travel. I am tired of hiding away in a bedchamber. I feel well."

"'Tis no' your health I am concerned about, lass." Angus glanced around at the men in the smoky tavern—all eyes on *his* wife.

He suspected that Edana being a woman had more to do with it, and not just because she was so bonny. Except for the tavern keeper's own daughter, Angus hadn't seen any women frequent the place. Una would join them in the morning before they left for Craigly Castle.

Against his better judgment that he should insist Edana hie herself up the stairs to their room, he moved her to a table sitting in the very back of the tavern with a view of all who entered. He was torn between having her sit with her back to the wall and having her seated where her back was to the view of any man sitting in the tavern. She took the option away from him as she moved the furthest from any men, making herself comfortable with her back to the wall.

Niall, her da, and three of her brothers joined them. Gunnolf took a seat at another table across the room. He didn't sit with the rest of Edana's brothers either. Something was wrong, but Gunnolf wasn't giving him any indication of what, as if he was distancing himself from Angus and the others. Angus suspected Gunnolf attempted to learn of some vile misdeed that would be directed toward Angus or some member of Tibold's family.

When Edana's hand touched Angus's thigh, he quickly looked at her, all thoughts of what Gunnolf was doing slipping from his mind. Edana gave him the most wicked of smiles. And he gave her one back. She leaned over to speak to him private. "You are worried about something?"

"Gunnolf."

She turned her attention on him, but kept

her hand on Angus's thigh. He covered her hand with his and moved her fingers higher toward his groin. She quickly turned her head to look at him. He smiled. "Your head is feeling better?"

Her brothers and father had been speaking of some matter, Niall listening raptly to their conversation, but all talk dicd when Angus asked Edana the question.

They watched her, and of course she blushed all the way to the roots of her dark red hair.

"Aye," she said softly, and sipped her mead.

He didn't kiss her as he would have liked. Not in the tavern filled with men, many he didn't know. But he leaned close and whispered, "Think you we should have retired to the room after all?"

Again a fresh blush. She looked charming.

He hadn't made love to her in the last three days, all because her head had hurt too much. He'd tried to just pleasure her, but even that had not worked well.

He was all too willing to try again if she was up to it this eve.

No one said a word, all the others at their table smiling at Edana.

She frowned. "Dinna let me stop your important talk," she said to her da and brothers.

"We only wished to know if you felt all right," her father said, but a smile still remained.

"And then we wondered why you blush so fiercely," Kayne said.

"And why Angus smiles so broadly," Niall said.

"Och, you would think you were a bunch of gossipy women," Edana said. And she blushed all the more.

Gildas smiled, but then spoke to Tibold, changing the subject. "If you have already sent men to tell our cousin, McEwan, that we will be late in arriving, mayhap we should help you to escort Edana to Craigly Castle."

"Nay, 'tis important you meet with McEwan. He needs our help and you shall give it," Tibold said.

Angus was curious about the business, but didn't want to ask if Tibold wasn't interested in sharing it with him.

"Drummond isna made to do it," Kayne said, sounding disgruntled.

Now Angus truly wondered what was going on. He thought the brothers would be eager to do their father's bidding. This reminded Angus of James's sending him in search of Edana.

"He is better, but he still isna entirely well. He will remain with me. Besides, he got the rest of you in trouble. God knows what he might do if he tags along further." Tibold finished his ale and motioned to the serving wench to give him more.

"Huh," Kayne said in a sarcastic way. "Kiss a woman, get us all thrown into a dungeon, and now he gets out of this task. How does he ever manage? I swear he is the only one who can do such a thing—consistently."

They all glanced back at Drummond sitting at a far table, smiling at the tavern keeper's daughter. Halwn sat across from him, smiling, shaking his head. Drummond patted his lap, indicating to the girl that she should sit there, but she leaned over and whispered in his ear, and he laughed out loud.

"He is bound to get himself into more trouble," Edana said, on a sigh.

"I will keep a tighter rein on him." Tibold gave her a fierce look.

"Aye, but if he causes dissension at Craigly Castle, then what?" she asked.

"I will ensure he stays out of trouble."

Angus wasn't certain anyone could.

The girl soon served fish stew and brown bread and everyone quit talking to eat.

Angus liked Drummond. He was just the kind of man who livened up life in a…mostly good way. Once Angus saw that Edana had finished her meal, he said, "You look exhausted, lass. Do you need to rest?"

"Aye."

He helped her to stand and she refused to look at anyone sitting at their table. The chatter died down in the tavern and all eyes were upon her again.

"Oh, do talk amongst yourselves," she implored her table companions, and then she left with Angus.

He hurried her up the stairs, unsure what they were going to do, but he was just as eager to lie quietly with his new wife, if that was all she was ready for.

He glanced in Gunnolf's direction. His friend bowed his head ever so slightly. He was watching their backs. But who posed the threat this time?

# Chapter 19

Edana loved Angus. He'd been so kind and gentle while caring for her, and he'd only hinted once about being upset with her for not staying with MacRae in the forest. She had expected him to say something more about it now that she felt better. She would insist she had only his health and that of her da and brothers' in mind and would have done nothing differently if she had a chance to do it all over again. How could she have known the man riding in front of her would disappear with the torchlight she'd been following? Or that she would have veered off too much from the correct path to take?

Before she could even remove her brooch on her brat, Angus helped her with it.

"Why is it necessary that your brothers visit McEwan? And why did Kayne say what he did about Drummond getting out of the task?" Angus asked.

She laughed. "He doesna wish to be tied down to a wife. No' yet."

One of Angus's brows arched. "Their visit is about taking wives?"

"One wife. She is the laird's ward. McEwan was tasked to find a husband for her. And quickly. My da said he would send his sons. If any were agreeable, the match would be made."

"This McEwan. He is married?"

"Nay. Da says his heart is lost to another."

"Ah. And your brothers are no' happy about seeing the woman?"

"None of us knows what she looks like. Not one of us has any idea how she behaves. What if she is a shrew, or...terribly shy?"

He smiled at that.

"I am no' shy," she said. "No' like that. I mean, of men, in general. What if she has a sharp tongue? Or in some other manner wouldna suit one of my brothers as a wife? She is like me, older, and no' so young. Three and twenty? She canna be choosey about a husband. But my brothers can be about a wife. I would have enjoyed seeing her since she will be like a sister to me if one of my brothers does take her to wife, but my da wouldna let me go with them."

"Good thing that. If you had gone with them—"

"I might have had trouble with Oppida myself. Ended up in the dungeon with my brothers also."

Angus took a deep, settling breath. "Aye. The woman was the devil." He helped Edana out of her léine. "So why has McEwan's ward no' married yet?"

"I dinna know. My da didna wish me to know anything further on the matter."

As soon as Angus had pulled off her chemise, he smiled, his gaze taking in every inch of her.

Her whole body heating, she quickly slipped under the covers of the bed and smiled back at him. "'Tis chilly."

"Will you always be shy with me, wife?" Angus asked, quickly dispensing of his own clothes.

"Nay, I am no' shy," she said again, hoping he would not think it was a bad trait. She couldn't help it. Not this early in their marriage, anyway.

He winked at her, grinning broadly. He appeared not to believe a word of it, and thankfully, he seemed to enjoy that about her.

"You surprise me, lass," he said, pulling the covers aside and like the rogue that he was before she'd been injured, he gave her another long, heated look before he settled gently right on top of her and pulled the covers over them.

"How is that?" she asked, as his mouth kissed her throat and then he moved lower, licking her nipple.

She tensed, the feeling of his tongue on her, making her needs rise up with an alarming rapidness that she hadn't expected as if she'd been starved for his sensual touches when she no longer felt the ache in her head from the injury.

"Are you all right?" he asked, his face anxious as he quickly stopped licking her.

"Oh heavens, aye. Do you have to stop?"

He grinned most roguishly.

"Wait," she said, wrapping her hands around his head and lifting it to look into his lust-filled gaze. "What did you mean by I surprise you?"

"You are so sweet and innocent, lass, yet your kisses..." He left the rest up to her to finish.

"My kisses? What about them?"

"They are no' so sweet and innocent." Before she could worry that he didna like them, he cupped her breast and kissed it. "I canna help wanting to fight the man who kissed you like that, when I wished to be the *only* one you bestowed such kisses on with so much ardor."

Her jaw dropped. "The man...what man?"

He stared at her for a moment, then closed his own gaping jaw. "Did a man no' kiss you? A lad when you were younger, mayhap?"

She shook her head.

He frowned.

And then realization dawned. "Was I no' supposed to do it in that way? I saw Una kissing Seumas in such a manner. I thought that was what a man and woman did." She frowned. "No lad or man would come near *me* to kiss me."

Angus grinned, and she thought her comment must have pleased him. Although she had forever and a day wished someone had kissed her in that manner before Angus had come along.

Then he slid off Edana and pulled her onto his stomach. His hands cupped her face, and he said, "Edana, you are truly precious. Kiss me like that again. Ever since you were hurt and I wished to make love to you once you were better, 'tis all I have waited for."

"That is all? Just my kisses?" She was tickled.

His wicked grin said it was not.

At first they were kissing, all tongues and lips, his fingers combing through her hair, her hands on the sides of his whiskery face, her thumbs stroking him. She felt oddly intrigued as she lay atop him instead of buried by the virile, muscular strength of him. She didn't feel in charge of their lovemaking like this. The experience was just...different. Any moment, she expected him to move her onto her back and climb on top of her in his male dominant and possessive way, but he seemed to enjoy having her atop him, the way he was fondling her breasts, eyeing them with interest, his eyes half lidded, a small smile curving his lips.

She felt his hard staff pressing against her belly and moved against it, just slightly, earning a groan from him.

She'd learned which groans meant she was stirring his male need, and which meant he was in pain. Well, mayhap he was in pain, but more of a sweet pain requiring release.

"Sit up," he said, his voice hoarse.

Maybe she had been wrong, and she had hurt him with her weight moving against him. She had never been in this position before, after all. When she tried to move off him to sit up, he seized her arms so quickly, she nearly squeaked. "What is wrong?"

He laughed. "You must stay on top of me. To see if you enjoy this as much, we are trying a new way to find pleasure, lass."

"You are tired of the *old* way?" She feared he became bored too easily. They hadn't even made love to each other long enough for the other approach to have become old—to her way of thinking. What would happen when he tired of the new way? What in heaven's name would he think of next?

"Nay, lass, I will make love to you in any manner your heart desires. But you will have to try them first to know which you like best, aye? Unless you are too shy as of yet."

"I am no' shy." She sat then, making him groan again. Maybe she sat up too suddenly. But as soon as the covers dropped from her back, she realized she was sitting on him, naked, exposed to his ravenous gaze, the *rogue*.

She could not change her mind at that point, not wishing to prove his words were true. Wanting to see if this was a way of making love that would appeal, she waited for him to do something.

He pulled her down again, only part way

and he kissed her mouth, his hands stroking her breasts. She realized when he wasn't resting on top of her, his hands were freer to fondle her. She liked this new way and didn't feel as exposed when she leaned over him like this. But she did feel naughty as she kneeled against the mattress, her feminine folds spread open to him just waiting for him to fill her, instead of him lying between her legs, covering her until he entered her. With her breasts swinging free, she felt carefree and impish.

One of his large hands moved from her breast, and he stroked between her legs, touching that part of her that was wet and achy for his touch. She hadn't meant to, but she moved against his fingers, wanting him to stroke faster. She wasn't able to say a word as the need grew deep inside her like a wave growing, and she felt as though she would break.

She hadn't needed to say a word. He watched her reactions, heightening the exquisite sensation building in her, stroking faster, harder, and she swore he looked nearly as satisfied as he was making her feel.

Then that intensely fulfilling sensation roared up and over her and through her and she cried out in exaltation. And felt horrified. She was certain the talk in the tavern below had grown much quieter as Angus quickly distracted her, impaling her on his staff. She was again overcome by the thrill of this new experience. He gently laid his hands on her hips and encouraged her to ride him!

Angus was certain all the men in the tavern had heard his bonny wife exclaim his name out loud during the throes of passion. He had been amused, loving her for her passion, and hoped she wasn't too embarrassed. He suspected he'd never be able to bed her in such a manner in another tavern for as long as they lived.

She continued to ride him, looking eager to please just as much as he craved pleasing her. He still couldn't believe she had thought making love to her while he was on top had become tiresome. He would never tire of their lovemaking no matter the way in which they did it.

Even now as he watched her breasts bounce and her roll her hips while he continued to hold onto them, her soft rounded arse pounding against his hips—taking him even higher in his need to reach the end—he was filled with wonder for her.

No matter how much he tried to keep the

momentum going, how hard he attempted to delay coming quickly, he couldn't. She moistened her dry lips. He wanted to kiss her again, but before he could, he exploded into her. Like a burst of hot white flame, he felt the heady release, claimed it and luxuriated in the sensation. Then he quickly rolled her onto her back, continuing to thrust deeply into her, thinking even now she could be well on the way to carrying his child. That thought pleased him to no end.

Finishing with a sigh of pleasure, he began kissing her again, his hands tangled in her hair, and to his surprise, she came again, only this time, he muffled her lovely cry of pleasure.

Settled together after that, her arm draped over his stomach, her head resting against him, she sighed, her warm breath stirring the light hairs on his chest.

"I will never be able to show my face downstairs again," Edana said, serious as could be.

# Chapter 20

Later that night in the tavern and groggy with sleep, Angus heard a light rap at the door to his room. Slipping out of Edana's arms, he quickly left the bed, threw on his tunic, lit a candle, and said as he approached the door, "Aye?"

"'Tis me, Niall."

Angus opened the door and saw Niall holding a lantern, his brow furrowed. "What is the matter?"

His cousin's dark curly hair had droplets of water clinging to the strands, more rainwater puddling atop his wool plaid, but Angus didn't hear the sound of rain outside, so he assumed the showers had stopped.

"Gunnolf sent me to tell you that he saw Keary speaking to two of his men, his voice hushed, before he left with the rest of them and headed in the direction of Lockton Castle. The two men attempted to keep out of sight of the rest of us, but they followed us here to the village. Gunnolf backtracked to shadow *them*, attempting to listen in on their conversation while traveling, but they didna say a word. Now they are sleeping at one of the crofters' huts. We are taking turns getting some rest and watching the men in the event they leave earlier than we do."

"You think they are following us? What are they about?" Angus asked.

Niall shook his head. "That is what Gunnolf is attempting to learn. I stayed with him for a while, but he wanted me to return to the tavern and let you know what is going on."

"Does he suspect it has something to do with Edana? And Keary?"

"Aye. He believes Keary was more interested in staying close to Edana than he was with regard to having his vengeance against Oppida. 'Tis true he wanted to tell MacRae about Oppida's evil doings to protect MacRae's son, Pol. But Gunnolf believes that Keary told MacRae such, as he wants to earn Edana's respect. Gunnolf thinks Keary still wants her for his wife because he received her da's consent."

"She is married to me," Angus said, more

vehemently than necessary.

"Aye, 'tis true. Unless you no longer live."

Giving that some thought, Angus rubbed his bristly chin. "Can you ask some of..." He shook his head. "'Tis my place to ask him if he can spare some of his men to help spell you and Gunnolf." Angus would do it himself, but hc wasn't about to leave Edana alone in the room.

"Nay, we will have your backs."

Drummond clomped up the stairs and paused as he saw Niall speaking to Angus. "Is this a private matter?"

Angus shook his head. "Gunnolf and Niall believe Keary has some intention of having me killed so he can wed Edana."

Drummond's brows arched. Then he hpmfed. "Does my da know this?"

"Nay, I have just learned of it," Angus said, angry that Keary didn't know when to quit, if what Gunnolf assumed was true.

Drummond nodded, then went to the door next to Angus's and rapped hard.

"Who is it?" Kayne said, his voice grumpy.

"Drummond."

Kayne opened the door to his room and glanced at Angus and Niall. "Is there a celebration going on and I havena been invited?"

Angus truly liked Edana's brothers.

"Aye, Keary wants his head," Drummond said, jerking his thumb in Angus's direction, "so he can have our sister for his wife."

"The devil he can," Tibold roared from the bed.

Angus smiled, very much approving of his father by marriage also.

"What is this all about?" Egan asked from somewhere in the unlit room.

Just like that, Angus had the support of Tibold and all his sons, two of whom had quickly dressed and were about to go with Niall to see the croft where Keary's men were holed up. Angus hadn't really considered how he would be gaining Edana's family when he wed her, but he was pleased to be part of her family as well.

Before they left, Niall said to Angus, "You really dinna need to worry about the lass. If something untoward happens to you, I will step in and take her to wife."

Used to Niall and his brothers' good humored jests to lighten a dark mood, Angus slapped his cousin on the shoulder. "Aye, but she would have to agree, and I would have to be dead. No way am I dying anytime soon."

Satisfied he'd have enough protection for him and for Edana, Angus shut and bolted the door. Then he pulled off his tunic, snuffed out the candle, and returned to bed to snuggle with his wife before the long journey home tomorrow. Though he kept his sword close at hand.

A short time later, he heard something rattling at the small window to the room—the shutters moving a bit, Angus thought. A high wind, or something more sinister?

He climbed out of bed and threw on his tunic, then reached for his sword. No man in his right mind would attempt to kill him in his sleep, he didn't think. Then again if it was one of Keary's men, he may have learned that Tibold and his men would be helping to escort Edana to Craigly Castle and Keary wouldn't get a better chance to murder Angus without anyone suspecting who had done the deed.

What he couldn't understand was where Edana's brothers and his own friends had gone that one of the men had slipped beyond their notice. Unless the two men sleeping in the croft were not the only two in the village working for Keary. Maybe even Keary and a substantial number of his men were here now, keeping out of sight. Perhaps he hadn't gone to Lockton Castle as he said he would.

The room was nearly pitch black, which made Angus wonder how the man thought he would manage to kill him. What if he injured Edana instead? Surely he would have realized she would scream and alert Tibold and his men.

Though the cover of dark would hide who the attempted murderer was—if that was what this was all about.

The shutter ripped part way off its hinges when a soft body slid next to Angus, brushing up against his arm. "Edana," Angus whispered, his voice hoarse, trying to keep the anxiousness from it. "Lass, go to your father's room." He reached down to feel her clothes to see what she was wearing. She had only managed to slip into her chemise.

"If I open the door, they will see the light in the tavern silhouetting me. They will see you and know just where to attack," she said, just as hushed.

She was the most irritatingly obstinate woman at times, especially when her words made sense and he didn't wish to see it that way—mainly because he was concerned for her safety.

The shutter creaked as it moved aside. The man had made enough noise to wake everyone in the room, had they still been sleeping.

"Lass..." Angus again prompted her to leave.

"I have my *sgian dubh*," she said, standing slightly behind him.

"Go to the corner of the room, or hide under the bed," he said.

She moved away from him then, but he didn't know if she did what he asked or if she remained close at hand. As dark as it was in the room, she could easily stab him, thinking he was the would-be attacker. And the man breaking into the room could do the same to her, not realizing she was Edana. He prayed she had done as he said.

A dog barked in the distance, setting off two more.

A dark figure started to climb in through the window, and Angus charged him, unwilling to allow him entrance, fearing Edana might be injured. With a warrior's yell, he vowed bloody vengeance.

Angus struck the man in the head and he cried out as he lost his hold on the window. He fell to the muddy earth below, making another holler in shock. Two of them then. One to take Edana? Or silence her?

Pounding on his door caused Edana to shriek.

"Open up!" Tibold yelled. "What the hell is going on in there?"

Edana ran to the door, unbarred it, and pulled it open. In the candlelight, Tibold looked from her to Angus. "I was awakened by Angus's yelling and then the other man cried out as I tried to reach your door. You are both well?"

"Aye," Edana said. "Angus tossed one of them out the window. Hopefully, he landed on the other one's head and cracked both their skulls."

"Did you no' know the lass is bloodthirsty when it comes to protecting her own?" Tibold asked Angus.

"She had my very own thoughts in mind," Angus said, turning his attention to the backside of the tavern where Drummond, Niall, and Egan were fighting the two men in vicious swordplay, someone having set a lantern down nearby.

He wanted to tell them to allow them to live so they could question them about their motives and plans, but the men weren't giving up, and his cousin and Edana's brothers continued to fight.

Several questions sprang to mind. Were the two men sleeping in the croft that Gunnolf was watching still there? Or had they slipped out the backside of the croft when Niall came to get reinforcements?

Tibold joined Angus at the window as Edana rebarred the door, then climbed back into bed.

Keary's two men finally collapsed in the mud. "Did you want to question them, or shall I?" Tibold asked Angus.

"Will you stay with Edana?"

"Aye."

"I will speak to them." Angus threw on his plaid and boots and stalked over to the bed to kiss Edana. "I will return momentarily."

And then he left the room, leaving her father in charge of her, hoping she wouldn't have the sudden urge to join Angus behind the tavern.

The mud sucking at his boots, he finally reached the injured men around back. "Were these the same two who were sleeping in the croft?" Angus asked Niall and Edana's brothers.

"Nay," Niall said. "Though I did think

mayhap the two men slipped through a window out back while Gunnolf guarded the front of the croft when I came to speak with you. But they are no' the same two men."

"Then there could be more." Angus glanced up at the second-story window to his room. Tibold was watching them. Angus poked one of the men with his boot. "What did you hope to accomplish in yonder room, eh?"

The man was holding his stomach, and Angus was certain he didn't have long to live. "Keary sent you to kill me, did he no'? He couldna have hoped to steal the lass away."

The other man shook his head. Angus turned his attention to him. "Nay? Then what? Kill me and come for her at Craigly later?"

"Let me live and I will tell you," the man said, his voice pained.

"Why should I? Would you have allowed me to live? What if you had injured Edana in the process?"

"We wouldna," he said.

Angus hmpfed. "In the dark, how would you know? And she was ready to defend me. If you had harmed me, she would have injured you. Then you are telling me you wouldna have retaliated?"

"I wouldna have...cut her. Keary is mad with wanting her. When her escort came to the castle and told him she was missing, he searched for her. He had every intention of taking her to wife as soon as he found her. He recalled having seen her as a young lass and remembered how bonny she was even then. But then you arrived with her and he still thought he had a chance to wed the lass. He didna believe you or she intended to marry. Laird Lockton had the notion even to get her da's permission before you had a chance. She had thoroughly bewitched Keary. No' only because of her fiery hair. He sees her as the kind of woman he wants to call his own."

"So he doesna intend to steal her away," Angus said, worried that Keary had that plan in mind.

"Nay. He intends to come for her at Craigly Castle, after you are dead. He will propose marriage again to her da, as she would be a widow and...free to marry."

Niall snorted. "I have already spoken for the lass. She will be mine first before Keary can get his hands on her."

Angus looked at Niall. He thought his cousin was truly serious. "Need I remind you,

Cousin, I have no intention of dropping dead anytime soon?"

Niall smiled self-assuredly. "Aye, Angus, but in the event Keary thinks he has a chance, he doesna. And you heard Gunnolf—he wishes her to be his warrior bride. So if something happens to me..." Niall shrugged.

Swords clanking in the distance made them all turn in that direction. Angus looked again at the wounded men, the one appearing to have expired. To the other, Angus said, "I will let you go for speaking freely to us. Should you attempt to harm me or mine in the future, I willna go so easy on you."

The man nodded and Niall and Drummond helped him to his feet. He waited, holding his bloodied wound, his tunic sleeve sliced halfway up the arm.

"I wouldna speak to Keary about any of this. Rather, if I were you, I would disappear." Angus truly hoped the man would do the opposite of that, and tell Keary he had no chance with Edana ever. Did Keary truly believe no one would connect him to an arbitrary murder? And that Tibold would again grant Keary the right to wed Edana?

"Aye," the man said.

"Go," Angus said.

Keary's man stumbled off, holding his bleeding arm. Angus glanced up at the window. Tibold was still watching them. Angus wanted to join the fighting to see if he could be of assistance, but he didn't want to leave Edana with just her father.

"Return to her," Niall said. "We will watch your back until you reach the room. Then Drummond and I can look into the other fighting."

"Aye." Angus hated to think anyone had to stay to protect him.

When he returned to the room, he found it empty, but before full-fledged panic could set in, Tibold opened the door to his own room. "Kayne moved Edana to my room. My sons and I will sleep in yours since the shutters no longer protect the window."

Angus agreed that the plan was sound and retired to Tibold's room with Edana, sword ready for any further disturbance.

Later, Egan banged on the door, "'Tis me, Egan, and Gildas ending our shift for the night."

Angus quickly opened the door to them so that they would not wake Edana. "Your father and Kayne are sleeping in our room next door."

"My thanks," Egan said. "Sorry to disturb you."

"Did you see any sign of Keary? Were any of our men injured?" Angus asked.

"Two of Keary's men were wounded and one killed. Our own men are well. Keary was never seen. We are going to suggest to our da that we stay with you until you and Edana are safely tucked away at Craigly Castle."

Angus dipped his head and the men said their goodnights and banged on Tibold's door. Kayne let them in and Angus barred his door and returned to a sleeping Edana. At least she had not been disturbed by *all* the night activities.

Or so he thought until she reached for him and said, "Make love to me, husband."

***

A couple of hours later, the dawn's pink ribbon of sunlight appeared, turning to orange, then yellow. The sky had cleared and it looked to be a beautiful, blustery day.

After breaking their fast, they were on their way to Craigly Castle, Una riding beside Edana, and looking much more refreshed than his wife after the harried night they'd had.

Gunnolf quickly joined him to give news of

the night before as no one wished to disturb him earlier that morn and everyone talked of other matters for their journey ahead when they broke their fast. "Niall says that if something untimely happens to you, he will wed the lass next."

Edana said, "You know, I should have some say in this." She arched a dark red brow.

"My very thought, lass," Gunnolf said, grinning. "Should anything happen to Angus, I would step in to take you to wife."

She laughed. "You jest as much as my brothers do," she said, smiling.

"For the last time, I am no' leaving my wife to *either* of you," Angus said, of good cheer, knowing they would always be there for him no matter the trouble, just as he would be when it came to protecting them. "'Tis good I dinna question your loyalty, or I might think neither you nor Niall would protect me sufficiently because the treasure to be had would be too tempting."

Gunnolf laughed heartily.

"So what happened during the fighting?" Angus asked. "Egan told me briefly what he had seen."

"The two men who had been sleeping in one of the crofts must have heard the fighting with the ones who tried to enter your room at the tavern. The men we were watching tried to slip out of the place. Egan, Halwn, and I engaged the men. Both were wounded, but we gave them the same message as you and Niall had told the other man. Leave; Keary has no hope to wed Edana as she has a string of men—Niall and me, waiting to wed the lass should some mishap befall you. We hope the word will get back to Keary and he will cease and desist," Gunnolf said.

"Or want your heads also. I recall Keary was always like that when he was a lad," Angus said. "Wanting something, making a half-hearted attempt to get it, and stirring his father's ire."

"Aye," Gunnolf said. "Only it seems he is making more than just a half-hearted attempt this time." He looked at Edana. "What exactly did the lass do to intrigue him so?"

"You have to ask, Gunnolf?" Angus said. "You, who swear you will never wed?"

Gunnolf grinned at Edana, who blushed in response. "She is a warrior woman. She would serve me well."

Niall rode back to join them. "Horses have recently traveled this way. Mayhap ten?"

Keary's men? Lying in ambush? Angus cursed under his breath.

# Chapter 21

Tibold posted more guards that night to ensure Keary nor any of his men thought to rid themselves of Angus too easily. Though normally, Edana and Una would have slept in their small tent together and no male would have entered it, Angus joined them, the low height of the tent forcing him to stoop. A candle chased away some of the shadows as he laid out his bedding next to Edana's. Her eyes widened with surprise to see him moving in with them.

Una giggled. "Had I suggested a man sleep in the same tent that I did, my da would have exploded."

Angus smiled at her. "He understands that I am here strictly for security."

Una made a face. "Dinna let me stop you from enjoying the night with your wife."

Angus thought back to Edana's comments about how she had witnessed Una and the guard kissing, which was where Edana had gotten the notion tongues were used in the process. He certainly didn't want to give Una any further ideas concerning lovemaking for when the time came for her to have a husband.

"Nay, lass. What would your future husband say?" Angus placed his sword next to his bedding.

"Oh, I would turn my back to you both and pretend it never happened." Una unplaited her hair, looking way too eager to see him make love to his wife.

Edana shook her head, smiling. "You will have your day, Una. I didna see you speaking with Gildas. Did you no' tell him how glad you are that he is well?"

Una snorted and smoothed out her blankets. "Think you he has any interest in me? Besides, when he sees that ward of your cousin McEwan, he may fall in love with her and that would be that."

"I am no' certain about that. He hasna been happy about the prospect. What about you and Seumas?" Edana asked.

Una blushed. "My da gave him the devil for going along with Kipper to escort the two of us in the search for your brother, because your da gave my da the devil for allowing it to happen in the first place."

"Oh," Edana said, her voice contrite. "So because Seumas is in trouble for aiding us, he is not happy with you?"

Una looked down at her bedding. "Truth be told, I think my da said that Seumas has to wed me."

"Why?" Edana sounded horrified.

Angus wanted to tell the lasses they needed to sleep. He hoped they would not talk all night long. Did they do this back at Rondover Castle? It was good that Una would not share his bedchambers with them.

"Because I traveled alone with Kipper and Seumas for so long. 'Twas the same as you being with Angus and his cousin and Gunnolf. Alone." Una looked expectantly at Angus and Edana as if she shared the same secrets as they did and wanted to hear about it.

Edana glanced at Angus, but didn't say anything.

Angus smiled. "It was cold those nights?" Of course he knew it had been. He could just imagine the guard using the same ploy—to snuggle close, to keep the lass from growing ill. Not that it wasn't true—he just couldn't imagine the guard doing it purely out of the goodness of his heart and not wanting more. Una was a wee bit older than Edana, her hair a light brown and sparkling green eyes, bonny indeed. She was a cheerful sort and he could see she could make a man happy.

"Aye, 'twas cold, as well you must know," Una said, slyly.

"Seumas offered to keep you warm?" Angus ventured.

"Oh, aye. He is always very heroic."

Edana didn't say a word, but she was blushing beautifully.

"He didna want me growing ill," Una persisted.

Angus shook his head.

Edana glanced at Angus and he thought she was afraid he'd tell how she had slept with him. For Una to learn the truth, Edana would have to tell Una herself, not Angus.

"Most sensible of him," Angus said, and blew out the candle.

But the absence of light in the tent did not stop the two women from talking.

He'd considered kissing Edana to stop the conversation, but he knew he'd want more, and that Una would be listening instead to Edana's soft moans, and…well, none of them would get any sleep, anyway.

He pulled her into his arms and snuggled with her instead and prayed they would be quiet soon.

Edana loved Angus. She knew he wanted to kiss her to shut her up. He curled his arms around her with her back to him. He stroked her arm in a soothing caress as she told Una all she'd missed while she'd stayed in the village and Edana had found herself lost in the woods, the boar, all of it.

Una was like a sister to her and she couldn't help it. She wanted to know what had happened to Una also while she stayed with the crofters. She wanted to know how Una felt about Seumas. Would she marry him?

Several times they had lapsed into silence, and then one or the other or the both of them would ask another question and the conversation would start all over again. Poor Angus. But if he was supposed to be guarding, he wasn't supposed to be sleeping anyway.

At one point when she mentioned about Keary and his men having the audacity to attempt to kill the sow and leave the wee boar piglets orphaned, Angus chuckled softly against her hair. She smiled.

Later, Una asked, "Is he sleeping?"

"Nay," Edana said, though she couldn't be for certain. "He is guarding."

That earned her another dark chuckle from him as Angus tightened his hold on her.

"So, will you wed Seumas?"

"I want to continue to stay with you. Serve as your companion. But if I wed Seumas, he…" Una paused.

"He what?"

"He would want me to stay with him."

"Aye," Edana said. "'Twould be most reasonable that."

"Since you will be living at Craigly Castle and at Rondover Castle sometimes, surely, it would present a problem for Seumas."

Edana thought of it for a few minutes, trying to come up with a workable solution. She wanted Una close at hand. When they both had their bairns, they could help each other greatly.

"He could serve on my brother's guard staff," Angus said, proving he was wide-awake still and listening to everything they said. "James would have to agree. Whenever we travel to Rondover Castle, he could serve to protect us on our journey. Once under Tibold's roof, Seumas could resume his service for him again in the capacity of guard."

Silence for a heartbeat and then Una said, "Aye, that is the solution. I will tell Seumas it should work."

"He would have to agree," Angus said.

"He already has." Una sighed. "We discussed something similar."

"James and Tibold would have to agree as well," Angus warned.

"The chief has said yes," Una said eagerly.

Angus shook his head. "Then how can James go against the plan?"

Edana smiled.

"But when we retire to our bed at night, we will be alone," Angus insisted.

The ladies laughed. Then Edana worried they may be keeping others awake who were sleeping near the tent. "Goodnight, Una. We will talk again on our journey."

Angus sighed and Edana thought he was much relieved. Did the men never speak to each other at night?

\*\*\*

The next morning, Niall and Gunnolf helped guard the ladies while they washed up at a trickling stream running gently over moss-covered stones, the sun rising, casting a yellow and orange growing ribbon of color as it rose higher. A smattering of white clouds dotted the blue sky. The last day of their journey and it looked as though the day would be like yesterday and they wouldn't have to slog through another downpour.

Birds were chirping in the trees lining the stream, making Angus feel even more lighthearted.

Everyone seemed more chipper, knowing James would spread a great feast in welcome and they'd all have a roof over their heads this eve.

"Did you get any sleep?" Gunnolf asked Angus, the blond, blue-eyed warrior casting him a small smile.

Angus gave him a disgruntled look.

"I could have told you what it would be like to stay in the same tent with the lasses. They canna help themselves."

Niall chuckled. "Several men were sleeping closer to the tent to protect the lasses, then they moved farther away to get some rest before they had guard duty."

Angus shook his head. "The lasses will have a time staying awake on their mounts for as long as they talked last eve, I fear."

"Aye," Gunnolf said, "but I suspect you dinna wish me to take the woman on my horse for a spell if she grows too tired."

"Una? I believe Seumas will want the honor if the lass wearies too much. Edana? Nay, the lass will ride with me. But hopefully she will be rested enough until later so my horse doesna tire," Angus said.

As they rode through the gorse-covered heath, the vibrant yellow flowers in full bloom, the sweet smell like a nutty fruit, filled the warm breeze as it tugged at their plaids and hair. But within the hour, Edana looked as though she would fall asleep in the saddle, her eyes drifting closed several times, her head nodding off.

Angus stopped her. "Edana, ride with me, lass."

She looked like she was about to object, but then she agreed. He lifted her onto his horse. Niall took her mare's reins, having been prepared to catch the lass if she had appeared as though she would fall from her mare and Angus missed her.

Seumas and Gunnolf stuck close to Una for the same reason. The lasses who could not stop talking last eve, had not said more than a word or two to each other or anyone else they had encountered this morn, they were so tired. At least this eve, Angus would have his wife to himself. He didn't expect much talking to be going on then, either.

Later that day, they broke for a brief nooning meal near a fast-moving stream. They filled their flasks with fresh water and ate dried fish and bannocks.

Niall and Gunnolf had ridden ahead, looking for any signs of trouble earlier, and finally returned. Gunnolf shook his head. "No signs of Keary or his men, but horses' droppings and the trampling of grass indicate they are no more than a couple of hours ahead of us. If that is who it is."

"I thought they would ambush us way before this. We are getting too close to Craigly and word would reach James if a battle ensued. What is Keary thinking, if it is him?" Angus asked.

Edana spoke up, refreshed from her nap. "Would it be like before? When he slipped around us and went to talk with my da? To ask for my hand in marriage before we arrived at Rondover Castle?"

Tibold joined them, hearing something of

their conversation. "I didna know you had already wed Angus. And in that case, he had come to *me*. James would have no say in who you married."

Then Angus shook his head. "What if the brigand believes his men killed me back at the village? What if he intends to be there when Edana is delivered to Craigly Castle and asks you again for her hand in marriage?"

"While she is newly widowed?" Tibold snorted and Angus assumed he had the same thought—the man was crass if he had such designs.

"He would pretend to be unduly sad for her husband's passing, offer alliances to James and you. Mayhap pay countless visits to the lass with condolences until she softened to the notion of marriage," Angus said, thinking aloud.

"Then we can play his game," Tibold said. "If he and his men are there, you willna show yourself. See what the fool does then."

Angus smiled. "I like the way you think."

Niall spoke up then. "Despite the lass's loss, I am afraid I will have to let Keary know I am next in line to marry Edana."

Gunnolf said, "Me also. Just so he realizes that she has many suitors and no' only Keary."

Edana smiled at Angus. "Despite what your friends say, you canna be so easily replaced."

They all laughed.

When they arrived at Craigly Castle, the portcullis still up as Gunnolf and Niall rode ahead to let James know of their plan, should Keary be there, Angus kissed his wife, then headed around the back of the castle to the gate the servants and merchants normally used. Four of Tibold's men accompanied him to ensure he didn't meet with foul play this close to home.

Angus had thought the notion of pretending he no longer lived a good one until he had to leave his wife in the care of her father and the rest of the men riding with them while he took the servants' stairs to speak with James in private.

When he reached James's chamber, Angus heard a babe crying in the adjoining lady's chamber. He closed his gaping mouth and turned to James as his brother bade him to enter his solar.

"The bairn has come? Already?" Angus asked, astounded. He knew the bairn was due soon, he just hadn't realized he'd been gone that long.

"Aye, Angus. A son with healthy lungs as

you can well hear. And Eilis feels strong. Now tell me about this marriage of yours and what Keary is up to. Niall briefly explained what the rogue was about."

Angus described to his brother most of what had gone on in a sketchy way. "Did you assume I would wed the lass?" he finally asked.

James smiled. "In truth? I had no idea. Though from the way you had been so intrigued with Edana in the past, I assumed you might be even more so once she was full grown. So you are truly happy?"

"Aye, but Keary isna."

James laughed. "Well, he will have to get over it."

"I am ready to rejoin my wife in the great hall."

James shook his head. "Patience, brother. My advisor is overseeing the matter for me and will send word as soon as we are to join them. Come, sit, and have something to drink."

Angus couldn't sit. He was too anxious. He wanted to show Keary he couldn't get rid of him that easily, and see his face when he showed himself—healthy and very much alive.

# Chapter 22

Edana was having a devil of a time meeting every one of James's clan who welcomed her and her da and his men as soon as they entered the keep. She was supposed to pretend to be a widow in mourning of only a couple of days, yet cheerily greet everyone who met her.

If she'd truly been in mourning, she would have displayed the grief freely. She couldn't act both ways and be in the least bit believable.

Did everyone at Craigly Castle know that it was all a ruse? They had to.

Only Keary and his men would not be told. She hadn't seen him yet, but had spied a couple of the men who had been with him when he found her in the tree and his men had tried to kill the sow.

She thought the ploy had been a good idea until now. She wished Angus would soon show up and put Keary in his place with regards to her.

Edana was somewhat anxious to meet James. She recalled the day so long ago when he and Malcolm, Angus's two oldest brothers, had carried her back to Rondover Castle as she had fought them with all her might. She had not wanted to return to the keep after the girl's drowning, knowing full well the others would believe Edana responsible for the lass's death.

James had been firm with her, but as gentle as he could have been under the circumstances. She still felt uncomfortable seeing him, believing he would think her nothing more than a wild hellion.

Any thought of that matter fled when her father escorted her into the great hall, and she came face to face with Keary.

He was unarmed and greeted her with stoicism. "Where is your husband?" he asked, looking perfectly innocent, *the bastard.*

Her father stiffened beside her, his hand on the hilt of his sword, but her brothers closed in ranks behind her and Gunnolf and Niall were nearby also.

Men and women stood around in the hall, more of Angus's kin, she assumed, as they watched the newcomers.

"He fought bravely," she said, and waited quietly for Keary's reaction. "Who had the audacity to fight him?"

Keary glanced at Tibold and his sons. "I didna think all of you were escorting Edana here."

Unable to help herself, she smiled just a little. "My brothers wouldna have attended me if Angus had not been attacked. But when that happened, my da ensured my brothers and his men all accompanied us. 'Tis good thing that. Seven other men have asked for my hand in marriage."

"Seven." Keary's voice almost sounded defeated. Then he frowned. "'Tis too soon for men to be asking for your hand, when you are grieving, lass."

"Oh, aye. If Angus had been murdered, you are verra much right in your assumption."

"*Had been.*" Keary's frown deepened. "I…was…under the…mistaken impression that Angus was murdered at the hand of a thief."

"The only treasure Angus had with him was me. Had the thief intended to steal me?"

Keary looked a little puzzled. Then latching onto her words concerning having more suitors, he turned to her father. "You promised her to me."

"Aye, but I wasna thinking straight. Know this—" Tibold said, but he didn't say anything further as Angus stormed into the great hall, sword readied.

Many stepped back. James's advisor, Eanruig muttered under his breath, his face tan, a dark beard covering much of it, black hair hanging loosely about his shoulders, and he looked just as ominous as Angus, "I should have known you wouldna wait for word from me first."

"I am unarmed," Keary quickly said, raising his hands to prove it, his face ashen.

"I am verra much alive, no thanks to you, Keary," Angus said.

Some of James's men watched Keary's men, should they think to defend him in any manner. "If you ever think of killing me, be a man and come for me yourself. But you will never wed the lass," Angus said.

"I offered friendship to James, and this is the kind of treatment I receive in return?" Keary asked, attempting to sound affronted.

"Your men told us everything, Keary," Angus said. "You canna lie to us to save your hide. I am willing to let this go, if you are allied with my kin and Edana's. But if you or your men attempt to kill me in the future..."

Edana noticed James had entered the great hall. Arms folded across his chest, he scowled at Keary—probably furious that Keary had arrived before them, pretending to be allies of the MacNeills when he'd tried to have James's youngest brother murdered.

"I didna know what some of my men were up to. I had let those men go because they were stealing from me. Mayhap they decided to take revenge and pin your murder on me," Keary said.

From the hard expressions on the men's faces, Edana didn't think anyone believed him. What would they have gained from the murder? A price on their heads.

"We will take our leave. And you have my promise to remain your ally," Keary said, looking highly annoyed, then he quickly left the keep with his men.

When they were outside, Angus wrapped his arm around Edana's shoulders and introduced her to his brother, James.

James's wife joined them, carrying a wee bairn in her arms. He was red-skinned and sleeping, puckering his mouth as if he was suckling on his mother's breast. He was adorable with brown hair as dark as James's.

Angus stared at the infant and Edana smiled. "You must be Lady Eilis." She thought how different the lady looked from her, red gold silky tresses, sea green eyes—when Edana had pretended to be her at Lockton Castle with her dark red hair and blue eyes. "What a lovely bairn."

"He is our first bairn," Eilis said proudly. "And you must be the sweet lass who bewitched Angus. No small feat that."

Edana smiled at Eilis and the baby. "Your son is beautiful. And Angus? Aye, as much as he made me see he was the only one for me." Angus and Edana's gazes met and she believed he was hopeful she would give him a son also. He offered her a small smile. She felt her cheeks heat.

James escorted his wife to the head table as a nursemaid took the bairn from Eilis.

The Chattan guard, Seumas, hurried to approach Tibold, spoke briefly, and Tibold smiled broadly. "Seems because of Keary's mishandling of his clan on a fool's errand— namely, pursuing my daughter when she was already wed to a clan chief's brother and possibly causing a war between both my clan and the MacNeills' with his, one of Keary's other brothers has taken over the clan with their people's blessing. One of his men rode all the way here to warn him of the news and my man overheard him."

"There goes the alliance between the Laird of Lockton and us," Angus said, sounding disappointed.

"Mayhap we can still encourage an alliance with the new laird," James said.

"And if you see Keary in these parts again?" Angus asked.

James snorted. "I would take him prisoner as I once did. Only this time, he would stay in our dungeon as he incarcerated you and our cousin in his."

As they took their places at the high table, James sat next to his wife on one side, Tibold on the other. Edana was seated next to her father, while Angus sat to her left. Edana heard James say to her father, "All turned out well."

"Aye. I canna express enough how grateful I am to you for sending your brother to find Edana. I couldna be more pleased with the way things worked out." Tibold smiled at Edana.

"Sounds like you both planned this," she

said, raising her brows.

An older woman strode across the hall to join them at the table and everyone in the room rose to their feet. She was all smiles, her eyes and hair as dark a brown as Angus's, only light strands of gray intertwined with the brown in braids down her front. Edna thought a strong resemblance existed between the two. His mother? She recalled the story Angus had told her about his father and how he'd had numerous liaisons with women when he was married to his mother.

She was so pretty and cheerful, Edana couldn't imagine her husband being so cruel.

Angus hurried to introduce his mother to Tibold and Edana. "Lady Akira, Tibold, chief of the Clan Chattan, and his daughter, Edana, my wife. James said you were tired. I didna think you would join us."

"I learned too late you had returned with a wife. Eilis's baby kept me up half the night. You know how it can be when a grandmomma wants to tend to her first grandbaby? How could I no' come and greet your new lovely wife?" She gave Edana a warm embrace as if she was her mother. "I seem to be missing out on too many of my sons' weddings, but I am much pleased

Angus was lucky enough to find you." She turned her attention to Tibold. "I dinna believe I have ever had the pleasure."

Edana's da looked positively dumbstruck. She poked her finger into his side to get him to respond and he quickly said, "The pleasure is all mine, my lady." He bowed over her hand and to Edana's shock, kissed it!

"This is my cousin, Fia," Lady Eilis said, as the dark-haired and dark-eyed woman hurried to join them. She looked about Eilis's age, but other than that, barely showed any family resemblance, except for their smiles.

But Fia considered each of Edana's brothers and smiled even more broadly.

"How long will you be here?" Lady Akira asked Tibold as seats were shuffled and she was seated between James and Tibold.

"My sons have a mission to see their cousin McEwan."

"I thought you wanted me to stay with you longer," Drummond said, sitting farther down the table and sounding a little panicked.

"If you can fight Keary's men, you are no longer too ill to journey with us," Gildas said, his smile smug.

Edana thought with her older brother

making such a statement, her da would agree and force Drummond to accompany the rest of her brothers to travel to see McEwan.

Lady Akira frowned. "If your son has been recently ill, he may stay here with us until you wish to return to Rondover Castle," she said to Tibold.

Egan and Gildas groaned. Kayne said, "I knew Drummond would worm his way out of it."

Edana watched her father speaking with Lady Akira. She was so animated and the way his blue eyes never strayed from her, a small smile curving his lips, he seemed to enjoy soaking up her attention.

Fia slipped onto the bench next to Drummond. "So you are staying here longer, aye? How did you come to be ill?"

"A stay in a cold, drafty dungeon after he kissed a chief's mistress," Kayne said, sounding disgruntled and not about to let Drummond say anything differently. "Which, I might add, got us all into the same predicament."

Edana thought Fia might be taken aback by the revelation, but instead she leaned toward Drummond, her brown eyes wide, and said, "Truly?"

Kayne laughed and shook his head. "He can fall into the swine's slop and still come out smelling sweet where the lasses are concerned."

Her brothers all laughed.

Angus took Edana's hand in his and kissed it. "You appear to be deep in thought. What are you thinking?"

She snuggled closer to him and again looked in her father's direction. "That I have found my true love, but I do believe I may have found a solution to my da's needing a woman's comfort."

Angus looked at Tibold and his mother. She was more vivacious than he'd seen her in a long time, and Tibold actually looked to be enjoying her company. "I think mayhap you have something there, Edana. We might even be able to persuade my mother to travel with us to visit Rondover Castle later."

Edana smiled. "Aye. I didna know you were a matchmaker at heart."

He chuckled. "If it meant our parents' happiness, aye."

Then Edana frowned. "Could be a problem if the scullery maid, Zenevieva, attempts to cause trouble between them if anything should come of our parents' relationship."

"Your father said he would no longer see the maid."

"Aye, but that doesna mean the woman might not seek revenge if my da shows interest in your mother. Because of your mother's bad experiences with your father, mayhap she would think mine is the same way."

Edana's brother, Halwn, said to Niall, "Now that we are all family, of sorts, would you want to come along with us?"

"Because your cousin McEwan needs a man to marry his ward?" Niall asked.

Kayne shook his head. "Who told him the truth of the matter?"

Everyone laughed.

Angus realized then that not only had he married into Edana's family, but that her family was happy to become part of his as well. He had never foreseen his mother might be interested in Tibold, nor that the chief might be intrigued with his mother. If the man could give his mother the kind of love she deserved, Angus would do everything in his power to help their relationship along.

"Now *you* seem to be deep in thought, Husband," Edana said, slipping her hand into his lap, squeezing his thigh.

He considered her smiling face. "I should have spoken to you all those years ago. I should have kissed you."

"But what if I had run away?"

"I would have chased after you and never given up."

She grinned. "What if I had chased you?"

"I would have made myself an easy catch."

She laughed. "Can I ask you something?" she said, leaning close to him.

Intrigued, he said, "Aye, lass, anything."

"You said you wanted to show me other ways of being intimate. How many ways are there?"

He smiled down at her. "Have I told you how much I love you?"

Her bright, happy expression told him how much his words meant to her. His bonny lass, who had only sunny smiles for her family, now had them for him, just as he'd wished he'd had from her so long ago.

He leaned over and kissed her upturned mouth. "There are as many ways as we can come up with to make love, my wife. Anything you wish to try, I am game."

She seemed to ponder that a bit, then whispered to him, "Una said one of the maids tied her man up."

Angus laughed out loud. He couldn't help it. He'd never considered such a thing, but his bonny wife had?

Several stopped eating and talking to look their way as he'd had his outburst. Edana's face flushed beautifully.

Angus grinned and spoke for her hearing only. "Aye, if 'tis your desire. But I believe in reciprocating."

She thought about that, then nodded. "Aye, I agree."

The festivities would not end soon enough before he could escort Edana to his bedchamber to see what else she had in mind. He thought he was the one who would have to come up with all the new ways of making love. "What other methods did you hear of?"

She only grinned. "I will tell you later—in the privacy of our bedchamber, since everyone is watching us because you laughed so loud."

"I couldna help it. I wasna expecting you to say what you did." He took her hand and kissed it, then rested it back on his thigh.

James, Gunnolf, and Niall saluted him with their tankards of ale in a silent message of—*well done.*

Angus saluted them back, wishing he could make some excuse to slip off with Edana to his chamber without anyone being the wiser.

"Do you know where we can get some rope?" she asked.

He laughed again. His bonny lass was truly a treasure. "We will use something softer so that our wrists willna be roughened up."

"Oh, aye," she said so seriously, he couldn't believe how much she was thinking about binding him to the bed.

Already his staff was hard as steel. "More ale," he called to a servant, wanting to cool his heated blood.

"I dinna know how to tie a tight knot. Can you show me?"

He wasn't sure he wanted her to tie him so well he couldn't free himself. "Aye."

"And should I tie your ankles also?" She didn't speak quietly to him this time and her father looked in her direction.

Smiling, Angus whispered to her, "Whatever you would like to do, but we should discuss this above stairs."

Then he hoped his sweet wife would not share such a thing with Una who very well might share with some other maid, and then everyone in the castle would know that his wife bound him to their bed to have her way with him.

"You are blushing, Angus. What are you thinking of?" she asked, in a teasing tone.

Just how much he loved his wee wild Highland wife!

# Chapter 23

The idea of engaging in bondage with his sweet wife intrigued Angus. Though no matter what, he didn't want anyone to learn of it! He could just imagine what his brothers, cousin, and Gunnolf would say if ever any of them heard about it.

When James called for dancing and there was so much activity as servants took the trenchers of leftover food away and everyone else helped move the trestle tables aside to clear the great hall, Edana whispered to Angus, "Let us go now, before anyone notices we are slipping away."

He was certain someone would spot them leaving the great hall. Many, in fact, as everyone in his clan was interested in the lass he'd married, and her own people—her brothers and da—had been curious as to how well she would be received by his clansmen and how he and the lass got along.

As soon as the hall was cleared and the

musicians started to play, he and Edana would surely be missed.

Her hand in his, he hurried her out of the great hall. He expected someone to say something, but then he assumed the talk would begin in earnest *after* he and Edana were out of earshot and everyone realized they were gone for the eve.

"I dinna know if I will do any of it right," Edana said, all of a sudden sounding a little shy as he moved her up the stairs.

"I dinna think there is any right or wrong way. Just as long as we both find enjoyment in the deed. This is all new to me, lass." He wanted in the worst way to reassure her that whatever they did, they would take pleasure in the act and in each other.

She smiled brightly at him and quickened her pace.

He adored her.

When they reached his chamber, he quickly pulled her inside, barred the door, and lit candles. She looked around at his chamber—the big bed cloaked in brown curtains, a couple of spare plaids hanging off hooks, a table, two chairs, rushes on the floor, and one Turkish rug hanging against a wall that he had brought back from the Crusades.

Digging around in the bottom of his wooden chest where he had stuffed a very worn tunic, he finally found it and used his dirk to shred it into strips of cloth. She watched, her blue eyes sparkling with intrigue, her tongue licking her lips—in anticipation? Or nervousness? He couldna tell.

"Here, lass," he said and showed Edana the way to tie a knot. Or at least one she could easily untie or he could, when they were done. He didn't want her to have to cut him loose should anything go awry!

When he showed her how she could yank on one tail and that would undo the knot, she looked up at him with wide eyes. "But you can get free."

He laughed. "Aye, lass. But I promise I willna try while you do whatever you wish to do with me."

Then he unfastened his belt and set his sword and *sgian dubh* aside. She undid her brooch and placed it on his table, laying her brat on top of a chair.

"Do you want me on the bed?" he asked.

"Aye, where else would I want you?"

He smiled and shrugged. "The chair,

mayhap."

She looked at the chair. "I dinna think that would work."

"If you sat on my lap."

She glanced back at the chair and frowned. "Aye, mayhap." Then she smiled. "Another time."

He couldn't wait. The anticipation of what she intended to do to him near killed him. "Do you want me naked?" He thought she would, but he wanted her to feel as though she was making all the decisions.

"Aye." She pulled her léine off and set it on top of her brat.

He quickly divested himself of his clothes and stretched out on the mattress, his staff already hard as his sword, his body desiring her something fierce. She was in no hurry, the wicked lass.

When she began to look around the chamber, still wearing her chemise, he asked, "What are you searching for?"

"Something soft."

Not him. He was hard and getting harder.

"Are you no' going to disrobe as well, lass?"

She sighed. "Mayhap later."

He groaned. "I love to see you naked."

"Later," she said, very much in charge and he loved it. She unbraided her hair and shook out the wavy strands so that they fell softly over her shoulders. Then she took one of the strips of linen and looped it around his hands and tied a knot that he couldn't slip out of.

"You knew how to tie knots already!"

She smiled. "Aye. I thought mayhap you would show me a different kind that I didna know."

He laughed, but then sobered. "But what if you canna untie it when the time comes?"

"I will call for your brother or cousin to help you out."

He felt his face heat with mortification. She gave him the most wicked smile, right before she kissed his mouth, her hair tickling his shoulders.

Then she lifted her chemise so that she could straddle his legs and to his surprise, she draped the linen over his fully aroused cock, hiding it from their view. But as she leaned forward, he felt her soft belly rubbing against it. He had to admit just how intriguing she felt.

She licked his abdomen all the way up to his right nipple, and with a wee nibble, touched her teeth to him. Then she slid her tongue over his aroused nipple. His bound hands were already caressing her head as he moaned in ecstasy.

Her body was soft, smelling of sweet woman, her tongue wet, and her breath warm. He'd never considered having a woman in his bed, and now he would never see his bed again without thinking of Edana in it on top of him or underneath him, buried in the furs.

As she moved to kiss his other nipple, she slipped her hands under her chemise and touched the top of his staff. With a jolt, he bucked. Unable to see what she planned to do to him was his undoing.

He gritted his teeth as she swept her fingers over the top, and then down, and finally taking hold and tightening like he'd shown her. Then she pumped him, making him want to come in the worst way—but inside of her.

He groaned and moved his hips, his eyes closed as the sensation built of need and want and a craving he had to have satisfied. Before he could help himself—*he told himself it wasn't his fault that he liked to be in charge*—he grasped her arm and pulled her forward just enough that when he moved again, he could align himself with her sweet heavenly body and bury himself in her. At least he hoped.

And when he did, she grinned, and yanked off her chemise and rode him. He was glad she had not tied his hands above his head as he worked to bring her to completion. His fingers massaged that sweet spot that had firmed and begged for his touch, her luscious breasts bouncing, her nipples blushing and peaked.

She cried out with pleasure, though no one would hear her this time as everyone was dancing down below, the sound of a lyre and even a Celtic harp playing way off in the distance, serenading them. She seemed satiated as she leaned down to kiss his mouth, softly. He took advantage of her, slipped his hands over her head and rolled over so that he was on top, filling her, kissing her mouth. His hands were pinned beneath her, but he'd caught her, too, and she wasn't getting away.

He pounded into her until he couldn't hold onto the sweet ecstasy of the moment any longer, and came, filling her with his heat and love. Then he rolled over onto his back so that she was once again on top of him. He caressed her skin with his tied hands as she lay against his hard chest, her hair spread out over them.

"I verra much liked that," she finally said. "Did you?"

"Oh, aye, but next time, I will enjoy tying *you* up."

She didn't say anything for a moment, then nodded. "I think I should have done it differently though."

"Nay, lass, 'twas a verra nice way to make love to you." He couldn't imagine having done anything differently to have made the experience any more grand.

"I think I should have tied your hands to the bed so that you couldna take charge." She grinned at him.

He laughed. Mayhap she learned *too* quickly.

Edana cherished Angus. He was just the man for her and she hoped she would always be the only woman for him. She valued that he *hadn't* insisted she remove the cloth binding his wrists after they'd made love, and he seemed just as happy to lock her in his arms like this.

"When will we try the chair?" she asked, tracing his nipple with her fingertip.

He chuckled. "You will be the death of me, lass, in the most pleasurable way."

She smiled. "'Tis good you are strong and

braw and can manage then."

"Lass, I am yours to command."

This time she chuckled. And she was certain she would have to remind him of his words another day.

###

## The Highlanders Series

*Winning the Highlander's Heart*, Book 1
*The Accidental Highland Hero*, Book 2
*Highland Rake*, Book 3
*Taming the Wild Highlander*, Book 4

## Time Travel to the Past

*A Ghost of a Chance at Love*

## Medieval England

*Lady Caroline and the Egotistical Earl*

## The Werewolf Highlander Series

*Heart of the Highland Wolf*
*A Howl for a Highlander*
*A Highland Werewolf Wedding*

# Acknowledgements

I wish to thank Vonda Sinclair and Judy Gilbert for critiquing and Loretta Grucz Melvin and Donna Fournier for beta reading the book!

# About the Author

*USA Today* bestselling and an award-winning author of urban fantasy and medieval romantic suspense, Terry Spear also writes true stories for adult and young adult audiences. She's a retired lieutenant colonel in the U.S. Army Reserves and has an MBA from Monmouth University. She also creates award-winning teddy bears, Wilde & Woolly Bears, that are personalized that have found homes all over the world. When she's not writing or making bears, she's teaching online writing courses or gardening. Her family has roots in the Highlands of Scotland where her love of all things Scottish came into being. Originally from California, she's lived in eight states and now resides in the heart of Texas. She is the author of the Heart of the Wolf series and the Heart of the Jaguar series, plus numerous other paranormal romance and historical romance novels. For more information, please visit www.terryspear.com, or follow her on Twitter, @TerrySpear. She is also on Facebook at http://www.facebook.com/terry.spear .

More Highlanders on the way. There canna be only one!

*The Highlander*, book 5